DANGEROUS SLEUTHING

A roar sprang up. Beams approached way too fast from behind. I swore and slowed. I checked the mirror again and was nearly blinded.

"Mac, watch out!" Gin cried.

My car's lane control system beeped frantically. I whipped my gaze forward. At the last minute, I steered sharply to the right where the road turned. The other vehicle sped past, nearly clipping my side mirror.

"What kind of idiot was that?" Gin screeched.

The road straightened and widened. A streetlight appeared not far away. I swallowed and pulled onto the shoulder under the light, pressed the hazard-lights button, and shifted the car into park.

"Idiot, yes," I said. "And maybe a murderer following us and trying to put our questioning to a permanent end . . ."

Books by Maddie Day

Country Store Mysteries

FLIPPED FOR MURDER
GRILLED FOR MURDER
WHEN THE GRITS HIT THE FAN
BISCUITS AND SLASHED BROWNS
DEATH OVER EASY
STRANGLED EGGS AND HAM
NACHO AVERAGE MURDER
CANDY SLAIN MURDER
NO GRATER CRIME
BATTER OFF DEAD
FOUR LEAF CLEAVER
DEEP FRIED DEATH
SCONE COLD DEAD
CHRISTMAS COCOA MURDER
(with Carlene O'Connor and Alex Erickson)
CHRISTMAS SCARF MURDER
(with Carlene O'Connor and Peggy Ehrhart)

Cozy Capers Book Group Mysteries

MURDER ON CAPE COD
MURDER AT THE TAFFY SHOP
MURDER AT THE LOBSTAH SHACK
MURDER IN A CAPE COTTAGE
MURDER AT A CAPE BOOKSTORE
MURDER AT THE RUSTY ANCHOR
MURDER AT CAPE COSTUMERS
MURDER AT THE TOY SOLDIER

Local Foods Mysteries

A TINE TO LIVE, A TINE TO DIE
'TIL DIRT DO US PART
FARMED AND DANGEROUS
MURDER MOST FOWL
MULCH ADO ABOUT MURDER

Published by Kensington Publishing Corp.

MURDER AT THE TOY SOLDIER

Maddie Day

Kensington Publishing Corp.
kensingtonbooks.com

KENSINGTON BOOKS are published by

Kensington Publishing Corp.
900 Third Avenue
New York, NY 10022

ISBN: 978-1-4967-5942-9

ISBN: 978-1-4967-5943-6 (ebook)

First Printing: September 2026

10 9 8 7 6 5 4 3 2 1

Printed in the United States of America

The authorized representative in the EU for product safety and compliance is eucomply OU, Parnu mnt 139b-14, Apt 123 Tallinn, Berlin 11317, hello@eucompliancepartner.com.

For Julie Hennrikus, a dear friend,
a talented author, my former Wicked Authors blogmate,
and the executive director of Sisters in Crime.
In her years with the organization, she has guided it
into the modern age and helped shape it into
a supporter of underserved voices and an educational
and advocacy platform for all crime fiction writers.
You're the best, Julie!

ACKNOWLEDGMENTS

I wrote the first third of this book while on a writing retreat in the area of Cape Cod where fictional Westham is set. This is my fortieth mystery novel, and I have to pinch myself to believe it!

Ruth Behling was the high bidder on my donation at Left Coast Crime in 2025 for the right to name a character in my next book. Ruth decided to honor her mystery-loving late mother, and I'm delighted to include Patty Harbach as a character in this book. I hope you love your mom's fictional self, Ruth, and thank you for supporting the Brink Literacy Project charity!

Many apologies to the citizens of the fair state of Rhode Island. I invented an entirely fictional senator and mean no disrespect to the two amazing actual senators.

Pruning the Dead by Julia Henry is the first of five Garden Squad Mysteries about a group of friends who do guerrilla gardening as well as sleuthing. It's one of my favorite series and is written by Julie Hennrikus (Julia Henry is a pseudonym). She's one of my favorite people and a former blogmate at WickedAuthors.com. The Cozy Capers are their own kind of double-purpose squad, so having the group read *Pruning the Dead* in this book is a perfect fit. I highly recommend you read Julie's series and all her other books!

I'm ever grateful to Jennifer McKee for assisting with many non-writing aspects of my business. You're the best, Jen. Once again, Amy Glaser gave a close look at this manuscript and sent along many insightful comments, which improved the story considerably. Bless you, Amy. As always, my partner Hugh Lockhart is happy to provide tidbits of astrological knowledge when I ask him.

Note to readers: the ideas and words in this novel were generated entirely by the author without contribution from an AI application. I wish I didn't have to include that statement, but you should know where your fiction comes from. In addition, no one has permission to use this book to generate AI content.

I thank John Scognamiglio and Larissa Ackerman and everyone at Kensington Publishing who makes the process of getting my books into print seem nearly seamless. Eight books into this series, I'm as happy with my publishing home as I always have been.

Many thanks to my new agent, the fabulous Jessica Faust. She was the first agent I ever queried way back in my baby author days. She turned me down then (wisely, I'm sure) but recently changed her mind. I'm delighted to have her and the BookEnds Literary Agency represent me.

Please check out my posts on the second and fourth Fridays and the eleven other talented author-cooks at Mystery Lovers' Kitchen, where you can find an original recipe (and regular giveaways) every day of the week. As always, I'm at my Maddie Day/Edith Maxwell Facebook page and at my web site, MaddieDayAuthor.com.

To my family, I love you. And to enthusiastic book bloggers, librarians, and readers, I wouldn't be on this path without you.

MURDER AT THE TOY SOLDIER

CHAPTER 1

I pulled open the Toy Soldier's front door that late February afternoon and was greeted by the music of a string of jingle bells that hung from it.

A woman about my height stood with her back to me at the retail counter. She tucked a lock of dirty blond hair behind her ear as she spoke in a low tone to the young woman behind the counter. The young one was dressed in a violet sweater and had wavy dark hair to her shoulders, framing the porcelain skin of her face.

"I need more time to think about it," Dirty Blond murmured.

"Please," Violet Sweater pleaded with her. "It would mean so much to me."

I scuffed my foot on purpose. This didn't sound like a retail transaction, and I didn't want them to think I was listening in.

Dirty Blond whirled. "Mac?" the chef of the Rusty Anchor Pub asked.

"Yvonne, I didn't recognize you without your toque and your chef's tunic."

"It's my day off," Yvonne said, "and I was just leaving." She pushed past me and pulled open the door, setting the bells jingling again.

The young woman seemed to sag for a moment, then took in a deep breath and straightened her spine.

"Welcome to the Toy Soldier," she said, her voice low and throaty and a little quavery.

"Thanks." I took another look. Yesterday I'd seen this person elsewhere but hadn't interacted with her.

She didn't return my smile as she cleared her throat. "Excuse me. What can I help you find, ma'am?"

At the counter, I held out my hand. "I'm Mac Almeida, owner of Mac's Bikes at the other end of Main Street. Have you worked here long?" I hadn't seen her during the holiday season, when I'd been in shopping for toys for Ella and Luca, our newly adopted children.

"No, I only began last month. I'm Zia Carven." She shook my hand with her smooth, slender one, but it was a brief and unsure touch. She was two or three inches shorter than my five foot seven, and I doubted she was over twenty-five. Her eyes were a light brown, almost golden shade I'd never seen before, and her naturally arched eyebrows angled down toward the bridge of her nose as if she were actor Nicole Kidman's offspring.

"It's nice to meet you, Zia. I'm sure June is glad for the help."

"Yes." Her gaze darted over my shoulder toward the door.

When I didn't hear bells, I didn't twist to look. "My

daughter is turning four in a couple of weeks." Although the word "my" combined with "daughter" still sounded strange coming from my lips, I was now a mother of two. "Ella's been talking about gardening since last fall. Do you have anything like children's garden gloves and tools for digging?"

Zia finally smiled. "We do. Let me show you." She had a wide mouth, and the smile transformed her face from ghostly to lovely.

I followed her to a display of miniature gloves, trowels, hand rakes, and bucket hats painted with whimsical vegetables.

"Those look perfect." I picked up a *Made in the USA* two-pack of a trowel and a hand rake, which were plastic, but the packaging said they were made of recycled marine plastic. The handles looked easy to grip for small hands, and neither tool had sharp edges.

"Let me know what else I can help you with." Zia made her way back to the counter, casting a quick glance at the door as she went.

I brought the two-pack of tools, a pair of purple flowered gloves, and a hat decorated with pea pods to the register, along with a picture book about growing vegetables.

"These will make my girl happy." I pulled out a credit card.

"Good." Zia rang up the sale. "Would you like me to gift wrap them?" She gestured behind her at three rolls of wrapping paper featuring balloons, jungle animals, and kites in primary colors.

"Would you? All I have is Christmas paper at home."

"Of course."

"Thanks. Please do the tools in the animals paper, and the rest together in the balloon paper." My husband, Tim, and I could say the tools were a gift from Ella's baby brother, who was all of six months old and clueless about things like birthdays. I checked the time on my phone. "Actually, I'm on my lunch break, and I have to get back to my shop. I'll pick up the gifts at five, on my way home, if that's okay."

"Not a problem. We're open until six."

"Thanks. I'll see you then." I made my way to the door. As I pulled it open, I looked back at Zia. She again stared at the plate glass, those naturally intense brows drawn even closer together.

What was this young woman worried about? And what had she wanted from Yvonne?

CHAPTER 2

Even though I needed to get back to work, I pulled out my phone in front of the consignment shop two doors down from the toy store and pretended to read something. My peripheral vision was trained on the front of the Toy Soldier.

Zia seemed anxious about an unwelcome visitor she was hesitant to see or maybe afraid of. Should I contact June? Maybe she wasn't around, if she'd left her new employee in charge. June had owned the store at least as long as I'd been back in Westham, going on four years now, and possibly longer.

Brrr. I pulled up the hood on my winter jacket. The end of February on Cape Cod could be miserably cold and rainy or bitter cold and dry, sometimes with snow. This week was all of the above. This morning had brought freezing rain on top of last night's snow. The temperature had warmed enough to make slushies of the sidewalks, but it wasn't enough to feel remotely comfortable. The damp cold permeated to my bones. At least it wasn't precipitating in any form.

I turned away toward the other end of town when the scuff of a foot caught my attention. Turning, I caught sight of a hooded figure peering into the toy store window. The person gave a wave through the glass and set their hand on the door handle.

But the door didn't open. The person hammered on it with a closed fist, then glanced up and down the sidewalk. I raised my phone in front of my face just in time. I began to stroll away, switching my phone's camera to selfie-mode so I could see behind me.

The impatient knocker uttered a growl. When Zia didn't unlock the door—and who could blame her?—the person stomped away in the opposite direction. They were maybe three or four inches taller than me, but they were so bundled up in a dark, thigh-length coat with the hood up, I couldn't tell who it was.

I gave myself a shake. I'd delayed my return to my workplace and livelihood even more. By now it was one thirty, and my high-metabolism empty stomach was complaining bitterly of mistreatment. I always gave my employees their lunch breaks before I took mine, but I had run my errand in search of a birthday present instead of eating. My ham-and-cheese sandwich awaited me back at Mac's Bikes. I could sneak bites of lunch between customers if I had to.

As I walked, I thought about an incident I'd witnessed the day before. Every other Monday, at the end of the afternoon, I volunteered at Our Neighbor's Table, a free food market run out of the basement of the church where my father was minister. I'd just finished my shift and was gathering my things to walk home when my mother began a conversation with a young woman I now knew was Zia.

They were at the far end of the market area from the door, so I couldn't make out their words, but Mom seemed to be exhorting the younger woman about something. Zia wasn't having it, shaking her head and turning away. Mom didn't appear happy, either. My mother, aka Astra MacKenzie, was rarely confrontational, although she did hold strong opinions, which I admired. I decided to ask her about their conversation next time I saw her. I shook off the memory and picked up my pace.

I hurried past my husband's business, Greta's Great Grains, which was named after Tim's mother, who'd taught him to bake. Since we'd taken in his late sister's two small children last November, Tim had pulled back from full-time baking. He still managed the bakery but needed more flexibility in his hours to make sure the kiddos were okay and that we had healthy meals on the table most nights. He knew I wasn't capable of making the cooking part a success.

What I was succeeding at was loving up Ella and baby Luca, those two little beings whose birth fathers had never been in their lives and whose mom was too troubled to keep herself sober and safe. Tim had been named the children's official guardian in case of need, and we happily took in our niece and nephew. Their official adoption was in process.

Tim and I had planned to get our own family underway after we'd married over a year ago, but conception was so far proving elusive. I had turned thirty-eight last

September to Tim's thirty-five. If my husband and I also produced a child or two the usual way, so much the better. If we didn't, if my eggs were too old or something, we still had our own little clan meshing with my beloved family here in Westham.

My half-brother, Derrick, had been raising his daughter as a single dad since Cokey, now six, was three. Derr's new wife Neli gave birth last month to a baby boy they were calling Joey. Our parents and my grandmother lived in town too. My dad, Joseph, was the Unitarian Universalist minister, my mom worked as a professional astrologer, and my grandmother Reba was a tiny dynamo and town monitor of activities, legal and otherwise. Each week, all of us congregated at the parsonage for Sunday dinner, and I wouldn't have it any other way.

CHAPTER 3

Mac's Bikes was quiet when I walked in, which was what I'd expected. Who wanted to rent or buy a bicycle in wretched weather like this? Luckily my mechanic, Orlean, had her hands full with long-deferred tune-up and maintenance jobs. When it was too cold to ride outdoors, cyclists brought their bikes in for service. They could do without them for a few days.

"Delia, you're off at two thirty, yes?" I asked my part-timer, Delia Haskins, after I grabbed my sandwich from the fridge.

"Yep. Miserable weather out there, isn't it?"

"Totally. No wonder we don't have any business in here." I took a big first bite of my delayed lunch.

A dozen grizzled and weather-worn men in cold-weather bike togs clomped in, one after the other. I'd spoken too soon.

A tall dude in a yellow jacket grinned at me. "Nice and warm in here. Thank you, ma'am." He pulled off his gloves and rubbed his palms together.

"Welcome to Mac's Bikes." I slid the sandwich

back into its container and stashed it under the counter. "Have you all been out riding in this weather?"

"We're hard-core, ma'am," Yellow Jacket said.

"We're kind of like the mailman," a shorter man in a purple knit cap said. "Nothing stops us except ice storms."

"We rode in from Providence, and we're headed for Provincetown," the first one added. "It keeps us out of trouble of the liquid kind."

Whatever that meant. "I admire your dedication to the sport, but that's a long ride. What is it, a hundred miles?"

"A hundred twenty," Purple Cap said. "But we have only twenty more miles to go today. We're breaking the trip with a night in Hyannis."

"A wise choice." I smiled. "What can we do for you today?"

The men spread out through the store, with both Delia and me helping them find items from energy gels to wicking socks and patch kits.

After they paid and began to leave, Purple Cap hung back. "Isn't Westham a kind of murder magnet? I follow the news on Cape Cod, and your town's name keeps popping up with homicides."

I grimaced. "Unfortunately, we have had a few in recent years, but I wouldn't say we're a magnet for that kind of crime." The most recent murder had been four months ago on Halloween. With any luck, that would be the last one for the foreseeable future.

"I hope not." He held up his bag. "I'd better get going or they'll leave without me."

"Have a safe ride."

"Thanks." He disappeared through the door.

Delia sidled over. "Did you hear what the tall guy said about keeping out of liquid trouble?"

"Yes, but I don't have a clue what he meant."

"I bet that was a group that met in AA. My brother-in-law is in recovery, and he's a wicked serious mountain biker in New Hampshire. For him, conquering trails, even in the snow, keeps him sober."

"Getting a lot of focused, exhausting exercise to avoid drinking makes sense to me." I retrieved my sandwich and thought back to my toy store encounter. "You know June Jenkins, don't you?"

"Of the Toy Soldier? Sure."

"A young woman was working there when I stopped in on my break. I wonder if June is away."

"No, I don't think so. I saw her somewhere in town this week. Maybe it was yesterday."

"Okay. Have you met Zia Carven? That's who waited on me in the toy store." I took another bite of my sandwich.

"What does she look like?"

"Early twenties, slender, with dark wavy hair and the palest skin you'll ever see. Plus odd golden eyes. About your height."

"Yes, I've seen her in the pub a few times this winter, but I didn't learn her name." Delia tended bar at the Rusty Anchor when she wasn't working at my shop. "Nervous, right?"

"She was today, but I didn't pick up why. She seemed to have locked the door after I left."

"That's strange for a retail store that's supposed to be open all day."

"I know." I gave a nod. "Someone wanted to go in after I left, but the door wouldn't budge."

"Maybe she was using the restroom and didn't want to leave the front unattended."

"That's probably it."

Or maybe the thing she was scared of was the person who seemed angry that they couldn't get inside. In that case, good for her for staying safe.

"I'm pretty sure Zia isn't from Westham," Delia added.

"I suppose not. I don't recognize the last name, but that doesn't mean much. I was elsewhere for a decade and a half, between college, working in banking, my stint in the Peace Corps, and traveling after I got out."

"If she's in her early twenties, she would have been an infant when you were packing up to go to Harvard."

"True, and I didn't babysit when I was in high school. Or she could have recently moved to town."

I finished my sandwich and started puttering around the shop. Delia bundled up to leave half an hour later.

"Say hi to Lincoln," I said. "I haven't seen him in months, and that's a good thing."

She'd reunited last year with her former husband, the state police detective who had worked on most of the murders I'd become involved in solving. Lincoln Haskins and I had become friendly, and I was more than happy that he and Delia had resolved their long-ago differences, issues that had arisen after the tragic death of their young daughter.

"I will. See you tomorrow."

I perched on a stool behind the counter and switched on my laptop, then brought up the accounting software I used. Quiet days like this were perfect for accomplishing the administrative tasks of running a business. Orlean worked away in the repair room, providing background music of tools clinking, the air compressor humming to life, and the hiss as it filled bike tires.

The only customers for the rest of the afternoon were folks picking up their serviced bikes. I checked in with my mom about how Ella was. Mom and Pa cared for the little girl once preschool was out for the day at three o'clock. Little Luca stayed in the church day care until four thirty, when Tim picked up both kids. I texted him that I'd be home by five twenty at the latest.

At four thirty, I headed into the repair area. "Are you at a good stopping point?" I asked Orlean.

"Yup." She lifted a replica Schwinn off the repair stand. "Just finished this one."

"Is anyone else expected in to pick up their cycles?"

"Nope." Orlean was nothing if not efficient in her communication.

"Then let's close up now."

"Sure." She wiped her hands with a rag.

I smiled and turned away. The sound of running water followed as she scrubbed her hands at the industrial sink in her area. I turned down the heat and ventured outside to bring in the Open flag. *Brr*. The temperature was dropping again. I hurried to lift the pole out of its holder, then paused to sniff the air. Was snow on its way again? I couldn't tell, and I hadn't checked a forecast since yesterday.

A few minutes later, Orlean gave a mock salute as she headed for the door.

"See you in the morning," I said.

"Yup."

I didn't care how taciturn my mechanic was. She did good work. I knew how to do the bike repair and maintenance side of the business, but having her take care of it freed me up—and kept my hands clean—to run the rest of the retail and rental shop, which was about to close for the night. I had gift-wrapped items to pick up and a cherished family to eat supper with.

CHAPTER 4

My cheeks stinging from the cold, I paused for a moment to admire the display in the window of the Toy Soldier. Dolls and stuffed animals kept books and games company on a bookshelf. In front stood a half dozen soldiers dressed like Buckingham Palace guards, and a toy train emerged from a tunnel onto a track that encircled the shelf.

As I watched, one of the soldiers teetered and crashed across the tracks directly in front of the engine. If someone switched on the train, he was a goner. I hoped June or Zia picked him up before any children saw him run over.

I pulled open the door to the shop, glad it was unlocked. I wasn't sure it would be. Inside, I gasped. Instead of smiling at me from behind the waist-high counter, Zia Carven slumped over one end of it.

"Zia!" I rushed toward her.

She didn't move. Her right arm hung over the edge. My nostrils flared with alarm. She was too still. Her back wasn't moving with breath, not even a little. I tore off my fleece glove and gently pressed two fingers into her neck.

I stepped back, my eyes filling. Zia Carven would never move again. Her skin was cool. She had no pulse. In the space of a single afternoon, she'd gone from being a lovely, if nervous, young woman, very much alive, to this. Dead.

But why? How did she come to slump over a retail counter? Surely she was too young to suffer a heart attack or a stroke.

I shook myself out of my musings. I needed to call this in. As I pulled my phone out of my bag, my gaze refocused on Zia. I moved closer to the end of the counter and peered at the floor under her dangling arm. My breath rushed in all over again.

What appeared to be dried blood was pooled under a toy rifle on the floor. My eyes lifted. The hair on this side of Zia's head was matted. The poor girl had been attacked. Maybe by the upset figure I'd seen? I couldn't solve that. What I could do was press 9-1-1.

"This is Mackenzie Almeida at the Toy Soldier on Main Street in Westham. I came in a minute ago and found the young woman who works here dead. No one else appears to be in the store, and I am safe." By now, I knew the questions the dispatcher would ask. Unlike the first time I called in a body two years ago, I knew to specify the town, since Westham used a regional upper-Cape dispatch service. "Earlier this afternoon, the employee told me her name was Zia Carven. I don't think this was a natural death. She has blood on the back and side of her head."

"Someone will be there shortly. You need to step outside, ma'am, and wait for the police."

"There's a door to the back. Shouldn't I stay with the body?"

"No, ma'am. Please go outside now. Tell me when you have."

I pulled on my glove and pushed open the door. "I'm on the sidewalk."

"Good. Feel free to leave this call open."

Sirens wailed into life down the street. "That's okay. I can hear them coming. Thank you." I disconnected and waited, my thoughts working overtime.

Who was this young woman who had started her job a month ago? Someone whacked her hard enough to end her life. I hoped June knew more about her employee than I did, but she might not be aware of Zia's personal life. The police were going to have to inform June about Zia's death, and soon.

Maybe the attack had been the result of a robbery gone bad. I hadn't ventured behind the counter to see if the cash drawer had been ransacked. Judging from my own business, we dealt very little in paper money. Most customers used either a credit or debit card. My trips to deposit actual money into the store account at the bank were growing less frequent.

I turned my face toward a person approaching, but it wasn't the police. A bright spot of color in the gray of the falling dusk walked toward me with a brisk step. The woman wore a hot-pink puffy coat, a turquoise knitted beret, and a rainbow-striped scarf. Even her boots were an iridescent purple.

"Good evening, dear." She extended a hand toward the door handle.

"Ah, you can't go in." I reached out and touched her arm.

"And why ever not?" She tilted her head.

"There's been an, um, accident inside. The police are on their way. They won't want anyone in there when they arrive."

"Oh? Good heavens. I hope June is all right."

"It wasn't June."

The woman gave me another look. "Aren't you Astra's daughter?"

"I am. Mac Almeida."

She beamed. "My name is Patricia Harbach, but almost everyone calls me Patty. Astra and I have recently become friends. You have her eyes."

"It's good to meet you, Patty." I had Mom's light green eyes despite my hair coming more from my Cape Verde–heritage father and my American Black grandmother. People often wondered if my olive skin came from being Italian or if I had genes from another Mediterranean country. They were often surprised to hear I was more mixed-race than that.

A uniformed August Jenkins jogged down the sidewalk toward us. A young Westham police patrol officer, he was also June's son.

"Mac, I got the call. I was on walking patrol. Am I first on the scene?"

"Yes."

He glanced at Patty. "Were you also inside, ma'am?"

"No, young man. I just walked up. I need to buy a

couple of games for my nephews. What kind of accident was there?"

"I'm not at liberty to say, ma'am." He positioned himself, elbows out, with his back to the door. "You won't be able to shop today, though."

"No? What a pity." She shrugged and gave me an "oh, well" look. "Nice to meet you, Mac. I'll bring my bicycle in when the weather warms up."

"That would be fine. Take care." After she'd gone, I looked at August. "Is your mom around?"

"She took the day off. Unfortunately, I have no idea where she is."

"You can't reach her on her cell?"

"No." He frowned. "You're sure Zia was dead?"

"No doubt at all."

CHAPTER 5

I'd been about to text Tim about what happened a minute later when two police cruisers roared up. Officer Nikki Kimuri jumped out along with three other officers I didn't know. A fire department rescue vehicle followed in short order, with two uniformed EMTs climbing out.

"Is there a back door?" Nikki asked August.

"Yes."

She directed one of the others to guard that entrance.

"I haven't been inside yet," he added.

"I think Detective Johnson is on her way," Nikki said. "Or maybe the chief."

"Not Lincoln?" I asked.

"Sorry Mac, above my pay grade." She pulled on a pair of purple nitrile gloves. "Is the door unlocked?"

"Yes."

I thought Nikki was about the same age as August, but she seemed to outrank him. She directed another officer to guard the door and asked the EMTs to wait.

"Jenkins, come with me. You, too, Mac, if you don't mind."

Inside, I pointed without speaking. Being at a murder scene wasn't my idea of fun things to do on my way home. Seeing a life that had been cut short was deeply sad, especially when it was a young person, but by now witnessing a corpse wasn't unfamiliar and didn't shock me to the point of feeling sick to my stomach.

"Stay back, please," Nikki told me. "Did you touch her?"

"Only her neck, briefly. She was cool to the touch and didn't have a pulse." I stayed near the door.

Nikki and August approached Zia but didn't get any closer than two or three feet. When August stared at her head, every speck of color left his face. Nikki swallowed. She moved closer and confirmed the lack of a pulse.

"Did you know the deceased?" she asked August as she stepped away.

"I met Zia once," he said. "But this is my mom's store, and I'm not involved in its operation. I haven't been able to reach my mom."

"We need Haskins or Johnson here," Nikki said. "Any detective."

"Right. We also need the ME and a crime scene team. The works." He pointed to the toy gun and the blood on the floor.

In the meantime, I glanced around the store. I hadn't taken the time earlier to see if anything was out of place or damaged. Maybe Zia had struggled with her killer. Perhaps the angry person had forced the lock.

Several objects were on the floor in front of the counter near Zia's body, including a donation can for the local feline rescue society and a small straw basket. The two-inch rubber duckies the basket had held now sprawled forlornly on the floor.

I turned to examine the door latch and was startled when the bells on the door jingled as it opened. Nikki whirled, frowning. It was Lincoln Haskins slipping in, not a member of the public. Nikki's expression relaxed along with her shoulders. August let out a sigh of relief.

"Mac, why am I not surprised to see you here?" Lincoln's tone was bemused and gentle, not irate.

"It is what it is," I said.

"Do you mind waiting a bit?" he asked me.

"As long as I can text Tim that I'll be late and briefly why."

"That's fine." He turned to the officers. "Jenkins, Kimuri, what do we have?"

Nikki outlined the situation while I thumbed a message to Tim.

I found murder victim in toy store. I am fine, not hurt or in danger, police here. I'll be late. So sorry. XXOO to you and kids.

He texted back a quick **Love you.**

"Where's June?" Lincoln asked August.

"I can't find her."

"She'll turn up." Lincoln pointed to the door. "Jenkins, first close those blinds on the windows and door, then please tell the EMTs we don't need them. I put in a call for the crime-scene team and the ME. We can't move the body until he's finished."

"Yes, sir." August shut off visibility from the sidewalk, then headed out.

"While we have a couple of minutes, Mac," Lincoln began, "please tell me what you know."

I ran through coming in on my lunch break, meeting Zia Carven, and buying the gifts. "I didn't have time to wait for them to be gift wrapped and said I'd come back at five. But she seemed super nervous and kept looking out the window and at the door as if someone threatening was out there."

"Did you see anyone like that?"

"Possibly." I described the bundled-up person and how they'd pounded on the door after I was outside.

"Man or woman?"

"I honestly couldn't tell."

"Winter is wretched for eyewitness ID outdoors. Go on, please."

"Zia must have locked the door after I left, because the person never got in. They sounded furious about it but stomped away."

"In which direction?"

I pointed. "The opposite way from my shop."

"Anything else?" he asked.

"Those things are usually on the retail counter." I gestured to the objects on the floor. "Zia told me she began working here in January, but that's all I know."

"Thank you," he said. "You can go if you want. I know where to find you."

I wrinkled my nose. "Can I take my gift-wrapped

packages with me? They're paid for and are probably behind the counter."

"Zia wrapped them?"

"She said she was going to."

"Then I'm afraid not. The whole place is a crime scene, and if she handled the paper and the toys, that's evidence too. Are they for your little ones?" His eyes were kind.

"For Ella's upcoming birthday."

"I'll make sure we replace them if they can't be returned to you in time. I promise."

"Thank you, Lincoln. Good luck."

"I appreciate that. You can help by keeping all this under your hat for the time being." He gave me a stern look over the top of his glasses. "Yes, don't even discuss it with your band of sleuths that masquerades as a book group."

"Would I do that?" I raised my eyebrows and gave him an innocent look that didn't fool him for a second.

He rolled his eyes but didn't press the matter.

I made my way out of the no-longer-happy place, that a toy store usually was. Outside wasn't a happy place either, as it turned out.

June Jenkins stood with fists on hips. "What do you mean, I can't go in? It's my store, kid."

It might have been the fresh-faced fellow's first week on the job, but he stood his ground. "No, ma'am, you can't. Those are my instructions. No one allowed entrance except law- enforcement personnel."

She turned to her son. "Aug, tell him to let me in."

"Mother, I can't."

"Why in heaven's name not?"

"You'll have to wait for Sergeant Detective Haskins to tell you that." August lifted his chin.

It had to be hard to stand your professional ground with your own mother.

She blinked, falling silent for a moment. "Lincoln?"

He nodded.

"That means . . ." Her voice trailed off. She turned to stare at the building, at the blank windows, and then back at her son. "Did something happen to Zia?"

CHAPTER 6

"Hey, beautiful," Belle, my African gray parrot greeted me when I opened the door to the house at six, an hour after I'd intended to be home. "Snacks, Mac?"

Ella giggled from her seat at the kitchen table. "Mama Mac, it's so funny. All Belle thinks about is snacks."

I kissed the top of Ella's head. I loved the name she'd come up with for me. Ella, unlike Luca, had real memories of her mommy, and Tim and I both wanted to preserve them. I gave Tim a smooch.

"I'm sorry I'm late. It was unavoidable." I gazed into his big baby blue eyes. "Tell you later."

"I know you will. Now sit." He gestured at a platter of fish and chips. "We have plenty of dinner."

"Papa Tim and I made it ourselves in the oven," Ella announced, using the similarly invented name for her uncle-turned-father.

"It looks yummy, honeypie."

I washed my hands, sat at my place, and let Tim pour me a glass of chilled white wine.

"You still have dinner on your plate." I pointed at Ella's plate.

"Oh! I forgot. I love the tart sauce." She swirled a piece of fish in the little mound of sauce on her plate and took a dainty bite.

"Tartar?" I murmured to Tim.

He smiled and nodded.

"When I'm four, I get to have ketchup with my French fries. Papa Tim said so."

"I love the tart sauce," Belle said in a perfect little-girl imitation. "I love the tart sauce." She gave the wolf whistle she usually saved for when Tim entered a room.

I decided to ignore her for now. "What about Luca?" I gazed at the baby sitting peacefully in his bouncy seat. That kid had more of a Buddha consciousness than any adult I'd ever met. "Did he get a fry?"

"Silly Mama. He's too little, and he doesn't have any teeth yet. But Abo Astra says he can have soft food, like mashed up bananas and baby oatmeal."

Abo was the Cape Verdean word for a grandparent of either gender. My family used it and a few other Kriolu words because of my father's heritage from those islands, although he was born in the States.

"He can." Tim nodded. "Grandma Greta sent us a whole box of infant-feeding supplies, from baby spoons to a food grinder to bibs and silicone bowls. I've been reading up on the current science and best practices of baby-led feeding."

I swallowed a bite of delicious, crispy fish. "I remember being offered plenty of tastes of adult food when I was little. I was never a picky eater and didn't have any food allergies, either." I sipped the wine, which was exactly what the doctor ordered.

"We'll figure it out." Tim pointed at Ella's plate. "Now, young lady, are you going to finish? If you're done, it's time for your bath."

She popped the last three fries into her mouth and drained her glass of oat milk, which we stocked because of her lactose allergy. "Done!"

"Want me to do bath or baby?" I asked. So far, we'd been giving Luca a bath when he needed one, after his sister was asleep. She was way too energetic to share a tub with a little guy who was still figuring out how to sit by himself.

"Finish your dinner while you watch Luca. I'm the kind of monster who can handle a girl in a bath." He growled at Ella and picked her up out of her chair, slinging her over his shoulder as a daddy ogre would do.

Peals of little-girl laughter accompanied them all the way up the stairs. After the day I'd had, a sweet baby was more my cup of tea right now than an energetic preschooler.

By eight, our kiddos were, respectively, clean, teeth-brushed, and read to or changed, bottle-fed, and sung to. Most important, both were sound asleep, as was Belle in her covered cage. Tim and I collapsed onto the couch. He'd poured himself a beer, and I had a mug of peppermint tea.

"Do you love Ella's names for us as much as I do?" he asked, squeezing my hand.

"Yes, for sure. I also know you're more than interested in what happened this afternoon."

"Do tell."

I told. I described my first visit to the toy store and Zia's nerves and the irate person trying to get inside. And then, finally, about finding the poor girl dead across the counter.

"Say again what Zia looked like?"

"She had this white, almost porcelain skin set off by a cloud of dark hair." I pictured her in my mind. "Her eyes were golden brown, almost amber. It's a color I've never seen before. When she was frightened, she looked like a wraith. When she smiled, she was a beauty."

"I think she's been into the bakery a few times."

"Oh?"

"I remember that skin and those eyes. You kind of can't help but notice."

"She was pretty striking."

"How did she die?" he asked.

"Cracked on the head, I guess."

Tim flinched.

"I know," I said. "It's awful. What looked like a toy rifle with blood on it was on the floor, but it had to be plastic. I can't believe it was heavy enough to be the weapon. We'll have to wait for an update from Lincoln."

Tim twisted to face me. "Do you think we're safe here? All of us?"

"I do. Sweetheart, it isn't like the Toy Soldier has riches to steal and Zia's killer is out looking for other deep-pocketed prospects to rip off."

"Which would exclude us, at any rate." He laughed,

but it morphed into a yawn. "I'm sorry, Mac. I need to hit the hay. I'm baking in the morning."

"Go slumber, my sweet. I've got the early shift."

While we often worked as a team while taking care of the little ones, each of us was getting better at managing both alone. In the first weeks of instant parenthood, frazzled was the best description of how I felt after being on my own in the mornings, feeding and getting both Luca and Ella ready for day care and preschool. Tim often looked equally frazzled when I arrived home after he'd had them for a couple of hours on his own.

Now? We weren't exactly old pros, but the job was becoming easier. It helped that the children were mostly delightful. They seemed to adore being with us, and we were grateful we could give them a safe, loving home after Jamie's death.

CHAPTER 7

I finished my cup of post-dinner tea and pulled out my phone to check my texts. A Cozy Capers Book Group thread about Zia's murder was already underway. We were a cozy-mystery book group, but in recent years we'd also worked together to solve real-life mysteries plaguing our lovely coastal town. This time, finding Zia's body made me feel responsible for finding her killer.

I read throughs the messages. Norland Gifford had started the discussion. As the retired chief of the West-ham police, he had his ear closer to the local news than most. He'd noted that a Toy Soldier employee had been found dead in the store, it was a suspected homicide, and asked if anybody knew anything more.

Gin Malloy, owner of Salty Taffy's candy store, said she'd noticed the police presence but hadn't known what it was about. Gin and I had been seven a.m. walking buddies before the children came along, but now I rarely had a morning free to stride and talk with her.

Flo Wolanski, director of the Westham Public Library, also had crack search skills and mentioned that she thought she'd seen me walk away from the shop but wasn't sure. Tulia Peters, owner of the Lobstah Shack, asked if anyone knew where I was.

I had to chime in. Lincoln had asked me not to discuss the case, but these friends already knew about it. Between us, we'd been helpful to the authorities during previous homicide investigations. And I hadn't actually promised to keep the details to myself.

I was the one who found Zia dead. Maybe whacked with toy rifle or something heavier? She seemed scared earlier in the day.

Gin wrote back first.

Where was June?

I replied.

Not there. Aug said she took the day off and he couldn't reach her, then she showed up at front door. Lincoln on the case, told me not to share details with y'all. Too bad, LOL.

Flo added a comment.

Ha! As if.

Zane King chimed in, which made me smile. He and his husband were the fathers of infant twins, and Zane had been on a break from the group since the babies were born the previous September. He'd told us a couple of weeks ago that he was eager to rejoin. Even parents of much-wanted babies need a break away from the house for adult conversation now and then.

Am loving PRUNING THE DEAD. Shd we meet tomorrow noon to discuss case and maybe book?

The first Garden Squad mystery by Julia Henry was the group's current cozy and was more or less behind my presence in the Toy Soldier. Ella had seen me reading it and asked what the book was called. Then, being in the question-everything phase of childhood, she asked what a garden squad was. That prompted our chatting about gardening in the spring, and my idea to give her garden tools for her birthday.

I wrote back.

I can do that. Brown bag it at my shop or elsewhere?

Zane replied.

Liquor store back room is more private. I'll be working tomorrow. 12:30?

Cape King Liquor and Distillery was across Main Street from Mac's Bikes. He was right. We had nowhere in my shop to meet away from customers and barely room to sit.

I responded I would be there. Gin and Norland agreed. Tulia said winter business was so slow, she would close the Lobstah Shack for an hour. Flo added a message.

Have noon meeting. Will either postpone or make it snappy.

Good. Texting was fine for quick catching up, but nothing beat meeting in person. These days, both Zane and I had family commitments in the evenings—at least until seven or eight. A lunchtime check-in sounded perfect.

Our newest member, Ilsa Kimuri, texted.

I'll be there but Nikki is on case, so can't get too involved.

As Officer Nikki's mother, she had to maintain a prudent distance. She was also widower Norland's new lady friend since late fall, which was his first romance since his wife passed away four or five years ago.

The thread petered out after we agreed to meet the next day.

I wasn't quite ready for bed. I headed into the kitchen for a second glass of wine and an oatmeal-chocolate chip cookie bar. When I saw the state the kitchen was in, I focused on cleaning up first. In our family, the person who cooks doesn't have to clean up afterward. Since I didn't cook, to speak of, I could both eat well and satisfy my need to leave everything in order. I itched when things weren't put away and tidy, which led some to label me a neat freak bordering on obsessive compulsive. Against comments like that, I donned my imaginary Teflon cloak and wore it with pride.

I finally settled in at the table with my bedtime

snack. The book of the week beckoned, a story featuring a retired widow and her justice-minded friends. They not only did guerrilla gardening at night to benefit the town and needy residents, they also—like the Cozy Capers—had a knack for solving murders in their fictional coastal town. Could I be a senior like that in real life? My grandmother nearly was.

But instead of reading, I found my thoughts drawn to the mysterious Zia Carven. Maybe I could learn more about her. Where had she come from? Why pick a toy store to work in? Who would want her dead? My so-called compulsion to sort everything out and put all in its place had come in handy more than once in these amateur investigations.

I sipped wine, nibbled dessert, and put a search engine to work. Zia's first name was rare, at least among English speakers, but her surname was much more common. Was Zia a shortening of a longer moniker? *Huh.* One source said the name meant "radiant" in Hebrew, which fit the Zia I'd met—at least when she wasn't terrified.

Another asserted the origin was Arabic, with a similar meaning. That made sense. The two Middle Eastern languages had a common parent, despite their cultures' century-long conflicts. I couldn't see that Zia was short for anything but Ziya, which was nothing more than an alternate spelling.

Interestingly, I didn't get a single search result for Zia Carven on the internet, including the few social media sites I frequented. I checked directories for Westham,

Falmouth, Bourne, and Hyannis. The few residents with that last name were either too old, too young, or seemed unlikely to have a young relative in Westham. I gave up trying. Surely June knew where her employee came from.

What else could I discover at this early stage in the investigation? I poked around on Cape Cod news sites, but all I found were the briefest of mentions that a female had died under suspicious circumstances. Her identity was being withheld pending notification of family, yadda, yadda, yadda.

I came across video footage of the storefront, likely sold to a local news affiliate by a police chaser. Unfortunately, I was in the video. It was the moment on the sidewalk when June had appeared, and I was trying to get home. *Ugh*. At least I wasn't identified and already had my hood up against the chill of the evening.

I let out a big yawn. Who Zia was and why someone killed her wasn't going to get solved tonight—not by me and likely not by Lincoln and his team. I needed to get some sleep. Those kiddos would be up by seven tomorrow morning at the very latest.

But should I feel more distraught by Zia's death? My heart ached for how she must have felt when the attack came. She'd already begged Yvonne for something. Zia had been so frightened of someone else she locked the door to the shop. She didn't deserve to die at the hands of another. Nobody did.

I hadn't known Zia. I hadn't interacted with her before

the brief encounter on my shopping trip. And now, as a mom, I wasn't as eager to plunge into sleuthing as I had been before Ella and Luca doubled the size of our nuclear family.

Still, the itch to get at the truth remained. But it would be there tomorrow. I cleaned my glass and cookie plate and headed to bed.

CHAPTER 8

By eight forty-five the next morning, I'd succeeded in dropping off both children at their respective schools. I'd also gotten myself to work on time without missing any part of dressing or personal hygiene for any of the three of us, although my socks didn't match and neither did Ella's. One small parental victory at a time.

I busied myself preparing the bike shop to open. The weather had turned sunny and cold, the kind of winter I preferred over damp and messy. I was reaching up to slide the Open flagpole into its holder when my mother strode toward me on the walkway. Once the flag was securely in, I turned and hugged her.

"Hey, Mom."

"How are you, sweetie?" Astra pushed back but held me by the shoulders and gazed slightly up into my face. "I heard about your ordeal yesterday."

"I'm fine. It wasn't exactly an ordeal, but come inside, okay? I need to open in a few minutes."

She followed me in and unzipped her coat but kept

it on. "You did find a murdered person yesterday, didn't you?"

"I did, and it's super sad that someone felt like they had to do that. But, as you know, she wasn't the first homicide victim I've encountered. I'd only met her for the first time a few hours earlier."

"I sincerely hope she was the last," she said.

"You and me both. Hang on a second, okay? I'm going to get the cash drawer from the safe."

"Want me to front a few bikes for display?" she asked.

"Please." I smiled at her using "front," a noun-turned-verb normally employed only by retailers and marketing people.

When I came back, she'd selected a shiny red children's tricycle, a silver tandem, and a sturdy, yellow commuter bike with a basket.

"Nice choices." I surveyed the inventory and pointed to a high-end road bike. "Can you get that All-City Zig Zag, too?" In warmer months I displayed several bikes outside, but not during this time of year. I fired up the cash register app, then headed into the mini-kitchen to brew a pot of coffee.

"I wanted to talk with you about Zia Carven," Mom said when I rejoined her. "May she rest in peace."

"I saw you talking with her in Our Neighbor's Table on Monday. Did you know her very well?" This could be useful. As it now nine o'clock on the dot, I unlocked the front door.

Mom blinked. "Let me get us both coffee first." She headed back to the kitchen area.

I said good morning to Orlean when she came in, lunch bag in hand. She nodded and continued on her way. A moment later she offered way more words than I normally got as she greeted my mother. So be it. Mom returned holding two brimming mugs dosed with cream.

"Thanks. Have a seat." I pointed my chin at the stool next to mine. "Mmm. All I managed this morning was one small cup and a granola bar."

"Getting two kids out the door every morning and taking care of yourself as well is a lot to manage." She sipped from her mug.

"You should know."

"Yes. I'm not sure I did that well at the taking care of myself part. I was not well-suited to the job of minister's wife, and I held a great deal of anxiety and resentment until I decided to make a few changes."

"Like changing your name and becoming a professional astrologer with an office?" Her ditching the name Edna in favor of Astra and letting the church take over its own domestic duties had happened while I was working in Boston and not living at home. Pa—my father—had given her his blessing.

"Exactly."

"I didn't know you were anxious and resented the job, Mom. I knew about the changes you made, but I don't think we've ever really talked about how you felt before that." I'd supposed her actions were her version of a midlife crisis.

She gave a rueful smile. "I loved being at home with you and your brother when you were young, honey, and the church needed someone to do the other work. Once you both were out on your own, my feelings about it changed." She cleared her throat. "Now then, before you become swamped with customers, let me tell you about Zia."

"Please." I kept sipping my coffee while it was hot. It had never tasted so good.

"As Zia is now deceased, I think I'm no longer violating her privacy to tell you she was a frequent shopper at the free food market."

"Okay." I loved that Our Neighbor's Table was a no-questions-asked food pantry. Shoppers needed to register, but nobody had to prove their income was below a certain level. If someone felt they needed help with food, they got it.

"I met Zia there a number of times," Astra went on, "and learned she was living in a run-down rooming house in Bourne. I offered to help her find better lodgings nearby, but she pushed back my every attempt."

That must have been the disagreement I'd witnessed.

"Mackenzie, I confess I didn't understand it."

"Why do you think she did?"

"There was something guarded about her, as if she needed to keep her identity and thoughts completely locked up. She could be anonymous in her living situation, and she apparently liked it that way. I asked her in several ways about family but never learned a thing." She quirked an eyebrow. "On the other hand, she was a double Scorpio. Wanting secrecy comes with the territory for that sun sign, plus she had lots of Pisces influence, which only magnified the effect."

"I wonder if her name was made up," I said. "Last

night I tried to search for her on the internet and came up empty."

"I never thought of that. Zia is certainly an unusual first name."

"Let's hope the police have better luck, and that June knows something about Zia's past. Have you told Lincoln what you know?"

Mom shook her head. "I hadn't thought about it."

"Can you tell him? I think he'd be interested."

"I will," she said.

The door opened and a handful of cyclists walked in.

"Looks like time's up." Mom drained her coffee and stood. "Thanks, dear. Your father is getting Ella after preschool today."

"Perfect. Tim will pick her up at five or before, as usual. Love you." I also finished my drink and turned toward the customers. "How can I help you folks?"

CHAPTER 9

We had a busy first hour. Renters and shoppers kept me on my toes until ten o'clock, when Delia's shift began. She arrived on time. That she was accompanied by Lincoln didn't surprise me in the least. I figured I would be speaking with him sometime today. She headed back to greet Orlean and hang up her coat.

I finished ringing up the last customer and turned to the detective. "How's it going?"

"We didn't really have a chance to talk at length yesterday, Mac." He waited until the door shut behind the customer. "May I have a minute of your time?"

"Sure, as long as Delia's willing. If we get busy, though—"

"I know the drill. Your customers come first."

"Thanks," I said. "Let's go over by the rental area. It'll be quieter."

He leaned against the wall and slid his hands into his pockets. "If you will, please go over your interactions with Zia Carven in the store. When she was alive, I mean."

"Sure." I repeated what had gone down. "I tried to figure out who the angry person was or at least get a physical description, but I wasn't able to."

"Don't worry about it. I understand you were there when June Jenkins showed up."

"Yes. I'd stepped outside after you told me I could go home. June was super mad they wouldn't let her into her own shop. That young officer really stood his ground, as did August. It couldn't have been easy telling his own mother she couldn't go inside."

"Good to know," he said. "Those were my instructions. We try to train them well."

"I assume you finally let her in?"

"Actually, no. I went out and instructed her to go home."

"Wow."

"Her store is a crime scene." He flipped open his hands. "We still had a homicide victim in there. She hadn't been at the shop all day, so she already had her handbag and phone and didn't need any personal items from inside. We'll allow her back in when the time is right."

"I was trying to find information online on Zia and her background last night. My search was a total fail. Does June know about Zia's family or where she's been?"

"We are still in the process of acquiring that information. Is there anything else you might have learned, Mac?"

I remembered my conversation from earlier. "My mother knew Zia from the free food market. Mom told me she was trying to help Zia get into a better housing situation, but that she was resistant, as if she didn't want anyone to know her personal details, her past. That was my mom's impression, anyway."

"Thanks. I'll check in with Astra. Is that it?"

"Afraid so," I said. "I'll let you know if I hear more."

"That's all I can ask. Thank you, Mac. I'll let you get back to work."

"Again, good luck." I headed for the counter.

Lincoln made his way to the door, pausing to blow a kiss to Delia. Before he could leave, June stormed in with narrowed eyes and her lips drawn into a furrowed scowl.

"I thought I saw you come in here, Lincoln Haskins," she said. "You've got a nerve, keeping me out of my own private property."

The detective squared his shoulders and let out a breath. "Hello, June. How are you today?"

"Terrible." She jammed her fists on her hips. "I have a business I can't run. How do you think I am?"

"You'll have access as soon as we're done with the shop. You wouldn't want your fine law-enforcement officers not to be able to do their jobs, would you?"

June didn't answer as she turned toward the door. "Never should have hired that slut," she muttered.

Lincoln took a quick step toward her and pressed his palm against the door. "I heard that. Care to elaborate?"

"No."

"It sounds to me as though you have additional information you neglected to share with us yesterday. I'd like to speak with you about it, but let's adjourn to the police station. I don't want to disrupt Mac's business."

"Do I have to?" June folded her arms over her chest.

"Strictly speaking, no." His voice was gentle, as always, but it held an iron resolve. "However, it would be in your best interest to cooperate."

She raised her chin. "All right. If it'll get me back in business sooner, I'll do it." She preceded Lincoln out the door.

Delia and I exchanged a look.

"Yikes," I said. "That didn't sound good for June."

"Not at all." She gazed at the door. "I wonder . . ."

"What?"

"Huh? Oh, nothing. I was thinking out loud." She headed over to the shelves of shirts and began refolding garments that didn't need it.

"Mac, got a minute?" Orlean called.

I made my way back to the repair area. "What's up?"

"Heard that little kerfuffle with June Jenkins and Lincoln just now."

"We all did. I'm grateful we didn't have any customers in the shop to hear it."

"That Carven girl, the murder victim?" Orlean didn't look up from the derailleur she was cleaning.

"You know about that?"

"Yup. I've heard of the place where she was living, poor thing. Sketchy area. Wondered if it was connected with her death."

I stared at her. "Willing to share that with Lincoln?"

"Don't see why not."

"Thank you, Orlean. I'll let him know."

She kept on cleaning and not making eye contact. I didn't need more. What she'd told me was enough.

CHAPTER 10

The taking-care-of-myself part of my conversation with my mother earlier hit me at a quarter to noon. Yes, I'd gotten the kids and me fed and dressed and to our destinations on time this morning, but I had not made myself lunch. I knew one way to fix that problem: I shot off a text to Tulia.

Bring a fishcake sandwich for me to the meeting, pretty please?

She responded with nothing more than a thumbs up, which was all I needed.

"I have to be across the street for a meeting at twelve thirty," I called to Orlean, knowing Delia could hear. "Who wants to take lunch first?"

"You go, Orlean," Delia said. "I don't need to take a lunch break. I had a big breakfast, and I'll grab a bite at home at two thirty."

"Thanks," I murmured to her. I felt bad I hadn't told them earlier about my meeting.

After Orlean left carrying her cloth lunch bag, I remembered to text Lincoln about what she'd said.

I added that she was willing to speak with him about Zia's living situation. As much as Orlean was normally short on words, she was long on heart and passionate about justice.

Orlean was back in plenty of time, and we weren't overrun with customers. I grabbed my coat and bag and headed to Zane's shop across the road at half past noon with a clear conscience. I hadn't been outside since I opened Mac's Bikes that morning. The bright sunlight startled me, as did the sharply warmer temperature that felt like spring.

Go figure. This was New England in all its fickle glory, but nobody who'd lived here for more than a year knew better than to get their hopes up. You could kiss Spring's rosy cheek one minute and an hour later be slapped in the face by the return of Winter's cold hand.

"We're back here," Zane called from the open door to the storeroom.

I loved having a well-stocked wine and liquor store mere strides from my shop. Zane being an expert adviser on vintages and flavors was the maraschino cherry on the top, and his homemade art quilts on the walls added to the welcoming air.

I sank onto a chair in the circle of Cozy Capers and glanced around, giving a little wave to Ilsa, who sat next to Norland. He'd started wearing nicer shirts and getting more frequent haircuts ever since he and Ilsa had begun dating in the fall.

"Your lunch, ma'am?" Tulia handed me a paper-wrapped packet and a couple of paper napkins. Her weathered hands and ruddy cheeks attested to her lobstering in the past, although these days she produced scrumptious dishes from seafood rather than catching it.

"My stomach and I thank you." In turn, I passed her a twenty-dollar bill. "If that's too much, keep it for your counter people." Knowing Tulia, she'd pass the tip along in the form of free meals to certain hungry residents of our mostly affluent town. I unwrapped the sandwich and took a big first bite.

"Is everybody here?" Zane's bow tie today was pink with green shamrocks, and green socks peeked out from under his skinny jeans. He was always a natty dresser, even at work, and today seemed to be getting a head start on St. Patrick's Day.

"Hmm, not Flo." Gin resecured her thick, reddish-brown hair in a hair elastic. "She did say she had a meeting and might be late."

I ate more of the sandwich while I was able to, plus a few bites of pickle. The first taste had prodded my stomach into remembering how hungry it was. The fish cake was perfectly crispy, the lemony mayo on the toasted bun a nice touch, and the pickle spear was sour and a little spicy, exactly how I liked it.

"Who had a meeting?" Flo strode in, brandishing her signature yellow legal pad. "Let's get this underway." Moss wouldn't grow on that girl, as my grandmother Reba was known to say. Flo ran a hand through her spiky white hair, then positioned her pen above the pad. "Mac, want to start from the beginning?"

Did I want to repeat the story of discovering Zia deader than, well, dead? I did not, but I swallowed and nodded. I ran through the basic facts of my lunchtime visit to the Toy Soldier and then finding Zia's body after work.

"August Jenkins was the first officer to respond after I called it in," I added, "and he wasn't able to get hold of June. She finally showed up and was furious Lincoln wouldn't let her into the store."

Tulia nodded slowly.

"It seems like we need to know the following." I ticked them off on my fingers. "Where did June find Zia to hire her, and where was Zia before here? Who was Zia afraid of? Who was the angry person she didn't let in? Who did she hang out with when she wasn't at work? And, finally, who killed that lovely, frightened young woman?" We also needed to find out the reason June called Zia a slut earlier, but I would bring that up later.

Flo was writing as fast as she could. She looked up. "Well, the last point is the most important one. But if we know anything by now, it's that the killer can be anybody, from the most obvious to the meekest and least suspected person who had only a slight connection to the victim."

"True," Norland said.

"It might be hard to get information about Zia," I said. "My mom came in this morning and said she'd been trying to help Zia get better housing, but she resisted. Apparently double Scorpios, according to Mom, like to keep things secret, which might be why I couldn't find a speck online about a Zia Carven."

"I can action-item that one," Flo said.

"I can try as well," Norland offered.

"We should see if any surrounding shops have sidewalk cameras," Gin said. "Maybe they caught the face of the angry person."

"The police are probably looking into that right now," Zane said.

"Sure, but I can ask a few innocent questions, too." Gin grinned. "I'll pretend I'm in the market for a security cam and inquire if they like the model they have."

Flo jotted down that item.

"My mom knows where Zia lived," I began. "She said it was a run-down rooming house in Bourne. Orlean says the area is sketchy. I can get the address and ask a few questions there."

"Have you lost your mind, Mac?" Gin shook her head. "What if her killer also lived there? Our pact with Lincoln is that we stay out of danger, and that includes avoiding in-person investigating when there's a risk of tangling with a murderer."

"True." I sighed. "I am somewhat more frazzled than I used to be. I should have thought of that."

Zane held up a finger. "Also a parent of two. I totally get it."

"I could go and say I'm looking for a room, or that my niece needs a place to stay?" I glanced at the group.

"If you head over there, you're taking one of us," Gin insisted.

"I'll go with you, Mac," Ilsa said. "As I said in my

message, I can't get too close to any of this because of Nikki's involvement, but asking a few questions—innocent ones, like Gin said—can't hurt." She smiled.

"It's a deal." I smiled back.

"So noted." Flo wrote on her legal pad.

Norland squeezed Ilsa's hand. "Tulia, you and June both live in Mashpee. Do you think you can find out where she was yesterday?"

Mashpee was a nearby inland Cape town where many members of the Wampanoag tribe lived, including June and Tulia. Lincoln was also a member but lived in Falmouth, which was also not far.

"I can ask around."

"Action item for Tulia," Flo said.

"She does have a bit of a temper on her, that June," Tulia offered.

"Oh?" I asked.

"I've seen her blow up at people before about really small things." She held up her palm. "I'm not saying she killed the poor girl, mind you. But the discontent June holds inside flares up now and again, at no fault of whoever she's aiming it at."

"I heard her say something shocking this morning," I said. "Lincoln was in my shop a couple of hours ago. June stormed in, saying she'd seen him come in and berating him for not letting her back into her store. Being Lincoln, he kept his cool. But as June turned away, she muttered something about Zia being a slut."

"Whoa," Gin said.

"Lemme guess," Flo said. "Lincoln was all over that like a cheap suit."

"He was." I pointed down the street. "He convinced her to accompany him to the station to have a little chat about what she'd said and why."

"I daresay she wasn't happy about it," Norland began. "But she went, am I right?"

"Yes," I said. "She went."

Lincoln was an expert at persuading people to talk. I knew that for a fact.

The group disbanded a few minutes later, each back to our workplaces with our respective assignments. Various combinations of us had done this for, what, seven homicides to date? We weren't the police, but we'd become good at what we did as amateurs.

CHAPTER 11

I was back at work well before Delia had to leave for her pub job.

"Were you meeting with your detecting club?" she asked after I hurried in.

"I guess you could call it that. I confess we didn't even mention the book of the week."

"You must have been talking about Zia's murder."

"We were," I said. "You'll let me know if you hear anything about it at the Rusty Anchor, won't you?"

"I'll try. It's a little tricky, being involved with Lincoln. If he tells me anything about the case in confidence, that's where it stays. But if I happen to overhear a tidbit at the bar, I'll pass it along to you."

"Sound like a plan. I appreciate that."

She pointed to my cheek. "Looks like you had a yummy lunch, but you might want to wipe off that smear of mayonnaise."

I smiled and shook my head. "Can't take me anywhere. Be right back." I headed for the restroom.

When I returned, personal hygiene accomplished,

Delia was speaking with a customer. I took a second look. The woman wore a scarf in rainbow stripes around her neck.

"Patty?" I asked.

"Hey, Mac." Patty smiled. She wasn't wearing the beret of the day before, and her white hair skimmed her shoulders. "Today's weather reminded me that cycling weather isn't that far off. I decided to bring my bike in so it's ready for spring. I thought it would be better now than later in the season, when you'll probably be swamped."

"That's a wise plan."

Two more customers pushed through the door.

"I'll help them," Delia said.

I gave her a thumbs up. "What's the bike needing?" I asked Patty.

"Probably everything. Air, lubrication, adjusting? I had surgery last summer and didn't ride it at all. It's been at least a year and a half since it got any use."

"I'll have my mechanic take a look and text you an estimate. Let me get your information." I pulled out a repair slip and had her fill in her name, address, and phone. I scanned it when she slid it back across the counter, and a little bell rang in my head. "You live in Bourne?"

"I do. It's funny, I grew up on a farm in Southern California, but I've been here so long I feel like a New Englander now. Bourne is a lovely place to land."

"Do you know of any rooming houses in your town?

A young person I know needs an inexpensive place to live."

She wrinkled her nose. "I do, but I wouldn't recommend North Lodging to anyone. It has a reputation of being worse than seedy. The town's been trying to close it down for a while."

"Ah, okay. Thanks. I'll make sure she looks elsewhere." I took note of the name, though.

"Do, especially for a young woman. I met a girl who lives there, and she alluded to having a couple of bad experiences."

Could the girl have been Zia?

Patty glanced around and leaned one elbow on the counter, lowering her voice. "I heard someone was killed in that toy store where I met you yesterday."

"Yes. It's terrible news."

"Do you know who it was?"

At that moment Delia saved me from answering. She approached the counter with her two customers. The woman carried a child-sized helmet and the man one of our pedal-less beginner bikes.

"I'll let you get back to work," Patty said.

"Thanks. If you'll leave the bike by the side door," I told her, "we'll store it safely until Orlean can get to it. We'll be in touch."

More customers came in. Delia left at two thirty. I worked steadily by myself, sometimes frantically, answering questions, ringing up sales, and booking a few rentals for the weekend.

During a lull at about four o'clock, I considered my

tentative agreement to check out the rooming house with Ilsa. That was never going to work. It would be stupid to go at night, especially if the place was sketchy. My weekday mornings were booked. And my weekends were the only chance Tim and I had to relax with the kids. Both my mom and Orlean knew about the rooming house beyond what I'd learned from Patty.

I thumbed open the group thread about Zia. I needed to let Ilsa, and everyone else, know I was backing out of that action item.

I shdnt have volunteered to check out rooming house, don't have time. Customer frm Bourne says it's called North Lodging and is seedy. Orlean says sketchy. Town trying to close it. If anyone goes, be careful. Or let police do it.

I felt better having done that. My time used to be my own, more or less. Now I had serious and joyful family obligations, and no way was I reneging on those to track down a killer.

CHAPTER 12

At about four thirty an incoming text dinged on my phone at the same time as a family of seven arrived. The new message was probably from someone in the group. It could wait.

The mom, who approached the counter, said they were there to pick up their rental bikes. It took until nearly five o'clock to get the family all set with the right sizes of bikes and helmets. The kids looked to be of either elementary or middle-school ages, and I kind of wondered why they wouldn't be in school for the next week.

The mother signed the contract while the dad corralled children and bikes and got everybody out the door.

"Thanks." The woman smiled. "Fingers crossed for good weather."

"Absolutely." I smiled back.

"My husband homeschools the kids, and we have big plans to visit historical sites, marine museums, and more for the week."

"Perfect. Safe riding to you all." Homeschooling explained their rental during a non-vacation week. Making sure your kids learned what they needed to would have to be that parent's full-time job, especially with five children. The mother must earn a lot to support a family that size on one income these days.

After the door closed, I headed back to Orlean's area. She was already cleaning up and tidying her tools.

"We've had a full day," I said.

"Yep."

"Let's head out, yeah?"

She planted her feet and stared at me. "Heard you talking with that woman about the roomin' house. Need me to ask a couple few questions over there?"

"About Zia?"

Orlean bobbed her head.

"It would be interesting to find out who her friends were," I said. "If she had visitors, who they were. If she tangled with anyone, what it was about. All of that. But Orlean, I don't want to put you in danger. The police can do that kind of in-person poking around."

"Seriously, Mac?" she scoffed. "You think anybody's going to talk to the likes of them? Folks who live in places like North Lodgin' don't care for the cops. Not at all. They'll button up quicker than a novice at the convent. Plus, WPD and the staties, they're all short on money. Officers are stretched too thin."

"I'm sure you're right," I said. "Well, as long as you stay safe, Orlean. Thank you."

She turned back to her end-of-day routine. I did, too.

After she left, I finally got to that text. Maybe Tim had been trying to reach me. But it wasn't from him or the book group. Instead, Delia had sent a message.

Police at Anchor, want to talk to Yvonne, might suspect she's a rel of Zia.

Wait, what? Yvonne was the manager and chef at the Rusty Anchor Pub. She was a veteran and lived with her girlfriend, and I didn't think Yvonne had any children. Zia might be a niece or a much-younger cousin.

I tapped a reply.

WPD still there?

I waited, but it was half an hour since Delia had written, and she didn't reply. Just as well. I didn't need a detour on my way home to my family, especially not one that involved the police and thoughts of homicide.

While I had my phone out I texted my mother that Lincoln wanted to speak with her. At another nonresponse, I stashed the device. I finished my closing routine and had the door locked by ten after five. I shot Tim a text that I was on my way and set foot on the sidewalk, hustling since the gloaming was already upon us.

Delia's message bugged me. Why would the police be talking to Yvonne? They clearly knew something I didn't.

They could simply be trying to find Zia's next of kin and had received a tip that Yvonne was part of the victim's extended family. They had—or would have at some point—DNA evidence from poor, dead Zia, and they might have some left over from when Yvonne was briefly suspected of murder last spring. That would be enough to show the two were related. The police never wanted to release a victim's name before the family had been identified. The press must be breathing down their necks to learn the ID so they could broadcast it. As it was often said, names made news.

Delia had mentioned that Zia had been into the pub and sat at the bar several times. I didn't think she'd said if the young woman had been there alone or with company. Surely the authorities weren't looking at the chef as a person of interest in the homicide, but they weren't the only ones wondering who Zia knew outside her work life and where she came from.

As I approached the pub, the lights pushed out into the falling darkness, and I was tantalized by the smell of fried food almost as much as I wanted more information about Yvonne and how shc might be connected to Zia.

Did I go inside? Nope. I had a date with my three most-favorite people at home, and I was keeping it, come Hades or high water.

That didn't stop me from thinking as I continued home. My steps dragged when I considered an alternate option about Yvonne and Zia's connection. What if Yvonne had become pregnant with a man about twenty-some years ago, carried the pregnancy to term, and given the child up for adoption? Yes, she was living as a lesbian now, but I'd known more than one woman who'd been married and borne several children before deciding to come out of the closet and live as her true self.

One possible reason Zia had come to town could be that she'd been adopted and was searching for her biological mother. If it was Yvonne, would she want a relationship with the person her relinquished baby had become? Yvonne's partner might or might not be happy about that.

CHAPTER 13

Luca and I made it to his day care, the Nest, by eight thirty the next morning. The weather remained clear, cold, and sunny. He wasn't yet too heavy to carry in the soft pack, but I opted for the stroller, which made it a lot easier to carry his formula and diapers along with my bag and Ella's. We first dropped Ella off at the parsonage, where one of my parents would deliver her to preschool at nine.

I'd never thought about how much gear children use on a daily basis. Even if you kept things simple, they still needed lunch and snacks or bottles, plus a change of clothes or two and a way to transport them, not to mention weather-appropriate outerwear. For both kids, every single thing needed to be labeled with their name.

I hoisted the baby out of the stroller and kissed his sweet nose, then carried him inside until I reached the baby gate at the inner door. Beyond that was strictly no shoes, and I needed to get to work. Evan Selyuk, one of the lead teachers in the baby class, held out his arms.

"Good morning, Luca," he said. "And good morning, Mac."

I slipped off Luca's coat and tucked his warm hat in one of the sleeves before handing him over. My son—another phrase I was still getting used to—tried to grab at Evan's gold hoop earring, but the teacher redirected him.

"Bye, sweet honeypie." I leaned over the gate and kissed him on the forehead, inhaling his baby smell. "Have a good time, and I'll see you tonight."

"We're going to have fun with our friends, little buddy, aren't we?" Evan asked.

"Everything's in his bag." I handed it to the teacher. "Where's Kim?" The place usually had two teachers on duty.

"They had an early doctor appointment. They'll be in by nine." Evan laid Luca on the rug under a mobile. He straightened and faced me. "Can I ask you something, Mac?"

"Ask away. We're not late on payments or anything, are we?" Tim's dad was generously contributing half the amount of the day care and preschool tuitions, which were steep.

"No, of course not." He switched to a super-low tone. "But I heard you were the person who found Zia. She was a good friend, and I know you've investigated such things before. Will you try your hardest to find the person who"—he gazed around at the half-dozen babies and crawlers in the room—"who did that horrible thing to her?"

That thing being murder. I blinked at his request and

considered it. I took a deep breath and let it out. "You have my phone number, right?"

"You and all the parents are on speed dial, so to speak."

"Evan, you must know I have no training and am not a professional in the field."

He nodded, looking somber.

"Okay," I said. "Text me how you knew her and everything you know. We'll make a time to talk, but I can't promise anything."

A one-year-old began crawling at high speed toward Luca. Another child stuck her finger up her little friend's nose, which caused the child to wail.

"I know. Thank you." In two quick moves, Evan scooped up the crawler and extricated the victim of the nasal incursion. "I'll be in touch. And thanks."

I hung the tiny coat on Luca's labeled hook in the entryway. I collapsed the stroller and stashed it in a corner of the front hall for Tim when he picked up the baby at the end of the day. The one time I'd left the stroller outside, rain had poured down and soaked it.

I made my way slowly the few blocks to Mac's Bikes. Evan was friends with Zia. Good friends, he'd said. Maybe he also lived in the rooming house or had known her before she started working at the Toy Soldier. Either way, I looked forward to whatever information he could offer.

CHAPTER 14

I glanced up at ten after nine and smiled to see a diminutive figure make her way into the bike shop from outside. I stepped around the counter and held my arms out to my grandmother, Reba Almeida. She always said she was five feet tall only when she wore shoes and stood up straight. I suspected she'd been shrinking in recent years, which wasn't unusual for an eighty-three-year-old. She toted her usual oversized shoulder bag and wore her signature rainbow-striped slouchy beret. She also carried a white paper bag that looked suspiciously—in a good way—like one from Tim's bakery.

"Abo Ree, good morning."

"And to you, darling." She set the white bag on the counter and lowered her shoulder bag to the floor. "I brought apple turnovers for the three of us." She tore open the bag to serve as a placemat and used a napkin to select one of the pastries. "I'll take this to Orlean."

Their murmured conversation lasted longer than

I expected, but eventually Reba returned and climbed onto the other stool next to me.

"Thank you." I smiled and bit into a pastry. I never, ever said no to one of Tim's creations.

"Quiet in here, isn't it?"

"Mmm." I swallowed the heavenly bite. "It's winter. No surprise."

"You might get a bit of business soon." She lifted her eyebrows.

"Why, is the president paying a visit to Westham?" I batted away the thought. "Never mind, that was the two previous presidents who rode bikes on their vacations."

"No, but a senator is in town with an entourage, and my grapevine whispered that he's a big fan of renting a bicycle wherever he goes."

"Not a Massachusetts senator, though." I wouldn't put a biking habit past either of our two senators, but I'd never seen pictures of them cycling in the news.

"No. It's Ross Kimball from our fair neighboring state. He apparently came here to campaign against the new marine wind power project."

"I'm happy to help him out with rentals, but I wish he didn't oppose the wind project," I said. "From what I've read, the turbines would be far enough out in the bay that we wouldn't be able to see them. Wind is free and clean power, right?"

"Who knows whose pocket Kimball is in? The oil and coal industry's, most likely. Now tell me what's happening in the case." Reba's eyes were bright, as always during a homicide investigation. "I know you and the group are on it."

I smiled fondly at her. "Nobody should be that excited about a murder, Abo Reba."

"You know I'm not excited about the poor girl's death. But doing detective work, following down clues, and keeping your ear to the ground? You can't beat it."

I finished my turnover instead of answering. Talking about staying out of danger was pointless. She'd nearly gotten herself in trouble with a murderer last year when she thought she was helping. We would all be devastated if something bad happened to Reba, me most of all. Maybe I could persuade her to stick to what she did best: gossip.

"I'll bet you've heard things about Zia Carven that I haven't," I began. "And if not, it would be super helpful if you'd keep your ear to the ground, as you put it."

She nodded. "Let's see . . . do I know anything to date?" She drummed her fingers on the counter. "Your mother was trying to assist the poor thing, to no avail. The girl shopped at the free food market. I guess she must have been short on funds. I saw her at the pub drinking with a young man a few times."

That was new intel. "What did he look like?" I didn't ask why Reba herself had been in the Rusty Anchor. She had lots of friends, old and young, and wasn't beyond enjoying a cocktail or a hot toddy.

"Thirty-ish, I'd say, although the older I get, the harder it is to tell the age of young folks. They all look twelve to me, including if they're forty and a medical doctor. At any rate, the fellow sported a hoop earring and pants that could have been a size larger, if you know what I mean."

"That sounds like Evan. He's Luca's day care teacher, and he told me this morning he and Zia were good friends. Did you talk to them at all at the pub?"

"No, sweetheart, I had no need to." She popped in the last bite of her pastry. "Mmm, hmm. That man of yours can bake like nobody's business."

Three middle-aged Black women in bike shoes and jackets clomped in smelling of fresh air. One was wiry, one muscular, and one full-figured. With pink cheeks from the cold and windswept hair, all three looked as athletic as the larger group who'd been in on Tuesday.

"I'll be running along." Reba hopped down from her stool. "Keep an eye on Astra, will you? I think something's going on there."

"What?" I frowned.

She gave a little wave. "Mornin', sisters," she said to the women, and hurried she out without explaining. What in the world did she mean, keep an eye on my mom? *Sheesh.*

I hit reset and smiled at my customers. "Good morning and welcome to Mac's Bikes. Let me know if I can help you find what you need."

My grandma must have been referring to Astra and Zia, but I had no idea why she thought Mom needed me to watch out for her. What I did know was that I would find out.

CHAPTER 15

By ten o'clock, Delia was on the job. The early sunshine had vanished behind a bank of dark clouds blowing in thoughts of a rainstorm sometime soon. At ten thirty, Lincoln dashed into the shop as the skies let loose.

A crack of lightning made me jump. Deep rolling thunder followed.

"You made it inside just in time, Lincoln," I said.

"'Morning, Mac." He shot a smile at Delia. "Hey, sweetheart."

She blew him a kiss.

"It's definitely pouring." He pointed at the west-facing window, where water beat on the glass and streamed down.

Delia whistled. "Hope none of our rentals are out riding the trail."

"No kidding," I said. "We have seven bikes currently rented, all to a family who picked up their bikes at the end of the day yesterday—a family with five kids.

I hope they're the kind of people who check the weather report before going for a long ride."

Lincoln had jammed his hands in his pockets and was jiggling one knee.

"I'd say you came in here not only to get out of the rain," I told him. "Do you want another quick chat?"

"Yes, if you can."

Delia nodded and turned away. I beckoned for the detective to follow me to the other end of the currently customer-free store.

"What's up?" I asked.

"Have you spoken with Astra today?"

"No." I scrunched up my face. "Why do you ask? Is she okay?"

"I haven't heard of her coming to harm." He seemed to choose his words carefully. "I would like to speak with her. She has been unresponsive to my messages."

"Lincoln, you're talking about my mother, right? She adores you. Why wouldn't she answer your texts or voice mail or however you tried to reach her?"

"I have no idea, Mac. You told me she said she knew Zia Carven, and I need more information. You understand that I wouldn't want to cite her in contempt for not responding."

Whoa. That seemed extreme. "I should hope not. I told her yesterday you wanted to talk with her. Give me a few hours to see if I can find her, okay?"

"Thank you. Any other new information, while I'm here?" he asked.

It was too soon to mention what Evan had said, plus he hadn't gotten back to me with more details. I really,

really didn't want my son's beloved day care provider pulled away for questioning about his friendship with Zia. Surely Delia had already told Lincoln about the Westham police trying to link Yvonne and the victim. The book group meeting yesterday had been about asking questions, not providing answers. I'd seen Lincoln right before that.

"Not that I can think of," I said. "Except, and this probably isn't related to the case, Senator Ross Kimball is coming to town or is already here. Reba told me. It's something about being against the Cape wind-energy project."

"Very well. I'll let you get back to work."

Before we could reach the retail counter, a thirty-ish man in a watch cap strolled in. Delia was busy with other customers who'd come in while I spoke with Lincoln. I waved at the newcomer and stepped up to greet him.

"Welcome to Mac's Bikes," I said. "I'm Mac Almeida."

"Cliff Vriesdorp." He smiled. "Good to meet you. This is your shop?"

"Yes. Might you be Piet's relative?" The Dutch owner of the local hardware store was a congenial man, but I didn't know him well. I didn't think this younger relative had been in here before.

"I am, for sure." He gave off a whiff of an earthy aftershave possibly mixed with cigarette smoke.

Lincoln had been studying the guy. He stepped forward. "Mr. Vriesdorp, I am Detective Sergeant Haskins with the Massachusetts State Police." He didn't extend a hand or say anything explanatory, only stood with his hands at his sides.

Cliff blinked, swallowed, looked away for a second and then back at Lincoln. "Good morning, sir." Cliff's sandy hair, while not military-short, was neatly trimmed off his ears and collar. His posture went from relaxed to a shoulders-back alert, with his own hands at his sides. He said nothing further.

I glanced from Cliff to Lincoln and back. Both seemed to be at a stalemate, or maybe it was a standoff. I had a business to run, so I cleared my throat.

"What can I help you with, Cliff?" I asked.

He roused himself and turned his face toward mine. "I need a tube kit, please."

"Sounds like you have a flat," I said. "We can fix it here at no charge beyond the kit, if you'd like. Is the bike in your car?"

"Thanks, but no. The bike is at home." His gaze never wavered from mine. "I'm good with simple repairs." He checked over the countertop display of odd bits. "I could use a tube of this gear smoother. What do you recommend for—"

"Sorry to interrupt, Mac. I'll be in touch." Lincoln had that iron look directed straight at the younger man. Lincoln turned and headed out, storm or no storm. He created plenty of emotional climatic havoc around him.

I blew out a breath. "Apologies for our law-enforcement types intruding on local businesses, Cliff. When there's a Main Street homicide to deal with, I can't blame them. Now, you were asking what I might recommend for what?"

He moved his mouth around as if he tasted gear oil. "I can't remember. Only the tube kit, please." He stared at the door.

"Of course." I rang him up and handed him the bag and his receipt when we were finished. "You know about the murder this week, don't you?"

"Yes, I suppose I do." He flipped up his hood and left without saying thank you or goodbye.

All righty, then. This Cliff was a strange bird, as it turned out. Or a guilty one? Possibly, judging by Lincoln's reaction. It seemed as if he'd recognized Cliff's name. If the younger man was guilty of something, was it the homicide or another crime? Did he have a connection to Zia?

So many questions. So few answers.

CHAPTER 16

Mom didn't return my call or text. Not at eleven and not now, at noon. I texted my father. All he replied was that he thought she was working all day. All right, I'd give her that. That could be why she hadn't gotten back to Lincoln. Sometimes she had back-to-back astrology consultations, and she always silenced her phone when she was working.

The rain had blown through nearly as fast as it came in. When I opened the door, the sun was peeking through scudding clouds. I'd already taken a lunch break, but it consisted of eating my sandwich in my tiny office in the back and catching up on ordering merchandise to restock our shelves. I could scoot over to Mom's office in five minutes flat, except if she was with clients, I didn't want to disturb her. She'd get back to me and, more important, to Lincoln, when she could.

A black Mercedes SUV with tinted back windows pulled into the parking lot. A woman slid down from the driver's seat. She had a no-nonsense haircut and wore sensible shoes to match along with a short leather jacket and khaki pants. A dude in his twenties or thirties in a blazer and sneakers climbed out of the passenger seat in the front and opened the back door.

The man who emerged might be Senator Ross Kimball, as Reba had mentioned. Who else drove around in a big fancy vehicle with a chauffeur and a separate person to open his door? The back seat fellow wore his brown hair combed back from a low hairline, with a streak of silver at both temples. He was clad in joggers along with nylon exercise pants and a zipped-up windbreaker. He looked ready for cycling, although it would be a chilly ride.

I smiled and held open the door to the shop as the men approached. The driver remained leaning against the vehicle.

"Welcome to Mac's Bikes," I said. "Thanks for bringing the sunshine with you."

"That was quite a downpour earlier." The man in the windbreaker extended his hand. "Senator Ross Kimball from the fine state of Rhode Island, ma'am."

"Good afternoon, Ross. I'm Westham bike shop proprietor Mac Almeida." I shook his well-manicured hand, which he kept out there even though he'd blinked light brown eyes when I used his first name. I stepped back. "Come on in."

His helper followed him in. The driver stayed by the car. Kimball began browsing the high-end section of the retail bikes on display.

Orlean slipped by us holding her lunch bag, giving me a quick wave. Delia was busy ringing up a customer's purchase.

The aide turned to me. "The senator would like to rent two of your best bicycles, ma'am."

"He's welcome to, but they're all the same. It's not the best weather for biking, though."

"That's all right. He likes to keep up his exercise routine when he travels."

To each their own. "I'm Mac. What's your name?" I asked. The senator hadn't bothered to introduce us.

"Brendan Lopes, ma'am." His skin was quite fair, but his dark hair had a tight wave like mine that made me wonder if he was also part Cape Verdean. With that surname he might be, or maybe his family came from the Azores.

"Nice to meet you, Brendan. How long would you like the rentals for?"

"We'll have them back on Sunday."

Today was Thursday. "So, three days. On Sundays we close at four. You'll have to return the cycles before that."

"Not a problem."

"Should I include two helmets?" I asked. The senator might be a fitness fanatic, but would he also be the kind of rider who scoffed at keeping his brain safe?

"I should think so." He glanced anxiously at his boss. He apparently decided to take initiative and add the protection rather than ask Kimball. "Yes."

"Good. Please come on back to the rental area with me. I'll need a signature on the contract and a credit card on file. I won't charge it until after you return the bikes."

All that seemed to make him nervous, too. He stood

patting his fingertips against the sides of his legs but finally accompanied me and read through the paper contract.

"Please fill out the contact information on the top." I pointed to the section. "Make sure you print clearly and include the full names of who will be riding."

When Brendan began writing, I was glad I specified printing. His penmanship was barely legible.

"Does Ross have business in Westham?" I asked in a low voice.

Brendan also looked taken aback at my addressing his esteemed senator the same way I would any other human.

"I can't, um, speak to that." He bent over the paper again. "There."

I checked over the form. Brendan's name wasn't one of the two.

"You won't be riding?" I asked.

"No, the senator's driver will accompany him."

"That's fine. I still need the credit card and the signature."

"Um, of course," Brendan said. "Be right back." He conferred with Kimball at the other end of the shop, then hurried back with the senator following. Kimball didn't hurry.

"I'm surprised you don't trust the account of a United States senator, Mac." He stressed my name.

"I run a business, and everyone who rents is required to run their credit card." I kept my tone light. I wasn't getting into the matter of trust in the government.

Kimball pulled out a slim wallet and extracted a credit card. "Very well."

I entered the quoted amount for two rentals for three days, plus helmets, on the tablet that doubled as cash register. "You can tap or insert your card now."

Because of the amount, the credit card device also required him to finger-scribble a signature.

"Thank you." I slid a pen and the last page of the contract toward him and indicated the signature line.

He signed without reading a word of the agreement. "There." He moved over to the row of bicycles and curled his lip. "These things are your rentals?"

The ire in my throat intensified. Who was this entitled prig? I swallowed.

"They're very popular. I'm happy to cancel your rental contract, if you'd like." I waited.

Kimball glared at his assistant. In turn, Brendan fiddled with a thread on the outer seam of his pants leg and looked like he might burst into tears.

"We'll take them," the senator said.

"How tall is your other rider?" I asked.

"What?" Kimball asked, as if it was an idiotic question.

"I said, how tall is the person who will be riding the other rental?" I spoke slowly and pointed to the line on the contract where Brendan had written E. Kobylarz. "That's not Brendan."

"What does it matter?" The senator turned away.

And this guy ostensibly knew something about bicycles? I was about to tell him why it mattered, but I changed my mind out of spite. The driver had appeared nearly as tall as the senator. I would select two frames and seat heights that wouldn't fit either of them.

Brendan glanced up from his phone with wide eyes. "Senator Kimball, did you know Miss Carven has died?"

Kimball whirled. "Zz . . ." He let the sound trail off, apparently registering my presence.

I was sure he'd been about to say Zia. I watched Ross Kimball carefully.

"Do you mean that young constituent who has been calling us?" he asked Brendan.

"Yes." Brendan nodded vigorously. "They're saying she was murdered right here in Westham, in fact."

"That poor unfortunate girl." He gave a slow *tsking* sound and pointed at his assistant. "Make a note to send a card to her family."

"Yes, sir."

Kimball turned to me. "Are you sure your little village here is safe to cycle in?"

"Completely safe," I said. "We have excellent law-enforcement teams hard at work on this terrible homicide. It sounds like you knew Zia Carven."

"Not at all." Kimball gazed at a spot over my left shoulder. "Miss Carven was a Rhode Island resident, that's all. Good day, Ms. Almeida." He strode to the door and out through it.

I helped Brendan to the door with our two smallest adult rentals and two helmets and let him take it from there. Then I texted Lincoln about Kimball and Zia's state of residency. I copied the text before sending and pasted it into a text to the Cozy Capers.

CHAPTER 17

After Kimball and his crew left and Orlean returned, Delia declined to take a lunch break. I cleared it with my own crew for me to head out for a quick errand. I promised not to be too long, although I hoped I could honor that. Amateur that I was, it was a lot harder to fit in bits of sleuthing now that I was also a parent.

Instead of turning right toward my mother's astrology office, I made a left and a beeline along the sidewalk to the Rusty Anchor. Maybe I could learn why the police wanted to talk to Yvonne, as Delia mentioned yesterday. The chef might be way too busy flipping lunch hour burgers to talk with me, but it was worth a shot.

The eponymous rusty anchor swung from its chains above the front door while a small group of women headed inside. Instead of following them, I took the passageway between two buildings to the alley. I turned the corner and peered through the screen door into the pub kitchen. Yvonne Flora wasn't working the grill.

Instead she stood near the screen door with her back to me and a phone at her ear.

"Absolutely not." She shook her head along with the words, although it didn't seem to be a video call. "No." She jabbed at the device and turned, pushing open the door.

I sidestepped in time not to be knocked over.

"Mac?" She tucked a piece of hair back under the multi-colored toque she always wore on the job. "What are you doing back here?"

"Looking for you." I smiled.

"Yeah, you and everyone else." When Yvonne smiled, she still looked a bit like she was frowning, but she wasn't smiling now as she pulled a pack of cigarettes out of her chef's-tunic pocket. "Sorry, nasty habit, I know. Right now, I'm not going to survive without a smoke."

"I understand." Not that I had ever smoked or vaped tobacco, but I understood. Stress could lead a person to want the thing that relieved it. "I don't mind cigarette smoke out in the fresh air anywhere near like I do inside, which basically never happens anymore."

She lit up, took in a long drag, and faced away from me to exhale. "That's better." She inhaled another long drag and held it, then let it out. She faced me. "So?"

"Do you mean why am I looking for you?"

"Yes, and make it snappy, my friend. I have a kitchen to run and dinner service to prep. At least I have reliable workers these days."

"That's good. So, you might have heard about another homicide in Westham this week."

When a shadow passed over her face, I glanced up at the sky. Not a cloud in sight.

"I did," she said.

"Well, I was the person who found the young woman dead. My mom seems to be a person of interest. My son's day care teacher was a friend of the victim. And—"

Yvonne cut me off. "You also heard the police want to talk to me about it, and you're wondering why."

"Yes, pretty much. I know you wouldn't kill anyone, but I'm wondering why the authorities think you might have information."

She barked out a laugh. "Don't tell the cops, but in real life I've been this close a couple of times to wanting someone dead." She held her thumb and index finger a millimeter apart.

"Getting that close and wanting something to happen, even in real life, is different than actually carrying it out. There must be more the police are going on."

"I don't know what they think they have. I got pestered with questions six ways to Sunday about where I was on Tuesday." She gazed at me almost defiantly, her greenish eyes unblinking for a long moment.

I'd seen her talking with Zia in the toy store only hours before Zia's death.

"When I saw you in the Toy Soldier, you seemed to know Zia Carven."

Yvonne turned away again to exhale the last puff on her cigarette. She ground the butt out under her toe, then picked it up. She set her hand on the screen door handle and didn't look at me as she spoke.

"I don't know anyone by that name. I have to get back to work, Mac."

"Take care." My words were eaten by the thwacking of the door closing behind her.

CHAPTER 18

As I made my way back to Mac's Bikes, I thought about Yvonne's wording. She'd said she didn't know anyone by the name of Zia Carven, but she hadn't met my gaze and had essentially slammed the door on me directly after that. Did she know Zia by a different name? From what I'd overheard, Zia had wanted something from Yvonne.

I didn't think many people in their early twenties changed their identities. Maybe Zia was in witness protection and Yvonne had recognized her from wherever the young woman had been before. Was that something Lincoln already knew?

The police asking Yvonne about where she'd been the day Zia was killed sounded like they were digging for an alibi. She told me she hadn't been at work but not what she'd actually been doing.

Speaking of alibis, I wished I could follow up on Ross Kimball's reaction to hearing Zia had been murdered. It seemed like he didn't want me to hear that he knew the victim on a first-name basis. Maybe the WPD would be better off finding out if the senator had an alibi for Tuesday afternoon instead of chasing down Yvonne's.

As I approached my shop, I wondered if I should continue on to my mom's office and find out what was up with her, but I decided against it. I'd always been responsible about my business and wasn't about to let a murder derail that.

Once inside, I plunged back into the world of bicycles and everything connected to them. When we had a quiet moment at about two o'clock, I approached Delia as she straightened stacks of folded biking shirts.

"Question for you," I said. "Do you happen to know a Cliff Vriesdorp? Maybe he has come into the pub, or you met him somewhere?"

"Isn't that the last name of the hardware store owner?"

"It is. Cliff was in here this morning, but you were busy with other customers. I wondered if you've served him at the bar or run into him anywhere."

"Cliff. Hmm. Tell me a little more. Age? Appearance?"

"Thirty-ish. Short sandy hair, lean body, maybe five ten." I thought back. "Possibly active or ex-military, from the way he carried himself. He's clearly a cyclist, because he wanted a patch kit and was considering buying other items from us, although I don't think I've seen him in here before today."

"I guess I missed him when he was here. But, yeah, he's been in the pub." Delia's eyes went wide. "Remember I said Zia had been drinking at the bar a few times?"

I bobbed my head, my interest at high alert.

"Well, most of the times she was with a dude who wears a hoop earring. Broad face, gentle eyes."

That would be Evan. I kept listening.

"They seemed to be good friends," Delia continued, "but one night she was sitting at the bar and hanging with that man you described."

Ooh. "Seriously?"

"Yes."

"How was their interaction?" I asked. "Could you overhear anything?"

"A bit. They seemed to be having fun at first, then it got a little dark, like she stopped having a good time. I might have heard the word 'father.'"

"You said she stopped enjoying his company. Do you think he was pestering her or giving her bad news?"

"Mac, I really don't know. It was Saturday night last week, and the bar was super busy. You know how it is. I'm forever back and forth between customers, mixing cocktails and pulling beers and updating tabs. All of that. I'm just telling you what I picked up in passing."

"I appreciate it. Since Zia's death, have you told Lincoln about seeing her with Cliff?"

Delia slapped her hand against her forehead. "Doh. I didn't think of it. I'll tell him, for sure, and soon."

"Good. Lincoln came in while Cliff was here and seemed to recognize the name. He might already be aware of their connection, but it won't hurt to let him know what you witnessed."

We got busy with customers after that, and Delia left at two thirty. I was interested in how Cliff was related to Piet, but I didn't have time to casually pop into the hardware store and ask—at least not today.

During a lull at around four o'clock, a text came in. I perched on a stool and opened the Cozy Capers thread. My eyes didn't exactly bug out, but I'd missed about a dozen messages while my phone was silenced.

Before I opened the thread, I checked to be sure I hadn't missed any texts from day care, the preschool, Tim, or anyone in my family. Exceptions to the silent setting were already in place for every adult in my family because when my device was muted I needed to be able to hear from my loved ones. I didn't know why I hadn't also set up exceptions on my phone for my kids' daytime situations. Probably because I was a new parent.

Tulia had started the morning's group responses. She wrote that nobody she talked to in Mashpee last evening reported seeing June around her home or doing business in the small, recently renovated downtown on Tuesday. So much for her action item.

Gin said she'd asked yesterday about cameras at both the businesses that abutted the Toy Soldier. Gifts from the Sea didn't have any video security. The manager at The Dairy, an ice cream shop, was happy to show her the hardware and the footage from that morning, but the software was old and didn't let the user replay a specific time. Gin would have had to sit with the owner and review hours of footage in reverse, and he said he didn't have time for that.

Another strikeout. I tapped out a reply to the group.

Just seeing these. Footage obv a job for WPD or Lincoln's team. Too bad re Mashpee intel.

I added what I'd learned.

Yvonne cagey about knowing Zia. Delia says victim seen at pub drinking with Cliff Vriesdorp, might have argued with him. Anybody know him? Related to Piet.

I added one more.

RI Sen. Kimball in shop today. Knew Zia as constituent, wouldn't admit to my face he knew her personally but seemed like it. Bears watching. He's anti-wind, is in town at least thru Sun (becuz bike rentals).

Did I want to add what Evan had asked me to do? Maybe later, when we next met in person, but not here and in writing. Evan was a more-than-gentle person who took care of our baby. I didn't want to think about police descending on the day care center to question him on the grounds that I'd mentioned to my sometimes-bumbling co-sleuths that he'd mentioned his friendship with Zia.

I didn't see an update from Norland or Flo about Zia's identity. What Yvonne had told me wasn't really worth a text either. Ilsa hadn't added a report.

When several customers hurried in, I closed the thread. I'd check it again later, after the kiddos were asleep.

CHAPTER 19

Tim's eyes and shoulders sagged during our family dinner that evening. He'd made turkey meatballs in tomato sauce over spaghetti, which Ella said she'd helped with. Tim rolled his eyes to me at the word "helped." From the evidence of red spatter on the white stovetop, her assistance might have made Tim's job harder, not easier.

While we ate, the girl was full of questions, as always, and Luca was cranky from his first teething. I took charge of the bedtime routine for two children and a bird and sent their dad off for some alone time.

By eight o'clock, children and bird were sound asleep, and I'd cleaned up in the kitchen. My beloved husband was also asleep sitting up on the couch, despite the television across the room presenting insightful commentary about national news by its host and the three guests whom he'd invited onto his panel for the hour.

I seated myself gently on the couch near Tim and picked up the remote. I lowered the volume but didn't switch off the device. I didn't want sudden silence to wake him. If the TV had been tuned to local news, I might have paid attention, but there was next to nothing I could do about the national scene. I was happy to ignore it, at least for the evening.

Instead I pulled out my phone and devoted myself to an effort I might be able to influence. I opened my eyes wide. The number of messages in the Cozy Capers thread had grown in the last few hours.

Norland wrote that he found several Carven families in Providence, Rhode Island, and surrounds. They were all too old or too young to have a daughter in her early twenties.

Flo forwarded a link to a news article about the killing but said authorities were still withholding Zia's name. I hadn't gone near local news sources today. They tended to be super sensational, plus I hadn't had a minute free until right now.

I wasn't about to turn on the television or radio news in the mornings while I fixed breakfast for a little sponge-like Ella. She would jump right to asking, "What's a homicide, Mama Mac? What does murder mean?" Yeah. No.

I debated whether I had anything to contribute to the thread. Lincoln wanted to speak with my mom but I didn't want to mention that here. She didn't kill anybody. I was even more annoyed than Lincoln that she hadn't responded to my messages, but that was a family matter. I would talk to her in the morning if I didn't hear from her before that.

Orlean said she would check into the rooming house.

I'd forgotten to ask her about that today, and she hadn't volunteered any information. She probably hadn't had a chance to get over there yet, but I could mention her offer to the group.

Orlean will check out North Lodging, says she'll get better results than any of us or the cops. I agreed. No news yet.

Norland wrote back immediately.

Good, thx. Ilsa and I didn't go yet.

I added another thought.

I'll try to stop by hrdware in early AM, talk to Piet.

I checked to be sure I hadn't missed a note or a call from Mom, but I hadn't. Then my phone dinged, and there it was.

Got your text, talk in the morning. Sorry.

Huh. I'd see what she had to say when I left Ella with her tomorrow. At least my mother had the grace to apologize. Now that I was also a mom, remembering to say "I'm sorry" was a good lesson to hang on to. A little grace can go a long way.

Tim listed to the side. I scooted over so he could lean his head on my shoulder.

"Mmm," he murmured. "Best pillow ever."

"One of my favorite parts of my job description." I stroked his dark blond hair.

He'd worn it shoulder-length since I'd met him, either tied back for work or loose at home, making him look the part of a surfer dude, which he was—or used to be. Since the children had come to live with us, he'd started getting his hair cut in a tousled, short look, saying it was much easier to care for that way. To my eyes, he was handsome and sexy with his hair any length. He would be gorgeous even if he were bald.

"I know another part of your job description, although it never seems like work for you." He glanced up with a devilish smile.

"If you're inviting me into your bed, sir, I am both able and willing." I summoned up what I hoped was my most sultry smile. "I thought you'd never ask."

CHAPTER 20

I brought Ella to the side door of the parsonage. The dwelling, which sat only a few yards away from the UU church proper, had a front door on the street, but that was where Astra had established her astrology consulting office. The shingles of the parsonage were cedar weathered to silver and were looking a little worse for the wear, but the building, which belonged to the church, was sound. You can't sneeze at free housing.

This entrance, on a wide covered porch, was where all good New Englanders entered homes, unless they lived in a Cape cottage like I did. My parents' side door led to the kitchen. Mom greeted the little girl and cooed at Luca. We stayed on the porch, since I didn't want to have to take the baby out of the stroller. The weather continued to be cold, and today was cloudy and blustery instead of clear. At least it wasn't snowing, but Luca was well bundled in his carriage and it was a lot of work to extract him and then strap him in again.

"Um, Mom, you said we were going to talk, remember?"

She glanced at her wristwatch. "Would you look at

the time? That little fellow is going to be late for day care, and we wouldn't want to delay you from opening the bike shop on time."

"What? You promised," I said.

"Little pitchers and all that." She tilted her head at Ella. So much for the parental apology and promise of talking.

"What's a pitcher?" Ella asked. "Is that like in baseball?"

"Come inside and I'll tell you, sweetheart. Say goodbye to Mac."

An exuberant little-girl hug later, Ella went inside with her grandmother. The door closed. I shook my head at my mother's avoidance tactics and headed for the day care. True, we wouldn't want Ella to pick up on anything she shouldn't, but my mother was going to have talk one of these days, to Lincoln if not to me.

At the Nest, I handed Luca off to Kim, a much-tattooed and pierced young person. I didn't care as long as they took good care of our baby, which they did.

"Is Evan here?" I realized he'd never texted me yesterday, and we could use more information in this case, especially from someone friendly with Zia.

"He had a dental emergency. He said he'll be in by ten. Don't worry, a teacher from the Chickens is coming to help out until Evan gets here."

"I'm not worried, but I'm glad you'll have backup. Can you please ask him to text Mac when he can?"

"Will do. Say goodbye to your mama, Luca." Kim helped him wave his little hand.

"Love you, baby. See you at dinner." I kissed the top

of the baby's head and made my way out. He'd been in day care since we took him in last fall, and he was used to the routine and the various adults he saw regularly. The Chickens were the next older class, and the two age groups often played together. Our son knew those teachers, and he would graduate to that class in the fall.

Two information dead ends in the space of twenty minutes might be a record. Without taking time for a chat with my mom or getting details about Zia from Evan, I was ahead of schedule for work. I knew exactly where I could drop in without being late to my livelihood.

A few blocks later, I arrived at Pete's Westham Mercantile, the best small hardware store on the Cape. Owner Piet had told me everybody messed up the spelling of his first name, despite it being quite simple. He'd said it was easier in this country to pretend his name was Pete. Bags of ice melt sat next to snow shovels on the sidewalk. Soon enough he would swap those out for hoes, bags of mulch, and garden stakes, to be followed by beach chairs and sand pails.

I pulled open the door, headed over to the pet food aisle, and selected a bag of parrot treats. I wasn't sure anyone in Westham other than me bought them, but Piet always kept them in stock for Belle. I was halfway to the checkout area when Piet hailed me.

"Mac, good to see you." He beamed. "Did you find what you needed for your darling Belle?"

"I did, thanks to you." I held up the bag of treats. "How have you been?"

"No complaints. You?"

"All good. Say, I met a relative of yours. Cliff?"

"Uh-oh, what trouble is he getting up to this time?" Piet's cheery mock criticism sounded forced.

"No trouble that I know of, but I'd never seen him before. I didn't know you had a son."

"I don't. Cliff is a cousin's child. He's my first removed cousin, or however you say it in English. The boy is visiting from DC and has made noises about making a move to Westham permanent."

"Is he staying with you?"

"For now, yes, and he has been here a month already." Piet rolled his eyes. "But it's not a permanent arrangement. No, not at all," he added, almost to himself.

"Thanks," I said. "I'll let you get back to work. I need to head over and open my shop."

"I'll ring those up for you."

I followed him to the cash register and tapped my card. Cliff walked in and hurried up to the counter, hair rumpled, holding a takeout coffee cup.

"Sorry I'm late, Oom." He sidled behind the counter.

Piet pressed his lips into a line but didn't speak.

"Hi, Cliff. Mac from the bike shop. It was terrible news about the murder this week, wasn't it? I was about to mention it to Piet."

"Tragic," Piet agreed.

Cliff set down his coffee and straightened a display of screwdrivers.

"I understand you knew poor Zia," I murmured. "I'm very sorry for your loss."

Cliff recoiled. The corners of his mouth turned down,

and something showed in his eyes. Alarm? Fear? Not sadness, surely. Piet turned to stare at him.

"I don't know who you're talking about," Cliff said.

"Oh? It's just that a friend saw you drinking at the pub with Zia last week."

"Was that her name? We found ourselves on adjacent barstools and got talking. That's all it was."

"I see. Well, thanks, Piet. See you both around." I headed for the door.

"Who is that woman?" Cliff muttered to his uncle. "She has spies in the pub and is all buddy-buddy with the police detective."

I slipped outside. I didn't think Piet knew of my sleuthing background, but he might. Either way, he would probably say I was nothing but a local businessperson, and that was fine with me.

CHAPTER 21

When Orlean arrived for work at a few minutes after nine, she paused at the counter.

"Went over to the rooming house last night. Asked around a little."

"Thanks for doing that," I said.

"Seems Zia might have been looking for her birth mother."

I'd had that same thought a couple of days ago. "Did she find her?"

"Nobody knew. At least not that they'd say." She shrugged out of her jacket. "Got a couple big tune-ups waiting." She headed back to the mini-fridge with her lunch bag.

"I appreciate you asking around," I called after her. I had many more questions, but I would save them for later. Orlean didn't like being distracted from her work. I took a lesson from her and focused on mine.

Delia came for her shift at ten, and I assigned her the task of unpacking and shelving a new shipment of helmets and shoes. I rang up a tire-repair kit and a can of gear lubricant for a woman and explained our rental options and choices to a white-haired couple.

"It's too cold for us to ride now, but we'll be back in our summer cottage in June," the man said. "We fly in from Vancouver, British Columbia, and no way we're bringing our bikes."

"I get it. If you want to rent bikes for the whole summer, we can talk later about a monthly rate."

He thanked me.

"Our daughter and her family live in Cataumet year-round," the woman said. "With prices as they are, it's better for us to rent than buy a place nearby, and we found a cottage in West Falmouth that gives us a good deal for the three months."

They moseyed out, hand in hand, which made me smile. My hope and dream were for white-haired Tim and me to be strolling hand-in-hand at their age.

My own elder relative scooted in next. I gave Abo Reba a big hug.

"Mackenzie, I heard something you're going to be interested in."

"I can't wait to hear." The shop was empty of customers. I resumed my place on one of the stools behind the counter. "Have a seat."

Reba plopped her huge bag onto the floor and unzipped her puffy purple coat, then slid onto the other stool. She drummed her fingers on the counter for a moment.

"Abo Ree, what do you know? We could get busy any minute," I murmured.

"Well, honey, I think your mother is up to something."

She matched my low voice. "She's been avoiding me and making up excuses."

"Hmm." I checked for where Delia was, then heard her and Orlean chatting in the repair area. "Lincoln wants to talk to her about the murder. Yesterday he said she hasn't been answering or returning his calls. Mom knew Zia because she shopped in the free food market, and she was trying to help her find a better place to live. For the last couple of days, Mom's been avoiding talking to me, too, and I don't know why."

"I met the young lady once," Reba said. "I stopped by the parsonage, and she and Astra were coming out of the market in the church fellowship hall. Your mother introduced us."

"How did Zia seem?"

"A bit nervous. She made an excuse about needing to leave, climbed into quite the beater, and drove off. That car was very nearly an antique."

"She shopped at the market," I said. "She must not have had money to upgrade her car. Working part time at the toy store couldn't have paid much."

"No. I saw her another time, as well." She gave me an impish side eye. "I happened to be inspecting Main Street with my spyglass, and I spotted Zia and a young fellow on the sidewalk near the Lobstah Shack. I do believe they were arguing, you know, from their faces and the way they stood and so on. Arguing about what, I couldn't tell you."

My grandmother's second-floor apartment was across the street and about a block away from the bike shop. Because she liked to keep track of what went on in town, one year we'd given her a telescoping spyglass for Christmas, mostly as a joke. She loved the brass device and kept it near her chair next to the front windows. After she reported a couple of crimes-in-progress to the police, they learned to stop treating her calls as those of a gaga old-lady busybody. There was nothing gaga about Reba Almeida.

"What did the man look like?" I asked.

"Around thirty. Light-colored hair."

"That sounds like it could be Cliff Vriesdorp."

"Piet has a son?"

"I was in the hardware store this morning, and Piet told me Cliff is his cousin's son," I said. "Cliff is working there and staying with Piet for the time being, but he arrived late for his shift. Piet didn't seem happy about that or about the long-term visit."

"Who would be?"

"True. It's interesting about the argument. Delia said Cliff was drinking with Zia in the Rusty Anchor last week, and Lincoln seemed to know who he was when they both were in here at the same time yesterday."

"I'll drop Lincoln a line about that argument I saw," Reba said.

"Good."

Reba's eyes brightened as she leaned toward me and spoke in a whisper. "Do you think that young fellow murdered the girl?"

"I don't know. Anything's possible, right?"

But why would he?

CHAPTER 22

Reba had been gone just a minute when Evan hurried in and approached me. I greeted him.

"I have to get to work, Mac, but I was passing by." His speech was thick and his cheek swollen. He swiped the corner of his mouth with the back of his hand. "I might be drooling. Needed a root canal."

"Ouch. I hope it doesn't hurt too much." I was lucky to have strong teeth that needed no more than a cleaning once a year. The only dental work I'd ever had done was to have my wisdom teeth pulled at the end of high school.

"I'm okay. Sorry I didn't get back to you." He pointed to his cheek. "Too much pain last night. I'll call later."

"Sounds good."

A group of adults in their twenties wearing cycling clothes burst in, laughing and chattering in a language I didn't recognize.

Evan's eyebrows rose, and he spoke to the customers

in the same language, albeit a bit thickly. After an exchange of greetings, he turned back to me.

"They're Russians."

"And you are too?"

He smiled and nodded. "I'll text you later." He made his way out. He didn't have a bit of an accent. He must have moved to this country as a young child, unless he'd been born here.

"Welcome," I said to the newcomers. "How can we help you?"

I was too busy until lunchtime to dwell on Reba's news of spying on an argument or my frustration at still not knowing how Evan knew Zia. Delia and I both had our hands full. The Russian group was replaced by a steady stream of customers in ones and twos and fives.

By one o'clock, we'd all taken our lunch breaks and things were quiet once again. I moseyed back to the repair area and leaned on the doorjamb.

Orlean didn't glance up but said, "Bet you want to know more about North Lodging."

"I'd like to. I'm curious about who told you Zia was looking for her bio mother. Can you share that?"

She finished tightening the rear brake and set down the wrench.

"Fella with a Russian last name said so."

"Was his name Selyuk?"

"Yes." She squinted at me. "How'd you know?"

"He's one of Luca's teachers and told me he was friends with Zia. Did you see him this morning? He stopped by, but it was quick because he was late for work."

"Nope. Anyhoo, he didn't offer up any more details about the dead girl. I talked to a couple other residents, but nobody wanted to get involved."

"Interesting. What did the place look like?"

"Kind of shabby, but not that bad. The price is right. Don't know why it gets such a bad rap."

Maybe that was the reason Zia had refused Mom's offer to help her find a new place.

"That's all I got." Orlean looked down at her work again.

"Thanks. I appreciate it."

She bobbed her chin. I turned away to a store that remained quiet.

I took a moment to see what I could learn on the internet. I'd searched for Zia's name before and came up empty-handed. Neither Norland nor Flo had reported learning anything new. What kind of name would Zia be short for? I was surprised to find a list of more than fifty names ending in -zia, which was disheartening. How could I search for all of them?

She could be Grazia Carven, or her parents might have given her the moniker Letizia, Pazia, Cinzia, or any number of other names. Maybe Zia was a shortening of Alicia or Cassia, or it could be the beginning of a name. I shook my head and gave up. Tracking that down was a task for an organization with resources, like the police, not a bike shop owner with a few minutes on her hands.

I checked the group thread. Zane had invited everyone to his house at eight o'clock that night to talk about the book. Another message from him came in. He added a note.

Babies are asleep by 7.

If I knew the Cozy Capers, we would also discuss the homicide. I wrote back saying I would check with Tim and let them know. Instead of texting, I stepped outside and gave Tim a call.

"Hey, beautiful."

I smiled to hear his voice. "Hey yourself, handsome."

"What's up?"

"The Capers want to meet tonight at Zane's, but not until eight. I'll be home for dinner and baths and bed routine."

"You should go. You know me, I'll be asleep shortly after Ella."

"I do know. Thanks. Love you."

"Love you, too. See you in a few hours," he said.

"I look forward to it." I disconnected the call and texted the group that I'd be there.

I crossed my fingers that one of them would have more information to share than I did. I was about to go in when I spotted June walking in my direction carrying a paper sack. I stayed outside and gave her a wave when she grew closer.

She spotted me, then glanced across the street as if she'd rather not speak to me. But she turned back.

"Hi, Mac."

I sauntered up to where she stood. "June, how are

you doing after Tuesday? I've been meaning to stop by and ask."

"Lousy, thanks. They only told me an hour ago that I can reopen tomorrow, and now I don't have an employee to help me."

"It was a horrible thing to happen to Zia, and to your store."

"I'll say."

"How long had she been working for you?"

"Only a couple of months. She was an okay worker, but now I wish I'd never hired her. I can't seem to get a break."

I looked at her sack, which bore Tulia's Lobstah Shack logo: a grinning lobstcr lounging on a picnic table in front of a shack that looked like it belonged on the Maine coast. "I'm holding up your lunch. I'll let you go."

"Best food in town. See you, Mac." June strode off as if she couldn't wait to get away.

I shook my head. She didn't express one word of sorrow about Zia. She also didn't ask how I was after the shock of finding the young woman dead only a few days ago. June had talked only about herself.

Well, focusing on herself might be her way of coping with the murder. She was probably worrying about losing customers. All the Main Street shops were small and owned locally. Most of us proprietors had the same concerns. I wouldn't stop shopping at the Toy Soldier because it was the site of a murder, and I hoped others wouldn't, either.

CHAPTER 23

I made it to Zane's by eight, and I remembered to slide the book into my bag at the last minute. I offered to pick up Gin. She said she and Eli were dining out and that he would drop her off, but she'd be happy for a ride home.

Tim and I had bought a low-mileage pre-owned Mazda SUV after the kids joined our family. Although he owned an older Volvo station wagon, we agreed that each of us needed a vehicle that could safely carry both Ella and Luca. My sporty red Miata was a two-seater, and I decided to trade it in. I loved that car with a passion, but my life had changed. It had been an indulgence while I was single and childless. All that was different now, and for the better. At least the new car was still red, and I'd had good luck with the brand.

I was the last to arrive at Zane's. My friends were sipping wine, tea, beer, or soda, and I selected a bottle of lime seltzer water. I was already feeling tired and needed to have my wits about me for the discussion and for the drive home.

Stephen Duke, Zane's husband and Westham's town clerk, popped his head in to say hello, then excused himself. I had met the twins at their annual Hanukkah party, and Zane and I had already talked about having play dates this summer with our three babies.

"Who finished reading it?" Gin held up *Pruning the Dead*. "I'm halfway through."

Norland and Ilsa held up their hands, as did Flo.

"I'm nearly done," Tulia said.

Zane and I exchanged a glance. I shook my head and he burst out laughing.

"Sorry," I said. "Two little ones at home and running my own business? I don't have much time for reading. The first third is great, though."

"I'm two chapters in," Zane said. "I wish I had more time to read."

"Do you have time to listen to it?" Ilsa asked. "I read the audiobook while I was walking and quilting."

"Not particularly, unfortunately," he said.

"Same here," I said.

"I enjoyed that the protagonist is an older person," Norland chimed in. "She and I are probably of an age."

"I like the older protagonist, too," I said. "Lilly Robinson and her garden squad double as sleuths. We're also a squad, right?"

"Exactly," Gin said. "A squad of both a book group and mystery solvers."

Flo whipped out her yellow legal pad. "Then let's talk about the homicide. Once that's behind us, we can get back to being a book group."

"Good idea," Tulia said. "I'll go. I had the action item

of finding out where June was on Tuesday. I asked around in my community. Someone thought they had seen her with a man, but that's all I got. I'll keep trying."

"I ran into June on the sidewalk this afternoon," I offered. "She didn't express one bit of remorse for Zia's death and mostly complained about her store being closed."

"That's harsh," Zane said.

"I know." I bobbed my head. "She said she finally can reopen tomorrow."

Flo jotted that down. "Who else?"

"I texted you all about Senator Kimball," I said. "His aide said Zia had been calling the office. Kimball claimed he didn't know who she was, that she was simply a constituent. He was dismissive when he said it but also a touch defensive, I thought."

"I checked him out," Norland began. "He's mostly been on the straight and narrow. Married, has a nice house and three daughters. He was a state senator before being elected to the US Senate. His past was murkier. It seemed he had a case of financial malfeasance dismissed by a high-power lawyer his father paid for."

"I'll ask my mom what she knows," Gin offered. "She grew up in Rhode Island and still visits friends there."

"Mac, do you have anything else?" Flo asked.

"I dropped by the Rusty Anchor back door yesterday to talk with Yvonne, since Delia told me the police were looking for her. When I asked her if she knew Zia Carven, she turned away and said she didn't know anyone by that name, then basically closed the door on me. She also wasn't at work on Tuesday. It's like her Sunday."

"You've been busy, girl," Gin said.

"Did your mechanic get over to the rooming house?" Ilsa asked.

"Luca's day care teacher lives there. Evan told Orlean that Zia was looking for her birth parents. Evan has promised to talk with me, but he hasn't found the time yet."

Flo whistled. "That's big. Maybe Zia found one of the bio parents, and they didn't want their past made public."

"She was in her early twenties, which means we're looking for someone who is at least forty and up to sixty, yeah?" Tulia asked.

"The father could be any age," Gin said.

"True," I said. "Yvonne or June could be the birth mom."

"Doesn't Yvonne live with a woman?" Flo asked.

"That doesn't mean she didn't give birth to a child earlier," Zane said. "Stephen has a daughter with his former wife. Some people take a while to decide to live as their authentic selves."

I'd never heard that Stephen had a child. I would ask Zane another time if Stephen was involved in the daughter's life. I hoped he was.

"Good point," Flo said. "What else do we have?"

"I signed up to dig into Zia's identity," Norland said. "It's hard to check for a birth certificate when you don't have a state. She doesn't have one under that name in Massachusetts, but I'm going to start checking surrounding states."

"How long have people been doing open adoptions?" Flo asked. "When I was growing up, many adoptive parents tried to hide it from their child, and there was never any contact with the bio mother or father."

"I believe it's been at least as long as Zia was alive," Ilsa said. "If she was given up for adoption and the records aren't sealed, that might make it easier to find her."

"I also said I would check into who she really is," Flo said. "I have a query out, and I'll add to the thread when I hear back."

"Sorry, I've been kind of a dud in terms of information," Zane said. "But I do keep my eye out through my store windows. That senator came in early this afternoon and bought my most expensive bottle of Cape King rum. He asked if I knew anything about the homicide. I smiled and told him I didn't. Pompous would be an understatement for him, but I didn't hear the guy confess to anything."

Not that Kimball would. I gazed around the circle. It felt good to have these disparate members of my community all keeping their eyes and ears open. We were a squad, and a darn good one. We'd get to the bottom of Zia's death sooner or later. Then we could all relax and focus on our already busy lives.

CHAPTER 24

It was nearly ten by the time Gin and I climbed into my car. The sky was dark, with no moonlight to guide us because of the gathering clouds. I tasted the cold, damp air before I closed my door.

"Is it going to snow?" I asked.

"Not that I've heard," she said. "I haven't ridden in this car before. Do you like it?"

"For a ride that's not Miss M, I love it. I can see now when I back out of parking spaces, and the children are protected in the back seat. Plus I have actual space to carry gear in the way back."

"Kids have a lot of stuff, don't they?"

I sighed. "Yes. Stroller, car seats, extra clothes, and diapers only scratch the surface. Plus books and toys and snacks and everything else."

"Wait until you start hauling around their friends and everybody's sports equipment. Softball was the worst. Bats, helmets, cleats, you name it." She gave a soft laugh. "But she was my only child, and I loved every minute of it. Well, almost every minute."

"Lucy is still in her twenties, isn't she?"

"Twenty-nine last month."

"Has it been extra hard for you this week, thinking about a young woman's life cut short?" I asked.

"Absolutely. My search for security cams neighboring the Toy Soldier didn't go anywhere, and I didn't get assigned any new action items tonight. If you can think of anything else I can check into, please speak up. I want to do my part."

"One thing I forgot to mention in our meeting was that Piet's sort-of nephew, Cliff Vriesdorp, apparently knew Zia. Delia saw them drinking at the bar together, and Reba observed them arguing on the sidewalk near her apartment."

"With her spy telescope?" Gin laughed. "I love that woman."

"You and me both. If you need something to do, you could look out for Cliff, engage him in conversation if you meet him. He's around thirty, sandy hair, and he's working for Piet at the moment."

"I think he might have already come into Salty Taffy's. I'll definitely be on the watch for him."

I yawned.

"You okay driving?" she asked.

"I am, but it's been a long day. Anyway, we're almost back to town." For which I was grateful. Zane and Stephen lived outside of Westham a bit, and the road was twisty and dark. The few houses on either side were tucked back into the woods. I'd seen headlights behind me a few curves ago, but they weren't in my rearview mirror now. At least nobody had come in the opposite direction to blind me with oncoming lights. My new car had strong, clear headlights, and I drove with the brights on when the night was dark like this.

A roar sprang up. Beams approached way too fast from behind. I swore and slowed. I checked the mirror again and was nearly blinded.

"Mac, watch out!" Gin cried.

My car's lane control system beeped frantically. I whipped my gaze forward. At the last minute, I steered sharply to the right where the road turned. The other vehicle sped past, nearly clipping my side mirror. I let out a string of the kind of bad words I'd gotten in the habit of never using at home.

"What kind of idiot was that?" Gin screeched.

The road straightened and widened. A streetlight appeared not far away. I swallowed and pulled onto the shoulder under the light, pressed the hazard lights button, and shifted the car into park.

"Idiot, yes," I said. "And maybe a murderer following us and trying to put our questioning to a permanent end."

Gin twisted in her seat toward me. "Mac, are you serious?"

"I hope that wasn't it, but yes, I'm serious." I laughed, but weakly. "I've been attacked before, but I can't believe I, or any of us, have been that obvious in our poking around this time."

"People who commit homicide are desperate not to be caught, though."

"Exactly." I thought back to the vehicle as my heart rate gradually slowed. "Did you catch anything about that car? Color, make, license plate?"

"We should be so lucky. Lemme think a minute."

"I feel like the vehicle was dark, maybe black, but I was too frantic and nearly blinded to think about the plate number."

"I agree about the car being dark, and maybe an SUV model bigger than this one, or possibly a van," Gin said. "The plate? I can't bring anything up right now, but I'll let the experience steep. Maybe an image will come to me."

"Thanks."

"You know how when you're gazing at stars, sometimes the one you want to see is elusive, but if you look to the side, it comes into focus?"

"Right." I took a deep breath and let it out. "Let's get home, you and me."

"I can't think of a better plan."

Once my contact lenses were out and I'd flossed my teeth, sliding into bed next to a slumbering Tim a little while later had never felt so good. Except, no matter how comforted and warm I felt, I wasn't able to fall asleep. Every time I thought about our drive home, my heart sped up again.

Maybe I should bow out of our group's efforts to find the killer. I had children now. I couldn't be putting myself in danger. Being tailed and nearly sideswiped like that had been terrifying.

But I also really wanted to know who it had been. If I let the image of the car that had possibly pursued us steep, as Gin put it, could I recall any details about it?

For now, I lay on my back with my eyes closed, slowing my breath. I pictured stars twinkling on in a dark sky, one at a time. I let my body be heavy, sinking into the mattress.

Finally, I turned, spooning with Tim, and stopped thinking about license plates.

CHAPTER 25

When I woke up after seven the next morning, I panicked for a second. Wasn't I supposed to be giving the kids breakfast because Tim was off at work? Was Ella making a mess alone in the kitchen while a wet, hungry Luca cried?

Wait. Today was Saturday. Tim had the weekend off, as did I. Now that I was oriented, I heard faint happy sounds from the kitchen. A baby banged on his high chair tray and a little girl giggled. I let out a sigh of relief.

I slid on my glasses and spent a little quality time with my phone. Not long after I dropped her off at home last night, Gin shared our near miss on the group thread. Zane responded almost immediately.

Oh no! Sorry girls. Glad yr ok.

Norland was next, with a message at five this morning. He'd told us about his increasing insomnia, something I was grateful not to be afflicted with.

Any ID of car or plate?

I wrote back.

Not yet. Hoping subconsc mem will kick in.

With no new texts, I checked local news. My eyes widened to see an item about June Jenkins being detained for questioning in the homicide case. The time stamp was a few minutes ago. I copied the headline and pasted it into the text thread.

When nobody responded, I put down the device and hit the bathroom. Today was family day. The wheels of justice would grind away, but they weren't my responsibility. My happily offered duties were with the man I loved and two equally loved little ones. The daylight through the window made the darkness of last night's chase seem less scary, less ominous.

After delivering Ella to my parents at ten to spend the day playing with our niece Cokey, Tim and I drove Luca to the beach for a winter stroll. I kept news of last night's close call to myself. The morning light, dim though it was with slate skies above, made me wonder if I'd imagined Gin and me being nearly sideswiped on purpose. With no actual information to offer, I hadn't let Lincoln know about what happened, either.

I wouldn't have related the incident to Lincoln unless I also told Tim. I'd withheld information from him before, but it was unfair to him and made me uneasy. The last thing I wanted was for us to be together and for Lincoln to ask about a situation where I'd been in danger and hadn't let my husband know.

Tim snugged the baby into the soft carrier on his chest. Luca was big enough to face forward, which he seemed to love, kicking his little legs and pointing to seagulls. Because we were on expansive Buzzard's Bay, the waves were never big. Today the wind scudded up whitecaps on the gray water, which lapped with vigor. I made sure the earflaps on Luca's knit hat were pulled securely down.

The bay was a changeable beast, or maybe it was a mirror. On sunny days, the shallows, which stretched quite a ways from the shore, could be a clear turquoise. Today the water reflected the frowning sky.

We headed down the slope from the parking lot onto the sand and turned right. When the tide was in, the walking space narrowed to nothing as it met the wall of rocks piled up to support a road atop the causeway that stretched ahead. Right now the tide was out, and the walkable sand was several yards wide.

Tim took my hand as we strolled. "How was your book meeting?"

"Good. As usual, we talked more about the murder than about the book." I glanced up and smiled. "Don't worry, we're leaving most of it to Lincoln and gang."

"I'm glad to hear it, Mac." He halted when the strip of sand narrowed where the seawall began to curve. "Um, I want to turn around." His face was pale, his eyes anguished.

"You're thinking of Jamie," I murmured.

He nodded and reversed direction, releasing my hand. I went with him and took his hand again.

This wasn't a freestanding breakwater like the one that jutted out into the town's harbor, protecting it from the Atlantic Ocean. But this seawall, which led to a private housing enclave on the last spit of land before the channel to a small harbor, was formed from the same kind of huge, jagged rocks that Jamie died on.

The other direction on the beach held no bad associations. I stooped to pick up shells and driftwood. I let Luca feel them but extracted them before he put them into his mouth. He screeched when two little girls ran toward us, but they weren't his sister and Cokey. Luca pointed at a sandpiper scurrying along the water's edge.

"Our kids are doing fine, aren't they, Mac?" Tim asked.

"They absolutely are. Don't you think so?"

"Yes, but I worry. We took on such a huge responsibility last fall. I didn't feel anywhere near prepared enough."

"If anything, you were more ready than I was," I said. "Think about it. Nobody who gives birth to their first baby really knows what they're getting into, either. They grow into it as the child does. We had two full-blown children land in our laps. I think that's part of the shock."

"I suppose."

"A friend was telling me what goes into adopting a newborn. The parent or parents have to take all kinds of classes, get security checks and references, letters from their employers, the works. We didn't have to go through most of it to adopt them, being family and because you were already named as Jamie's guardian in case something happened. Biological parents don't have to pass any exams or scrutiny."

"At least we both already had experience with little

ones," Tim agreed. "And we have income and family, all of it."

"See?" I smiled at him. "We're well equipped to parent them, and I think the proof is how happy Luca and Ella seem."

We strolled hand in hand in silence for a few minutes. When Luca's eyes closed and his head listed to the side, Tim snugged up the carrier's support on that side.

I slowed as we approached the abandoned motel facing the water. The building had been boarded up for years. A sign everyone ignored marked the beach a yard before the structure as PRIVATE, DO NOT PASS. Yeah, no.

Except today something seemed different. The same shutter banged on one hinge in the breeze. The same peeling paint decorated the window trim. The same weathered plywood covered the windows, and the stairs had the same warped, splintery treads and railings. What had changed?

I shivered. What was not the same was that a murderer roamed the streets of our town. Who knows, maybe the killer was hiding right here in this decrepit building, skulking out when night fell.

"Are you cold, my love?" Tim laid his arm over my shoulders and squeezed me into him.

I leaned into his comfort. "No, but the motel is creepy. Let's get past it."

We picked up our pace until the building was behind us. I wished a solved homicide could be behind us as easily.

CHAPTER 26

By two o'clock, it had grown quiet upstairs, and I crept up to see what was happening. Tim and Luca were both napping, with the baby in his crib and Tim stretched out on Ella's bed in the same room. Although we had two rooms upstairs, she insisted on sharing a room with her brother when they came to live with us.

After the trauma the little girl went through losing her mother, we didn't argue. It meant we still had an office up there. At some point the kids would want their own rooms, and we could accommodate that.

When my phone rang, I hurried back downstairs.

"Mama Mac, can I sleep over here with Cokey?"

"You mean at your grandparents'?"

"Yes!"

I heard my father's voice, then he came on the line.

"We thought we'd give the parents of babies a one-child family for the night. Is that all right?"

"You bet it is," I said. "Thank you."

"Do you want to bring by a few things for her?

I invited them to Sunday school tomorrow, and they both seemed excited about the prospect." He gave a low chuckle.

"Converting the vulnerable youth, are you?" I could hear the smile in my voice.

"Why not?"

"It's fine with me. I'll pop by with a bag for Ella within the hour. Is Mom around?"

"She is. She's doing her best to teach both girls how to play Uno."

"Great. See you soon." We'd had epic and cutthroat games of Uno as a family as I was growing up. Six and nearly four might be a bit young for the game, although if anyone could teach them, it would be Astra.

I stuffed a little backpack with PJs, toothbrush, blankie, fresh socks, two pairs of underpants—just in case—and a warm knit dress with leggings for Sunday. After I got myself ready to go out, I left Tim a note on the kitchen table about where I was headed. I wouldn't mind a second walk, and with any luck, I could corner my mother and find out what was going on with her.

When I entered the parsonage family room, Cokey slapped down a card and shouted, "Uno!" Ella jumped up from where she sat on the rug and ran to me, wrapping my legs in a hug.

"We're playing Uno, Mama Mac. It means one in Spanish."

"I know, sweetie." I ruffled her hair. "I brought your stuff for the slumber party."

"We're having a party? What's slumber?" she asked.

"It means sleep," I said.

"Slumber party is an old-fashioned way to say sleepover," Cokey declared, with all the wisdom of the older cousin. "Now come back and play."

Ella plopped down and picked up her cards. "I like the blue ones best."

"I think the green ones are the prettiest," Cokey said.

My mom gave me a helpless shrug. Pa appeared in the doorway holding a tray.

"Can you all take a break? It's snack time."

"Snacks," both girls shrieked.

"Did you know it was National Tiny Sandwich Day?" he asked, giving me a wink. "Come to the table, girls, and check these out." He set a plate of miniature sandwiches made of cheese crackers and peanut butter on the kid-sized table in the corner. He added one mug of hot chocolate for each girl, with mini marshmallows floating on the surface.

The girls slid onto their little chairs and dug in. "It's a good thing I had a late lunch," I said. "I might elbow the kids out of the way."

"Come to the kitchen, ladies," Pa said. "I have snacks for the adults, as well."

We left Cokey explaining to Ella how to blow on the mug to cool the hot drink. In the kitchen, three mugs and a bottle of Irish whiskey sat on the counter next to a steaming pot of hot chocolate with a ladle in it.

"Help yourselves." He pointed at a bag. "Marshmallows are there."

"I remember when the rule was that we could have as many as our age plus one," I said.

"I'm willing to bet you're not going to stuff that mug with thirty-nine marshmallows," Mom said.

I smiled. "I'm not, but I might have three."

Pa ladled the hot drink into a mug and excused himself. "I'll be in the other room reading over tomorrow's sermon, but I can be interrupted at any time."

"Let me know if you want me to give it a sanity check, dear," Mom murmured.

He gave her a thumbs up and disappeared through the swinging door.

Mom filled two mugs for us and lifted the whiskey bottle. "I'm going to dose mine up. You want some, honey?"

"Only a splash, please." I sat across from her at the kitchen table. "Ooh, we get tiny sandwiches, too." I selected one from the plate on the table. The grown-up version was open-face sandwiches of mini stoned-wheat crackers spread with a soft herb-and-garlic cheese.

"Everything good with you, sweetheart?" Mom asked.

"Yes, except for Zia's killer still being at large." I blew on my mug and took a sip, gazing at her over the rim. "I think you know something, Mom. Abo Reba says you're being evasive, and I'm willing to bet you never got back to Lincoln. What's going on?"

My mother ran her finger around the rim of her cup. She sipped from it and added another splash of whiskey. She then ate a tiny sandwich, obviously stalling. I did my best to be patient, but this was getting ridiculous. I had my mouth open to speak when she lifted her gaze.

"It's like this . . ." Mom cleared her throat. "I was trying to help the poor girl. I told you she was resistant."

I nodded, not wanting to interrupt her.

"We were on the sidewalk one day after the free food market closed. Her refusals annoyed and worried me, and I'm afraid I was impatient and raised my voice. Mackenzie, I simply couldn't understand why she wouldn't accept help."

I stared at her. "Mom, getting mad is really unlike you, especially at someone you barely knew."

"I'm aware of that, and I'm not a bit proud of my outburst." She downed a glug of her chocolate. "The thing is, she reminded me of myself at more or less that age."

"She did?" I blinked and sat back.

"Yes. I gave birth to Derrick in my early twenties. I had not established myself in a career, to speak of. When my husband died young without leaving me anything but his debts and a toddler, I was in a bad way. If my aunt and uncle hadn't offered us a place to stay on Nantucket and I hadn't gotten that job with the Steamship Authority, well, I don't know what would have happened to your brother and me. Then I met your father, who had an interim pastor job on the island, and everything turned out fine."

"I know it did." I reached for her hand and squeezed it. "I'm glad you had caring relatives to tide you over.

But return Lincoln's calls, okay? He doesn't bite, and he knows you'd never murder anyone."

"I should hope so." She gave a wry laugh. "If everyone who raised their voice in public were a murderer, we would have a much-diminished population."

True words. I left for home with a lighter step. Evasive behavior from anyone I loved made me queasy, and this question at least was in the rearview mirror.

CHAPTER 27

I arrived at the Lobstah Shack a few minutes before three. A painting above the door of the grinning lobster from the shop's logo showed the creature waving a claw and lounging on a picnic table. The clapboards on the front of the building were painted red, and it wasn't a shack in the least, but the name was catchy. Tulia always posted the mouthwatering menu in the front window. It all sounded delicious unless you happened to be allergic to seafood. I was grateful neither Tim nor I were.

I headed inside and saw she was alone in the place. The restaurant was mostly for takeout but included a half dozen tables for diners.

"Hey, Mac," she called from behind the counter. "Here for a late lunch?"

"Actually, I want to bring home dinner. We don't have Ella for the night, so Tim and I can indulge in a meal that doesn't have to be kid friendly." I had texted Tim about the idea on my way here, and he'd given his enthusiastic approval.

"Great idea. Let's see, how about a lobster bisque to start, then fish cakes and hot biscuits?"

"Perfect, except I don't know how to make biscuits."

"I got you covered." She smiled and pointed a finger at me, then pulled a package out of the glass-doored upright freezer. "The instructions are on the package. You preheat the oven, lay these on a cookie sheet, and pop them in to bake for ten minutes. Serve hot with butter. To die for."

"Okay. I suppose we own a cookie sheet, and Tim will help me with the oven thing."

"You suppose?" Tulia smiled and shook her head. "I totally don't get not knowing how to turn on an oven at your age, but whatever. You seem to have survived just fine."

"Hey, I live with a baker who also likes to cook." I lifted a shoulder. "Believe me, I know how lucky I am."

"A green salad would be perfect with this meal. Do you know how to do that?"

"Um, like buy a bag of lettuce and a bottle of salad dressing?"

"Never mind," Tulia said. "I'll add coleslaw for two to your order. How does that sound?"

"Heavenly."

She glanced at the wall clock. "Got a minute for a chat before I pack up your dinner? I think I'll close early."

"Sure. Have you learned something new?"

"I might have." She turned the sign on the front door to CLOSED and locked up. She switched off the lights over the tables nearest the front windows and pointed at a small table farther back, near the counter. "Want something to drink?"

"No, thanks. I'm good." I sat across from her.

She popped open a bottle of Moxie and took a long swig. "I know this makes me a New England dinosaur, but I love the stuff."

"I've never tasted Moxie. Isn't it like Dr Pepper?"

"Kind of, but not really. Anyway, I was thinking about the dead girl, and I remembered that she came in here near the end of December."

"To buy lunch?" I asked.

"No. She was looking for a job, but I told her I already had one helper on the counter and in the kitchen, and that's all I need in the winter. I said if she came back in May, I might have something for the summer season."

"A season she'll never see, sadly."

"True. The poor girl." Tulia ran her finger around the rim of the bottle. "Yvonne Flora was in this morning. I don't know why a chef needs somebody else's cooking, but whatever. She said her partner was jonesing for a taste of my chowder."

"Yvonne might be tired of producing bar food five days out of seven."

"Exactly. I figure, who am I to judge? But here's the thing: You know how Yvonne's eyebrows do that thing?" Tulia frowned and touched the bridge of her nose where her eyebrows nearly touched. "Like, they naturally point down toward her nose even when she isn't frowning?"

"Oh, yes." I gave a slow nod. "I do know. Yvonne's eyebrows are like Nicole Kidman's, and Zia's were identical." I slapped the table. "I knew something seemed familiar when I spoke to Yvonne earlier this week."

"Do you think they're related?"

"I have no idea. As I said last night, Orlean learned that Zia seemed to be looking for her birth parents. She must have come to town because she had information that one of them lived in the area."

"Like maybe Yvonne gave her up for adoption as a baby?"

"I had that thought."

"Wouldn't a reunion be joyful?" Tulia's mouth turned down. "Yvonne would never murder someone she gave birth to."

"Certain people don't want secrets from their past revealed. As we both know by now, normal constraints on what people will or will not do is out the window when it comes to murderers. Except I'm not sure how we'll find out. Has Lincoln been in here at all?"

"No."

"I don't think I've spoken with him since Thursday." I'd never asked him how he'd recognized Cliff Vriesdorp's name in the bike shop. I should.

There was rap at the front window. I twisted in my seat to see my grandmother pressing her nose against the glass and waving.

"One of my favorite people." Tulia smiled and jumped up to unlock the door.

And one of mine.

"How are our intrepid sleuths doing?" Reba joined us at the table.

"Good, and you?" Tulia asked.

"Just ducky." Reba pointed at me. "And you, querida?"

"I'm fine. What are you up to this afternoon?"

"I was toodling down to the Rusty Anchor. Can I treat you girls to a drink?"

"Not for me, but thanks, Reba," Tulia said. "I've got to finish up here and head home. I have my grandgirls tonight."

"I'd love to," I said. "Let me check in with Tim first. He's alone with Luca." Maybe Reba and I could also check in with Yvonne while we were at the pub.

Tulia stood. "I'll pack up your order, Mac. Since you're not going straight home, I'll throw in a cold pack to keep the biscuits from thawing too much and to keep the other food cool."

"Thanks." I handed her two twenties and a ten, enough to cover the meal and then some.

"Takeout dinner?" my grandma asked.

"You bet." I texted Tim about going for a drink with Reba and asked if he and the baby wanted to join us. The pub was nothing if not family friendly. He wrote back declining, saying Luca was having a long nap and he was getting a bit of bakery accounting done. I replied with XXOO and said I'd be home with dinner by five.

CHAPTER 28

A few minutes later my grandmother and I slid onto stools at the bar. A gas fire flickered in the middle of the restaurant, and the wood of the booths and tables shone warm and inviting. The barstools were cushioned and comfortable, with backs on them, although Reba's feet dangled above the foot rail.

I loved the smell inside the pub. Meat grilling, onion rings and battered fish deep frying, and malty, hoppy drafts being poured made for a stomach-growling combination. I didn't think I could ever turn vegetarian.

Reba twisted to face me. "What new developments are there in the case?" She barely restrained herself from rubbing her palms together in anticipation.

"I'm not sure we have any since we spoke yesterday."

Delia, who was busy pouring and taking money behind the bar a couple of yards away, held up a finger to indicate she'd be right with us. I gave a little wave in return.

"Did you get a chance to talk to Lincoln about Cliff and Zia?" I asked.

"Why, yes," Reba said. "He seemed most appreciative."

"Thanks for doing that. What else have you been up to?"

"Well, our local history club wrapped up our latest project."

"What club is that?" I asked. "I didn't know you were in a history group." My grandmother was nothing if not full of surprises."

"We organized it at the library, you see, after you and Tim found that poor, shackled bride behind your wall. Ninety years dead she was."

Tearing out a wall in the cottage to add a downstairs bathroom had presented us with a shock we'd never expected less than a week before our wedding a little over a year ago. A modern-day murder had nearly followed.

"The story of Westham's families and society almost a century ago intrigued a few of us oldsters," she went on. "We began meeting every week to peruse local records, census reports, documents, what have you. We often shift over to the historical society building and dig into their files, too."

"That's fabulous. Why haven't you told us about the project?"

"Oh, you know, it's simply a silly thing to keep our minds active."

"It doesn't sound silly to me," I said. "I think it's a valuable contribution to the town." I'd bet Flo was helping them find documents and peruse newspapers of the era.

"There's a new girl in the group. She lives in Bourne but wants to move to Westham."

"Patty Harbach?"

"Why, yes. Do you know her?" Reba asked.

"I've met her. But Abo Ree, she has white hair. Patty is hardly a girl."

"It's only a turn of phrase, sweetheart. I'd say she's about your mother's age, which means I'm old enough to be her mother. Calling Patty a girl makes sense to this old lady."

I gave her a fond smile.

Delia slid down to us. "What can I get you two Almeidas today?"

"Rum hot toddy for me," Reba said.

"That sounds yummy," I said. "Same for me, please, Delia." It was Saturday, and I was on foot.

"I approve," Delia said. "Anything to eat?"

"We'll share a basket of French fries, dear." Reba glanced at me. "I can eat them all if you don't want any."

"Anchor Fries?" I raised my eyebrows. "How could I possibly not eat any?" Their fries were coated in something that made them extra crispy and flavored like heaven. I would family-snack my way through the afternoon. Lucky for me I'd inherited Reba's hummingbird metabolism and had no worries about not being hungry at dinnertime.

"Two toddies and an Anchor Fries, coming right up." Delia turned away.

Two minutes later she returned with our drinks.

"Delia, is Yvonne too busy for me to sneak into the kitchen and ask her something?" I tilted my head. I had no idea what to ask the chef, but I thought I shouldn't let the opportunity slip by.

Delia wrinkled her nose. "She's actually not here."

"On a busy Saturday?" Reba asked.

"That was my thought when I heard," Delia said. "Her assistant is handling everything today. She didn't even call him, just sent a text that she had to be out."

"That's interesting." I frowned. "Do you know Tulia Peters?"

"I do," Delia replied. "We play pickleball together in the warmer weather."

"She told me Yvonne was at the Lobstah Shack earlier today buying clam chowder," I said. "Yvonne told Tulia her girlfriend wanted some."

"So she's not out because she's sick." Delia glanced toward the kitchen. "Your fries should be up. Let me go check."

"Thank you." My grandma pulled out her extra-large cell phone and poked at it with her knobby index finger. "Ooh, says here June Jenkins was hauled in for questioning about the homicide."

"I know, I read that this morning. You know June. What do you think? Would she murder a young woman she'd hired to help her? If so, why?"

"Those are the million-dollar questions, Mackenzie. I'm afraid I don't have a single answer."

"Yeah." I gave my head a shake. "Neither do I."

CHAPTER 29

As I checked my phone to be sure things hadn't changed at home, two people approached the empty barstools next to us.

"Are these free, ma'am?" a woman asked Reba, pointing at the stools.

Reba glanced up. "Why, yes. Help yourselves. Oh, hello, Senator Kimball." She beamed at the man.

That dragged my attention away from my phone. The pair was Kimball and his driver, or perhaps she was his bodyguard. I hadn't seen her close up. Did US senators have Secret Service protection? I had no idea. This could be a federal employee or a private security guard who doubled as a personal driver.

"Good afternoon, ma'am." He gave my grandma a wide smile, as slick as can be. "Who do I have the pleasure of addressing?" He slid onto the stool next to Reba, despite the frown and head shake from his person. They must have come by car, since his slacks, leather shoes, and a sweater over an open-collar shirt were hardly biking clothes.

"I'm Reba Almeida, and this is my granddaughter, Mackenzie." She held out her hand.

"I'm delighted to meet you, Mrs. Almeida." He shook her hand, but his gaze drifted over to me. "Ah, the Mac's Bikes proprietor. We've met."

"Are the bikes holding up okay, Ross?" I asked.

"Yes." His smile disappeared.

I leaned over and extended my hand to the as-yet unintroduced woman. "We haven't met. I'm Mac Almeida."

She pursed her lips a little before speaking. Maybe she didn't want anyone knowing her name. She apparently changed her mind.

"Ed Kobylarz."

Her handshake was almost too firm, leaving me with aching knuckles. Ed? Maybe it was short for Edith or Edwina or Edna, and instead of going Mom's route of changing her name entirely, she went with a curtailed version that fit with her athletic, tough-woman self.

"Good to meet you, Ed."

Kimball made a face as if his beer was sour.

When Delia returned with our fries, Ed ordered a cup of coffee and Kimball asked for an IPA and a menu.

"Senator," Reba began, "I understand you're in town to open a dialogue about the wind project."

He blinked. "Ah, certainly, ma'am."

"Well, then." She channeled her best innocent, welcoming face. "We're having a meeting about it at the senior center tomorrow afternoon, and we hope you'll make an appearance and have a nice chat with Westham's old folks."

I didn't quite snort my toddy out my nose, but I had

to focus on the crispy fries in front of me so I wouldn't roll my eyes.

"I'd be delighted, Mrs. Almeida." His tone was smooth and overlaid with a touch of condescension.

"Good. We'll see you at two o'clock, dear. The senior center is behind the library next to the pickleball courts." She again beamed.

He turned away to confer with Ed. Reba faced me and winked. She lifted her mug and clinked it with mine, then began digging into the fries.

Her invitation sounded like a trap to me. Reba and her energetic cohort of seniors were strongly in favor of the wind project. Kimball wouldn't stand a chance.

Delia delivered the beer and coffee to our neighbors. My grandma lifted her mug.

"Cheers, Senator," she said.

He swiveled back to face her and raised his pint glass. "Here's to your very good health, ma'am."

"I'm entirely in the pink, thank you, sir." She lightly touched her drink to his. "It's a great tragedy that young Zia Carven's health was stolen from her. Her entire life, in fact. I saw the two of you conferring last weekend. How did you know her?" Reba raised her eyebrows.

That woman could play innocent with the best of them, but I knew better. She was digging for information.

"I'm sorry, what?" Kimball shifted his gaze away from his diminutive questioner and toward Ed.

"I asked how you knew Zia." Reba measured her words. She didn't raise her voice, but her intention to receive an answer was clear.

"Well, I, uh, I didn't know her." He gazed past Reba's left ear. "Not at all. I represent the entire state of Rhode Island, though. The young woman claimed to be from there and accosted me on the sidewalk in front of my hotel." He took a deep drink of his IPA. "She had some fantasy about her past. I pitied her. Mental illness, you know."

Ed leaned over and spoke in a low tone to him. He took another long glug of his beer and stood. Ed laid money on the bar and slid off her stool.

"Excuse us, ladies," Kimball said. "Business calls." He followed his driver out.

My grandma whistled. "Somebody was in a big donkey's hurry all of a sudden, wouldn't you say?"

"I would. Did you really see him talking to Zia last weekend?"

"Would I lie?" She winked at me. "Yes, I actually did. Couldn't hear a word they said, but it didn't look like a friendly chat. Not at all."

CHAPTER 30

After Kimball and Ed were gone I told Reba I would try to get to the meeting tomorrow.

"Do," she urged. "It's open to the whole town. The invite is on the Westham Talks group page, too. I admit, I told a teensy white lie to the senator about us old folks, and I don't mind one bit. That man is more slippery than a greased pig on an oil slick after a rain. To my mind, he deserves to answer a mess of hard questions."

I moved briskly along Main Street twenty minutes later, dinner bag in hand. Now I saw the flyers tacked to telephone posts and on the announcement board in front of Town Hall. I doubted they had gone up only today and scolded myself for not being more observant.

At the Toy Soldier, I slowed and peered in the front window, where the poor fallen soldier still lay crosswise on the tracks. No lights were on inside, even though the posted hours said the business didn't close until six o'clock. It was only four thirty, and June had told me she'd gotten permission to reopen that day. Why was the store closed?

"Looking for June?" a man asked.

I turned to see Lincoln a few feet away. "No, but I was remembering finding Zia."

"A sad story, and a criminal one. Do you have a minute?"

"Not really." I held up the bag. "I have to get home with dinner and to give Tim a break. He's been alone with Luca all afternoon. But you can walk with me if you want."

"Perfect."

We set out.

"I thought it was strange that the toy store was closed," I said. "Saturday afternoon has to be a good time for a retail shop like hers. Yesterday June told me she'd gotten permission to reopen today."

"I think it's a bit strange as well. I was hoping to speak with her. She's another one who has been hard to pin down in person."

"Are you thinking she had a reason to murder Zia?"

"We aren't closing any doors at this time, Mac."

As we went down the sidewalk, we passed more flyers about the senior center event. They advertised a public airing of the proposed wind project's pros and cons.

"Do you know what that's about?" Lincoln pointed his chin at one of them.

"I found out a little while ago from Reba. Do you already know that Senator Ross Kimball is in town, apparently to campaign against the wind project?"

Lincoln nodded.

"Well, I was just in the pub with my grandma. Kimball and his driver, or whoever she is, sat next to us at the bar." I related Reba's invitation to the event. "Except she made it sound like the 'old folks' would welcome his input. I think he doesn't know what he's in for."

"I'm sure he doesn't." Lincoln didn't seem to find the news amusing. "You're being careful, aren't you, Mac? Kimball is a powerful man."

"I am. You might want to be at the meeting tomorrow for the fireworks." I thought back on the day. "Listen, I know you had a few suspicions about my mom and her argument with Zia."

"This is true, and Astra is still avoiding me."

I swallowed. "She told me a couple hours ago that she got mad at Zia because the girl reminded her of herself at that age. My mom was in a bad spot when Derrick was a baby and she was a young widow without a job. If she hadn't been offered help and accepted it, she thinks their lives would have spiraled downward. At least, that's my sense of what she said."

"She could have told me as much."

"I think it's still hard for her to talk about it." I blew out a breath. "Anyway, that's why she was trying so hard to help Zia, and why she got upset at her refusal."

"I see. Thank you for letting me know. I still want to speak with her."

"I know, and she's aware of that." I snapped my fingers. "There is something else. Orlean happened by the place in Bourne where Zia lived. She talked to a few people and learned that Zia was looking for her birth parents."

"She just happened by." He turned one of his stern-detective, over-the-top-of-his-glasses looks on me.

I shrugged and ignored the look. "I've been wondering if Yvonne Flora gave up a baby for adoption twenty-odd years ago. Have you ever noticed her eyebrows?"

"I can't say I have."

"When you get a chance, look at pictures of Nicole Kidman."

"The actress?" he asked.

"Yes. Zia had similar eyebrows. Yvonne does, as well."

"So noted."

"And did I tell you about when Kimball came into the bike shop?"

"I don't believe so," Lincoln said.

"His aide, a young guy named Brendan Lopes, mentioned that Zia had been pestering the senator's office with calls, wanting to meet with him. Kimball claimed she was only a constituent, but he protested rather too much. It might be worth checking out. Also, my grandma says she saw Zia talking with Kimball last weekend and that it didn't look friendly. While we were at the pub, Reba asked him how he knew Zia, but he claimed not to."

"Do you know where they're staying while they're in Westham?" he asked.

"No, but it might be on the bike rental agreement. I'll check for you on Monday."

A gust of cold wind made me shiver. I snugged my

scarf tighter around my neck, but the shiver reminded me of the abandoned beach motel.

"This morning we walked on the beach past that boarded-up motel out there," I said. "Do you know it?"

He nodded.

"It's pretty derelict," I went on. "I wondered if a killer was hiding inside."

"I'll make sure someone checks it out. Thanks."

We passed Salty Taffy's, also closed, and then the health clinic, outside of which Gin and I had found a murder victim a couple of years ago. The hardware store was ahead a few storefronts.

"When you saw Cliff Vriesdorp in my shop a couple days ago, you seemed to recognize the name," I said. "Can you say more about that?"

"He appears to have a connection with Senator Kimball, and Delia reported that he was drinking with the victim in the Rusty Anchor. That's all."

"Did you learn anything about how he knew Zia?" I asked.

"No. We don't really have a reason to question him, but we haven't given up."

I made a mental note to see what I or another Cozy Capers member could find out.

We approached where Blacksmith Shop Road ended at Main Street.

"This is my turn." I pointed. "Was there more you wanted to talk about?"

"I guess not. Thank you for sharing what you know."

"Seriously, Lincoln?" I smiled. "I always let you

know what I've learned. And before you say it, I'm always careful."

He did not hold back from rolling his eyes.

"Have a good night," I said.

"You as well." His gaze shifted across the intersection. "Super—the next person on my list has appeared."

I glanced in the same direction. Cliff stood in front of Pete's Hardware frowning at his phone, then began walking toward us along the sidewalk, still absorbed in his device. I was dying to stay for their conversation, but I really had to get home.

"Let me know what goes down, okay?" I murmured to Lincoln.

He gave me a quick thumbs up. I turned away and pointed myself toward my menfolk.

CHAPTER 31

At eight o'clock that night Tim and I were streaming a show, although I'd already detected light snores from him, when a call came in from my dad.

"Ella's homesick," he began.

"Should I come and get her?" I asked. She'd slept over at their place before and never asked to come home.

"She wants to talk with you. I'll put her on."

"Mama Mac," her little voice said. "I miss you and Papa Tim and Luca."

"We miss you, too, sweetie. Have you been having fun with Cokey and your abos?"

"Yes." She sniffed. "And we're going to make banana waffles in the morning."

"That sounds yummy." I heard her talking to someone away from the phone. "Ella, do you want me to bring you home?"

"Kind of, but Cokey says I can sleep in her bed with her and all the stuffies. She has ten!"

"That's awesome, Ella. You'll be nice and cozy. Sweet dreams, darling."

"Okay. See you tomorrow. Here, Abo Joe."

My father gave a low laugh. "Problem solved as fast as it arose. Talk to you tomorrow, Mac."

"Thanks, Pa."

I sat there for a moment. Ella might have picked up on the commotion in town, on my concern about finding a killer still at large, even though I hadn't talked about it in front of her. I was sure nobody else had, either, but her emotional radar might be on high alert.

Tim sat up and asked what was going on. I gave him a big kiss, said all was well, and suggested he might want to go to bed. After he returned the kiss and went, I turned off the television. With as much as we each had missed of the show, we'd have to watch it from the beginning again.

I buttoned up my cardigan, then got up to pour myself a tiny nightcap. The thermostat gave a tick and the boiler in the basement fired up. The house was drafty, having been built a hundred years earlier. While Tim and I didn't mind sleeping in cool air, we kept the heat higher overnight now because we didn't want the children to get cold. Luca slept in a warm sleepsack, since he was too young for a blanket in his crib, but Ella was prone to kicking off her comforter.

Once I was in the kitchen, another noise sounded, almost masked by the sound of the furnace but not quite. I stepped back to the wall and switched off the light. I stood still to listen.

It had been cold but not windy when I walked home. If a person had come to visit, the motion-detector lights outside would have sprung into action. If the visitor had good intentions, they would have knocked or rung the doorbell. If bad, well, maybe the focused illumination would convince them to leave. But neither the front nor back door motion-activated lights were on.

All the doors were locked. I'd checked them after dinner. All the windows were secure with had curtains or shades pulled. I kept listening but didn't hear the noise again. Maybe a mouse had found its way in through a crack in the antique foundation and sought refuge in the relative warmth of the cellar.

On the other hand, someone murdered Zia. Killed her as she worked in a toy store, of all places. I had a bit of a local reputation for looking into homicides. Heck, even my son's day care provider had asked me to put on my amateur sleuthing hat and look into his friend's death. The killer could be trying to break into our home, our refuge.

The thought made me more angry than fearful—more Mama Bear than shrinking violet. I flipped on the kitchen light, then heated water for herbal tea instead of pouring a couple fingers of whiskey. I wouldn't be cowed, but I wanted to be sharp in case I needed to act.

Back in the living room with my hot drink, I checked my phone for Cozy Capers texts. I smiled at one from Gin.

I miss our morning walks. Any chance of a stroll tomorrow? I plan on going to the wind power meeting. You?

Before the kiddos came into our lives, Gin and I would meet every weekday morning at seven for a power walk and a good chat. I wrote back that, yes, I would be going, I missed our walks, too, and we could head over together, as long as she didn't mind a stroller holding a baby as our third. We exchanged a couple more messages about arrangements.

I settled in to read about the Garden Squad. If that fictional gang could solve the murder du jour, my own squad could, too.

CHAPTER 32

Tim and I spent a quiet morning with breakfast, the baby, and the newspaper. When Luca went down for his morning nap at nine thirty, Tim headed out for a long run, with my blessing. Our son was usually good for at least a solid hour's sleep, which helped with getting a few things accomplished.

After I switched on the baby monitor, I took a quick shower, put in a load of laundry, and picked up a few toys and books in the family room. I stopped in my tracks, holding *Blueberries for Sal* in one hand and a toy airplane in the other. I'd had a lifelong obsession with keeping things neat and tidy, but I realized my Neat Freak crown had slipped in recent months. I no longer grew itchy when things weren't perfectly put away, with everything in its place. I smiled, crediting motherhood with a relaxation of my standards. Kiddos simply weren't neat creatures. It would be insanity to try to make them be.

I stashed the book and plane on their assigned shelves

and settled on the couch to spend a little quality time with my phone. Lincoln hadn't sent an update about his conversation with Cliff. Maybe he was taking Sunday morning off, too, or didn't feel obliged to share news with an amateur like me.

Gin had sent an interesting message an hour ago.

Was out last night. Yesterday end of day saw Linc and Cliff having chat on sidewalk near my shop. Cliff wasn't happy.

That must have been right after I turned to go home. I tapped out a reply.

Did you overhear anything?

No. Cliff stalked away after a few minutes.

So Lincoln hadn't detained him. Interesting.

Luca was still asleep when Tim returned home. He leaned over and gave me a quick salty kiss before starting his post-run stretches.

"All quiet here?" he asked.

"Very. Babykins is having a solid sleep."

"Good. I ran by June Jenkins on my way home. She was cleaning her shop's front windows so vigorously I thought she was going to wear a hole in the glass. She didn't look good. Has she been ill?"

"I don't know. Having your only employee murdered in your store can't be good for a person's mental health. Lincoln seems to have suspicions about her, too, which I'm sure is worrying her."

"I see. I didn't know that part." He did one last stretch.

"I'm going to head in for my shower while I can." He waggled his eyebrows at me. "Want to keep me company?"

"Ooh, that's an invitation I can barely refuse." I laughed. "You know I'd love nothing else, but we're pretty much guaranteed to have way too much fun and forget we have a baby sleeping upstairs. I'll take a rain check, my love. Now go, quick, before I change my mind." I made a shooing motion,, and he headed toward the bathroom.

At a bit before noon, my father dropped both girls at our house by prior arrangement. We caught up for a moment in the kitchen.

"We'll see you at family dinner," Pa said before he left.

"We're going to bring cookies," Ella told him.

"Did you have a good time at Sunday school?" I asked after hugs and kisses all around were accomplished.

"Yes," Ella said.

"We sang songs and learned about Noah's ark and the giant flood," Cokey added.

"The water covered the whole wide world." Ella's already large eyes grew bigger.

"But Noah built a gigantic boat and let two of all the animals on, a boy and a girl of each," Cokey said. "Even snakes."

"Even snakes. Even snakes." Belle had mastered

Cokey's voice along with everybody else's. "Whole wide world. Even snakes."

"Really?" I asked.

"Yes." Cokey nodded. "And when the sun came out, a bird flew up, holding a branch."

I'd wondered as a child if it had been one of the two doves on board and if not, how it had survived the deluge. I wasn't going to get into the often-shaky logic of myths with these two darlings.

"And we got pineapple juice and crackers for snack," Ella added.

Belle waddled up "Snack, Mac?"

Cokey giggled. "Can I give her frozen carrots, Tia Mac?"

"Sure." I poured some into a bowl and handed it to my niece.

"Are you girls ready for lunch?" Tim asked.

"I want to make cookies first." Ella looked hopeful. "You said we could, Papa Tim. Cookies we can take to family dinner."

"We will, sweetie, but baking is for after we eat." He handed Luca to me and began pulling things out of the refrigerator.

We spent the next hour together, eating and talking and laughing, the big people being entertained by the small ones. I soaked up the normalcy of the moment. Ella having a slightly older girl cousin nearby had been a huge help in her adjustment to life with us. In a couple of years, Luca and little Joey—Joseph Alcindo Searle, named for his grandfather and great-grandfather—would also become playmates.

This slice of the present had nothing to do with murder, and rightly so. My brain swirled with thoughts and questions, but for now I kept them firmly in the background.

CHAPTER 33

At one forty, I popped a bundled-up Luca into the stroller and tucked the packed diaper bag underneath. Tim and the girls were happily elbow-deep in cookie dough.

"I'll either be back by three thirty or I'll send a message and meet you guys at the parsonage. I'm not sure how long this meeting will last."

"Stay to the end if you want. I'll bring a bottle for the young gentleman." He pointed a floury finger to his lips.

I bestowed kisses on everyone and opened the door to find Gin waiting on the porch. She helped me lift the stroller down to the walkway, and we set out for the wind power meeting. With any luck, the little boy would fall asleep on the walk and take his afternoon nap in the stroller for the duration of the gathering. If he didn't and started fussing, I could always leave. I had no responsibilities there, only a keen curiosity.

For now, pacifier in his mouth, Luca fiddled with the

various bits on Dan the Dinosaur, a green activity stuffie we'd attached to the crossbar on the stroller. This wouldn't be a power walk, but it was good to have the company of my friend.

"Have you recovered from our drive Friday night?" she asked.

"I have." I shrugged. "We weren't hurt. The plate number hasn't come back to you, has it?"

"Nope, unfortunately."

"It hasn't to me, either. Have you learned anything new?"

"Not really," she said. "You?"

"Maybe. Reba and I ran into Kimball and his driver, Ed, at the pub yesterday. My grandma was chatting him up."

"As she does." Gin smiled.

"For sure. She invited him to the meeting today." I added the way Reba had framed the meeting as being a bunch of sweet old folks. "For some reason he seemed unhappy to see me with her."

"Do you think he knows we're looking into him?"

"I don't know how he could, but it's possible. Here's another thing. You know that abandoned motel at the beach?"

"Of course." She shook her head. "It's a real eyesore. The owner mismanaged it and then died. The property is apparently tied up in a dispute with the heirs. Until that's sorted out, it can't be sold or torn down."

"I had a super creepy feeling walking by it yesterday

morning. The thought occurred to me that Zia's killer might be hiding out inside. Do you think that's crazy?"

"Not at all. I hope you told Lincoln."

"I did, and he said he'd have someone check it out."

When we passed the toy store, the windows gleamed. Like yesterday, I saw no evidence of June being inside. A winter Sunday in a tourist town wasn't a big shopping day for anyone, and it was still thoroughly winter. Despite the lengthening days, today a cold, damp wind snuck in under my coat.

"Hang on a minute," I said to Gin. I paused to snug down Luca's earflaps. I tucked one of his hands back inside the warm, zip-up bag that fit into the stroller seat and had slits for the safety belts.

"Check this out." Gin stood in front of a light post near us.

We both perused a newly posted meeting flyer, which read, "Clear the Air for Wind Power. Come prepared with questions for Senator Ross Kimball. All are welcome. Westham Senior Center." It added the address, date, and time. Even though he represented Rhode Island, his state shared the bay where the project was to be located with this part of Massachusetts. It made sense for him to try and sway the opinion of people on this side of the state line.

Whether it was due to the cold, the movement, or naptime, Luca was sound asleep when we arrived at the senior center. It was single-story modern building of light-colored bricks tucked behind the antique Town Hall. A shed in the parking lot held loaner walkers, wheelchairs, and shower chairs. The row of handicapped parking spaces was twice as long as at other municipal buildings, and all the doors had square automatic door-opener pads.

I pressed one with my elbow, a hands-free habit I developed during the pandemic, and in we went.

CHAPTER 34

The baby, Gin, and I were easily the youngest people in the large meeting room so far. Reba and a white-haired woman busied themselves around the front table, which held a wireless microphone, several glasses, and a pitcher of water. A podium next to the table had a microphone sticking up from it. Rows and rows of folding chairs were neatly arrayed with an aisle down the middle, and half the seats were already filled. A microphone on a stand stood at the front of the middle aisle.

We grabbed seats at the end of the last row, and I set the brakes on the stroller next to my chair. I gently slid off Luca's hat and unzipped the bag so he wouldn't overheat as he slept. Two speakers were on stands in the front corners of the room, but this kid had a big sister. He was a great sleeper, including in noisy surroundings. If he woke up and fussed, I was close to the exit.

Reba was heading back to greet me when Brendan and Kimball made their way in. Brendan moved nervously,

Kimball with confidence. My grandma changed course and approached them.

"You have quite the little gathering here, Mrs. Almeida." The senator's voice boomed.

"And more are coming. Everyone is looking forward to hearing what you have to say, Ross."

In fact, people still streamed in.

Reba smiled at Brendan. "Who might you be, young man?"

"Brendan Lopes, ma'am. I'm the senator's aide."

"Excellent," she said. "We can all use one. I'm Reba Almeida." She held out her hand.

He gave it a quick shake and dropped her hand with a glance at Kimball, who seemed to be ignoring Brendan's very presence.

"Let me get you gentlemen settled." She waved toward the front. "We have plenty of residents with questions, and I'll be moderating."

Kimball blinked, but he followed her to the front. He slowed at the filled seats and began smiling and shaking hands with those on the aisle. Brendan trailed behind and grabbed a seat in the front row at the other end from the side I'd chosen.

A woman hurried in, slid around the stroller, and took the seat in front of mine. She twisted to face Gin and me. I was surprised to see Patty Harbach.

"How are you Mac? Isn't it great to see so many people interested? With any luck, we'll change this sleazebag's position on wind power."

"That's what my grandmother is hoping for," I said.

"Gin, have you met Patty Harbach? Patty, this is my friend Gin Malloy, who owns Salty Taffy's."

The two shook hands and exchanged greetings.

"I love your candy store," Patty added. "But speaking of Reba, Mac, you're lucky to have her in your family. I've become super interested in the history around here, and I'm part of the study group Reba and a few others began."

"I thought you lived in Bourne, Patty."

"I do, but I'm planning to move to Westham. It's a much more vibrant town." She glanced around the room. "Is Astra coming today?"

"I don't know."

Mom hadn't mentioned it, but it wouldn't be out of character. Pa, on the other hand, tried to stay away from taking sides in local politics. He didn't feel it meshed well with being a minister for everyone, regardless of their views.

Within five minutes, nearly all the chairs had filled with residents who spanned the adult age spectrum. Two rows were taken by teens wearing green T-shirts. I spotted Tulia's counter employee among them. If Kimball thought he was in for a little chat with push-over old folks, he was in for a shock and hadn't paid attention to the wording on the flyers.

At the last minute, Lincoln sauntered up, hands in his pockets, and stood with his back to the wall next to the stroller. I gave him a little wave as Reba lifted the microphone on the front table. Gin gently elbowed me.

"Good thing he's here," she murmured. "Just in case."

"Agree," I replied.

Lincoln gave the appearance of a casual observer, but I caught his keen gaze keeping track of everyone present. There was nothing casual about the detective in this moment.

CHAPTER 35

"Thank you all for coming out today," my grandma began, her voice loud and clear through the speakers. "My name is Reba Almeida, and I'll be our moderator this afternoon." She got an enthusiastic round of applause. "We're super pleased Senator Kimball has joined us to hear our concerns and answer our many questions about this important energy project." She faced him at the podium. "Ross, would you like to make a few remarks first?"

"I appreciate that, Mrs. Almeida. First let me offer my condolences to the community for the tragic death of Miss Carven earlier in the week. I've learned she was one of my Rhode Island constituents. Our state mourns her loss along with you."

That seemed odd. Zia hadn't lived in Westham, although she died here. Not many people knew her. Sure, Kimball had been her senator, but was he also Zia's biological father? I glanced over at Lincoln, who seemed to be more focused on the crowd than the speaker. The senator went on to speak about all the different kinds of harm a wind project in the bay could bring.

When he made a statement about the ample energy our region already had, one of the students stood and called out, "We need clean, renewable energy for our future!"

Reba, who had remained standing, grabbed her mike. "Thank you, young lady. Audience members will have ample time for voicing their opinions. Senator Kimball has the floor. Ross, do you have more to offer, or can we move to questions?"

He shot a look at where Brendan sat. The aide shrugged helplessly. Kimball nodded at Reba.

She lifted a pad of lined paper. "We'll start with several questions prepared by the committee, and then I'll open it up to the audience. People, if you have a question or concern, you may line up at the central microphone and wait your turn."

Audience members, including one of the teens, hurried to join the rapidly growing queue.

"Our group has learned you have accepted several large donations from fossil-fuel companies." Reba's friendly tone didn't change. "Please elaborate on your reasoning."

Good for her. I loved my grandma.

Kimball took a moment to adjust his collar, possibly trying to cover up his shock at the question. "Ma'am, we accept campaign donations from a wide range of the population."

"Except you are not campaigning, Senator. You were elected two years ago. You have four years to go."

A hoot and a smattering of applause came from the audience. Weren't politicians always campaigning? Representatives to congress certainly were, with elections every two years.

Kimball mustered a smile. "Next question?"

"Why are you so opposed to clean, renewable power sources?" Reba asked with her same sweet-but-steely smile.

"I am not opposed, but this wind project isn't the right answer. As I'm sure everyone knows, Buzzards Bay and Vineyard Sound spill into the waters of my fair state. We have them in common, and this project affects all of us."

She then asked him how long he had lived in Rhode Island. I found out why after he answered.

"The Kimballs have had a vacation home in Westerly, Rhode Island, for generations, and we began living there full time about ten years ago."

In order to have a better chance of being elected by living in a wealthy enclave near the Connecticut border? Possibly. He wouldn't be the first politician who changed his address to better his chances.

Reba turned the questioning over to the line of folks at the microphone. "Keep it snappy, please. We want to give everyone a chance, and nobody needs to hear five minutes of your opinion before you get to your question. I will cut you off if that happens," said the former high school teacher, experienced at keeping her charges in line.

The majority of those who came forward were in favor of the wind project. Interspersed were a handful who applauded Kimball for fighting it.

The green-shirted youth got her turn at last.

"It's our climate you want to ruin, and our future you don't care about. We need wind and solar now." She raised a fist in the air.

The others in green shirts stood and punched their fists in the air. They began chanting, "Wind and solar now. Wind and solar now," on repeat. The speaker re-joined them.

"People." Reba's voice was loud and firm through the speakers. "Thank you to the youth of our town. You have been seen and heard. Now sit down and let others have their turn," she said, in a tone that implied an "or else." When she came around the table and headed toward the group with a deliberate step, hands on her hips, they all plopped onto their chairs.

I chuckled to myself and glanced at Luca, who was still asleep. Gin grinned and gave me a thumbs up. She appreciated Reba as much as I did.

A familiar voice sounded. June stood at the microphone with three speakers waiting behind her. "June Jenkins, Mashpee. The waters of the Sound are sacred to my people." Her voice shook, but after she squared her shoulders and exhaled, it strengthened. "The fish feed us, the birds watch over us, the waters sustain us. None of it should be disturbed. This project must not take place. It will use machinery. It will construct vibrating devices. It will send out polluting ships to maintain the turbines, and more. We are strongly opposed."

"Thank you, June." Kimball spoke slowly and gazed intently at her.

June's face went pale. A smattering of applause swelled. Lincoln nodded and frowned at the same time. June turned and headed straight for the exit. Lincoln followed. *Good.* He'd been looking for her. Why had the color drained from her face when Kimball spoke directly to her?

Patty spoke next.

"What are you doing to help solve Zia's murder? Rumor has it you knew her better than you're letting on."

I stared. Where had she come up with that?

Kimball's nostrils flared and his face flushed. Brendan stood. The senator waved him away and lifted his chin.

"I understand the local authorities are diligently pursuing the instigator of that terrible deed. That will be all for today. Thank you, Mrs. Almeida, for inviting me. Thank you to everyone for coming out today," Kimball said. It appeared he was about to say more, but clamped his mouth shut. He shook Reba's hand and followed Brendan out through a door near the front.

Well, well. Somebody didn't want to answer a question about his own young constituent's homicide. Too bad Lincoln had already left, but I would make sure he knew what had happened. Luca opened his eyes and whimpered.

"I'd better go," I said to Gin, "before this turns into a full-blown wail."

"Take care." She waggled her fingers at the baby.

"Shall we go, sweet boy?" I pushed the stroller into the lobby and secured his wraps and my own before heading outside.

CHAPTER 36

As usual for Sunday dinner at the parsonage the kitchen smelled divine, today with Italian-themed scents. We'd shifted the gathering time earlier to four o'clock so the junior set could get bathed and to bed on time on a school night.

Patty's bombshell question that ended the meeting came after three o'clock. Since Reba had been busy schmoozing near the door with her friends and other attendees, I told her I'd see her at dinner, and I sent a message to Tim that Luca and I would meet them at the parsonage.

After I extracted the baby from the stroller, my mom took possession of boy and diaper bag, saying she would change him if he needed it.

"Thank you. Tim's bringing a bottle."

"You know I have supplies, too. Don't we, sugar pie?" She made a big-eyed smile at the baby, who smiled back. She carried him away into the family room.

"What's on the menu?" I asked my aproned father.

"Lasagna and salad. Neli's bringing an appetizer."

"And Tim and the girls will have a raft of cookies with them when they arrive, if any survived their baking adventure."

"Knowing your husband, he might have an extra dessert on call as a backup." Pa finished tearing lettuce into the wide salad bowl and unwrapped a long, slender cucumber.

"He totally might."

"Grab a glass if you'd like." He lifted his jelly glass of red wine and motioned toward the box of good-quality cabernet sauvignon on the counter. "Tell me, how are you doing, favorite daughter of mine?"

"I'm pretty well." I filled a jelly glass half full and took a sip. "I'm figuring out how to manage life as a mom, as you can imagine."

"I can, as a matter of fact. Don't forget I also inherited a toddler when I met your mother and Derrick."

"Right." I did sometimes let that fact slip to the back of my mind. "Did you feel prepared?"

"Prepared?" He laughed. "Only a little. I had babysat my sister's children when they were little, which meant I knew how to change a diaper. Having a son land in my life wasn't a shock as much as a learning curve. But love eases many burdens."

"True words, favorite father of mine." I smiled.

"How's the homicide case going?"

I made a low little groan in my throat. "Nothing is clear. I hope Lincoln and his team are moving faster than my group of amateurs." A text pinged into my phone. "Speaking of them, excuse me for a minute, okay?"

He nodded, and I turned away.

Norland had written to the group.

Learned a few things about Zia. Meet in person soon?

I liked the sound of his discoveries, and I was eager to get the facts. But I wasn't sure if I could easily meet again in person. Flo wrote next.

I have new info about her, too. Can we get together tonight?

Ugh. I didn't want to go out tonight. Sundays were for family, despite my little outing to the senior center. I always savored being home after family dinner and holding on to that gathering in my heart. Before I had a chance to respond, Gin added a message.

News here as well. Can't do tonight. Tomorrow lunchtime my shop?

That was a much better plan. I send a quick reply.

Yes to tomorrow. One pm best for me. I have a few bits, too.

Everyone else gave a nod to the meeting, and before I stashed my phone I sent a message to Lincoln.

After you left, attendee at meeting asked Kimball how he was helping solve murder of his constituent, accused him of knowing her better than he let on. He flushed, abruptly ended meeting. FYI. Accuser name Patty Harbach, lives in Bourne.

I hit SEND and slid the phone into my back pocket as Reba trundled in, cheeks pink from the excitement of staging a public grilling. She hung her parka on a peg and beamed at Pa and me.

"That was a success, don't you think, Mackenzie? If he thought he was drumming up support, he got a rude awakening."

"Yes, not that anyone was rude." I took down a glass from a shelf my petite grandma would never be able to reach. "Wine?"

"Please. Patty was rather direct, don't you think?"

"She was. I loved it." I handed Reba the glass and pulled out a chair.

"Who is Patty, and what was she direct about?" Pa finished slicing the cucumber and set down the knife.

Mom wandered back in with a wriggly baby in her arms. "Here. He's hungry." She handed him to Pa, stuck a glass measuring cup full of water into the microwave as a bottle warmer, and filled a bottle with the premixed formula she kept on hand.

Soon Pa was sitting at the kitchen table with Luca as the baby sucked down his warm snack. Mom helped herself to wine and joined us.

I told them about Patty Harbach and the question she'd asked. "She's a Californian transplanted to Bourne, but she said she'd like to move to Westham. I met her last week."

"She's one of my clients," my mom said.

"Yes, she mentioned that," I said.

"She'd be a lovely addition to our town, don't you think?" Mom asked.

I nodded.

"She already is," Reba said. "She's taken a keen interest in Westham's history. But I think the question really is, what does Patty know about the senator and the victim?" Reba nearly rubbed her hands together. "Ooh, *The Senator's Victim* sounds like the title of a movie or a crime novel, right?"

"Mother, perhaps we shouldn't get ahead of ourselves," Pa said in the gentle-but-firm tone he was an expert at.

He was right. Abo Reba had demonstrated her tendency to get excited about homicides in the past. Still, hers was a valid question. Patty's bike should be ready for her to pick up soon. I could try to subtly dig for information and then inquire why she'd asked Kimball about Zia at a gathering about the wind-power project.

CHAPTER 37

By four thirty I sat with my jelly jar of wine in the living room as the parsonage filled up with the usual happy chaos. Reba sat on the couch holding Luca. A pacifier in his mouth, he quietly watched the action. Wearing a diaper bag backpack like ours, Derrick brought a sleeping Joey inside in his car seat while Neli carried a board covered in foil. When Tim arrived with the girls, each of whom proudly held a closed cookie tin in her hands, the family gathering was complete. Two baby boy cousins, two older girl cousins, a dog, and seven of the three older generations made for a full house.

Ella handed Astra her tin and hurled herself at me. “Mama Mac, I made cookies all by myself.”

“You did? Was it hard?” I pulled her onto my lap for a snuggle.

“Tio Tim helped us,” Cokey said. “But we each got to run the mixing machine, and we scooped the cookies out ourselves. They’re oatmeal chocolate chip.”

I set Ella down. "You guys didn't eat any dough, did you?" I fake frowned.

Tim smiled and rolled his eyes. Ella gave Cokey a worried glance.

"We did," Cokey said. "It's okay, Ella. We do it all the time."

We bought eggs from a trusted local organic farmer so I didn't worry about the girls eating raw dough, and I knew Cokey tasted it at home, too. Scraping the cookie dough or cake batter bowl was a cherished memory from my childhood. I didn't want my kiddos missing out on it.

"Appetizers are ready." On the coffee table, Neli had uncovered the board, revealing three long puffy strips of bread about four inches wide topped with caramelized onions, cherry tomato halves, and ribbons of fresh basil.

"Mmm, that smells really good," I said.

"Thanks." She sliced the strips crosswise into individual pieces. "It's kind of like pizza, girls."

"Yum." I smiled at my sister-in-law. "How are you feeling, Neli?" She'd had a really long labor with Joey, who was her first baby. "You look great."

"Thanks. I'm always exhausted, and it seems like he nurses constantly." She had smudges under her eyes, but she'd had her braids redone and wore a new warm-yellow sweater that made her skin glow. Belinda, Neli's mom, was as dark as Reba, but Neli's father had been white, and her skin was more like Pa's—a bit darker than mine. So far Joey looked fairly pale, but that could change over time. I loved that our family was a mix of everything.

Including a dog. Tucker pranced up and sniffed at the board.

"It's not for dogs, Tucker," Cokey scolded.

"Tucker, kitchen," Mom pointed to the other room. She followed him, carrying the cookies. My parents had acquired the hypoallergenic Portuguese water dog as a puppy a year and a half ago. Now full grown, he was mostly Cokey's pet, but since Joey's birth he'd been living at the parsonage full time.

Tim emerged from the kitchen holding a pint glass of beer for himself and a soda for Derrick, who was doing a great job at living a sober life.

"What would you like, Neli?" he asked.

"A giant ice water, please. I always seem thirsty, especially as soon as I get all set up to feed Joey and can't move."

"Coming right up."

"Special drinks for special girls." Pa held two jelly glasses filled with something colored and bubbly, probably a mix of lime seltzer and cranberry juice. "Head into the family room and sit at the table."

They hurried away, with him close behind. Derrick set two slices of tart onto cocktail napkins and followed them.

Tim handed me a piece of tart and took one for himself.

I took a nibble. "This is so good."

Tim tasted it with the discerning palate of a cook and baker. "Puff pastry, yes? And ricotta mixed with Parmesan, if I'm not mistaken. Delicious. I want to recreate it for the bakery."

Neli blushed. "Yes to the pastry, and thank you. I saw the recipe online, and using store-bought puff pastry is easy and quick. I feel like I do nothing but feed the baby. It was fun to make something I could feed adults with."

Derrick came back and beckoned me. I rose and followed him into the kitchen where Pa was whisking up a salad dressing.

"I overheard something in the hardware store yesterday I thought you and the group might be interested in." Derrick had originally been in the Cozy Capers, but he withdrew when he went back to school and then met Neli.

"Please dish," I said.

"I was in Pete's Mercantile, and a man in his twenties was behind the counter."

"Yes, I've met him. His name is Cliff, and he's Piet's cousin's son, or something like that."

"I see," Derrick said. "Well, he got a call and turned his back, but I was browsing the nearest display, and I could hear his side of the conversation. He said something about not being successful. He apologized but said it had been a bad idea, and he still wanted to get paid."

"He didn't say what he'd failed at?"

"No, nor the name of who called him. But his tone and his stance were furtive, like he was trying to hide whatever it was. I pretended I hadn't heard a thing. I thought it might have something to do with the murder. It's still unsolved, isn't it?"

"Yes, unfortunately. Thanks, Derr."

Pa turned, the whisk in his hand dripping oil. "Listen,

children of mine. You are both parents now. You have to stay out of this sleuthing business. I will not have my grandchildren lose a parent, do you hear me?" Both his voice and his expression were as stern as I'd ever seen him.

"Yes, sir," Derrick said.

"I'm staying safer than ever, Pa. I promise."

Despite my drive to find poor Zia's killer, I had no intention of going anywhere near a murderer.

CHAPTER 38

At first Evan seemed busy with the babies when I arrived at the Nest with Luca the next morning. I had decided not to remind him that he still hadn't gotten back to me with more info about Zia. Luca had been up a couple of times in the night, probably from teething, and had fallen asleep in the stroller on the way over.

The other teacher took over the little ones and began a singing circle with them as I handed my snoozing son to Evan. He held Luca on his shoulder and gently patted his back.

"I know I owe you information," Evan began. "Let's step into the hall for a minute."

I followed him back out.

"So Zia moved to Bourne right after Christmas and got a room down the hall from mine." He swayed with Luca to keep him asleep. "I know people say North Lodging isn't a nice place to live, but they're wrong. It's kind of like a dorm for adults. We have a common room and a kitchen we all share. Residents can keep to themselves, or they can hang out together. And believe me, the price is right."

I doubted day care teachers brought in the big bucks, even though taking care of our precious little ones made the teachers golden in my eyes.

"After a while," Evan continued, "Zia opened up to me about her adoptive family. Her father was always loving, but her mom seemed to resent Zia. She thought it was because the Carvens weren't able to have their own biological children, and appearances were super important to the mother. Zia started researching her birth parents and thought her birth mom lived here in Westham."

"So she moved a couple of towns away and got a job at the local toy store."

"Exactly."

"Do you know who she thought her bio mom was?" I asked.

"No. She kept that to herself. A couple of times we met for drinks at the Rusty Anchor pub, though. She seemed extra interested in it. The thing is—"

A wail rose up from inside the day care. Luca started awake and began to cry.

"I better get in there," Evan said.

"Thank you." I gave my son a kiss and headed out. What had Evan been about to add? I hoped he would text me when he got a chance.

As I unlocked the door to the bike shop, I paused. It was certainly cold and cloudy enough to snow. But . . . come on, Mother Nature. We'd turned the corner into March. We should have crocuses blooming in sunshine instead of an impending snowstorm. At least the air didn't smell of snow. Yet.

I sighed and headed inside. I'd experienced more than one heavy snow even in early April. Poor Ella was going to have to wait a while to use her new gardening tools.

Speaking of her birthday, Tim and I had to get organized about the party. We'd settled on the next Saturday for a birthday celebration, although she actually would turn four on Monday, the eleventh. Ella had asked to invite three little friends from her preschool, plus Cokey. At this age, it also meant one or more parent and possibly other siblings would accompany the child. Our cottage would be full, but we'd manage, and Mom had planned a family-only party for Sunday afternoon.

I was stashing my bag under the counter when an early customer pushed in through the door. When he slid back his hood, I saw it was Cliff Vriesdorp.

"I'm sorry, we're not quite open yet." Why hadn't I locked the door behind me?

"That's okay." Smelling as if he'd just finished a cigarette, he folded his arms and leaned against the doorjamb. "I'm not here to buy anything."

I didn't know if he presented a threat, but I did know I didn't want to be alone in the shop with him.

"You'll have to help me set up, then." I grabbed the flagpole and gestured at the door with my chin. "After you."

He frowned but pushed the door open. I followed him outside and leaned my back against the closed door.

"Here." I extended the pole with the Open flag furled

around it. "Slide this into the holder there, would you please?" I was plenty tall enough to do the task, but many men enjoy being given a job to do that they perceive a woman wouldn't be able to. I thanked him after the flag began floating in the breeze. "You've helped me. How can I help you?"

"I know you're some kind of lady PI—"

"Hang on. I'm not a PI at all. I own a bike shop, as you can see."

"Yeah, sure." He tossed his head as if he didn't believe me. "Anyway, I wanted to tell you that I think that chef at the pub is up to no good."

"Oh? In what way?"

"She's been lying about everything. I saw her sneaking looks at poor Zia before she was so brutally murdered, and a couple times I saw them arguing. You'd better watch out for her."

"I hope you've told the police what you just said."

"Nah, they wouldn't listen to someone like me." His gaze shifted across the street.

"I don't see why not."

"Listen, it's pretty cold out here. I'll come inside and help you there."

"That's okay," I said. "I can handle everything." As I always did.

He swiveled to face me. "I insist." He wasn't smiling.

He could insist until the cows came home. I had no intention of moving away from the door. Maybe the guy wanted to help. Maybe he didn't.

An older-model Jeep pulled into the lot, and Orlean climbed out. Bless her heart for arriving at exactly the right moment, which was well before her usual starting time.

"Good morning, Orlean." I smiled at her.

"Mac." She bobbed her head. "Have to leave early today. Thought I'd get a head start."

"Let's get to it." I opened the door for her and angled myself so Cliff couldn't follow. "Have a nice day, Cliff."

"Right. You too." He slid his hands into his pockets, turned on his heel, and sauntered away.

Orlean hadn't gone back to her workspace. "What did he want?"

"I'm not sure, but I didn't get an easy feeling about it." I gazed at the closed and now-locked door.

"Good thing I showed up, then."

A very good thing.

CHAPTER 39

I busied myself readying my business to open. I checked over the receipts and rental returns from the weekend. *Huh*. The two bikes Brendan had rented for Kimball and Ed were still out. When I called the number Brendan had filled in on the form, nobody picked up. All I could do was leave a message that the rentals were late and we needed them back. The signed agreement specified the daily late charge, but the senator gave the impression he had enough money to cover it.

By nine thirty Orlean was hard at work, and the store was still empty. I sidled back there.

"Good weekend?" I asked.

She nodded, not looking up.

"I wondered about the status of Patty Harbach's bike," I added.

"Done. Texted her. She said she'll be in this morning."

"Great, thanks." I turned away.

"Hang on, Mac" she said. "Heard about the kerfuffle

with the senator yesterday. Want I should ask a few more questions over to the rooming house?"

I faced her. "Sure, if you can do it safely. Thanks."

"Can do."

I smiled to myself as I headed back to the retail counter. She hadn't once broken eye contact with the bike she was working on, which was not a problem for me in the least. I didn't know where she'd heard about Kimball's session with Westham-area residents, and I didn't need to.

As often happens when the weather isn't great for biking, we were busy with folks shopping and asking for repairs. By ten thirty, when Patty came in, I'd just finished up with a couple from Vermont, a bike club from Hyannis, and a family returning their rentals. The shop was again empty of customers. I thought Delia was late, then remembered she'd told me she had scheduled a teeth cleaning this morning and wouldn't be in until eleven.

I greeted Patty.

"Orlean sent me a message that my bike was ready," she said.

"It is. But first, do you have a minute?"

Her gaze shifted away, and she pressed her lips into a line. She faced me. "Sure, what's up?"

"I thought your comment yesterday to Senator Kimball was interesting. Would you be willing to share why you said he knew Zia better than he's letting on?"

"I guess." Her shoulders sagged. "My niece lives in Portsmouth, Rhode Island. When I reached out to her after Zia was killed to see if she knew her, she said they were friends. They'd worked at an ice cream shop together a couple of years ago and they'd stayed in touch. She texted me later saying she was worried about how important it seemed to Zia to get in touch with Ross Kimball."

"Did she say why she was worried, or explain the reason Zia was trying to contact the senator?"

"She said she didn't know, but she seemed unusually uneasy when she told me."

"I'd love to speak with your niece. Do you think she'd be willing to talk to me?" Maybe the niece knew more about Zia's past than anyone here had been able to uncover.

"I'll ask her." Patty glanced at her watch. "I really do have to run, Mac. I promise I'll get back to you."

"Thank you. I appreciate it. Soon would be best, okay?"

She didn't respond as she hurried back to the repair area, where Orlean explained what the bike had needed. Patty returned only to pay and then meet Orlean outside to get the bicycle.

Delia arrived a few minutes before eleven and flashed me a gleaming white smile.

"Wow, your teeth look great," I said.

"I am blessed to have strong ones."

"Did you have braces when you were young?"

"Nope. I guess I hit the dental genetic lottery. My teeth are straight, white, and they don't stain or decay."

"Lucky you." I'd a few cavities filled, but regular cleanings and my flossing practice went a long way toward avoiding the need for further work on my teeth.

"Has it been busy in here?"

"Off and on." I looked at the shoulders of her navy puffy jacket. "Looks like it isn't snowing yet."

Delia peered at me. "Mac, don't you ever look at a weather forecast?"

"Almost never." I laughed. "I don't have time. I figure I'll know it when the rain or snow starts, or when the sun comes out. I seem to be surrounded by weather maniacs like you to warn me if something worse is on the horizon."

"I'm like the poster child for weather nerds." Smiling, Delia shook her head. "Fortunately, Lincoln is also tuned in. You should hear us discuss storm blobs on radar maps."

"Speaking of him, did he tell you about the meeting with Senator Kimball yesterday?"

"No. What happened?"

I recounted what Reba told the senator about the old folks. "But the gathering wasn't a group of doddering pushover seniors at all. Almost everyone, young and old, challenged him on his opposition to the wind project."

"Hmm. Linc did say something about June Jenkins representing their tribe."

"She was one of the few voices supporting the senator in his opposition. She said the project would harm the water and fish and birds."

Delia flipped open her hands. "It might, you know?"

Yes, but way more important in the short term was the way Kimball had reacted to Patty's remarks, as well as what her niece might know about the powerful legislator. Meanwhile, our more immediate future was the group of ten bundled-up cyclists who blew in with ruddy cheeks. I smiled at the newcomers.

"Welcome to Mac's Bikes. How can we help you?"

Delia and I were both immediately busy with an assortment of items they needed and wanted, from tubes to helmets to souvenir shirts. Thinking about men wielding undue influence would have to wait.

CHAPTER 40

I sat on a bench in front of the Town Hall at a quarter to one. Lincoln and I had cross-texted each other an hour earlier, each asking for a quick meetup. Now he strode toward me at a faster pace than his usual amble and sat at the other end of the bench.

I twisted to face him. "It's still not snowing. Delia says you're as much of a weather nerd as she is, which is her word, not mine. Are we going to get some white stuff?"

"Probably, but it's a slow-moving front. Maybe it'll snow later this afternoon." He cleared his throat. "What did you want to talk about? I only have a few minutes."

"Same. Okay, I told you about what Patty Harbach said to Kimball at the meeting yesterday after you left. This morning she was in to pick up her bike, which she'd left for a tune-up. I asked what she knew that made her say that. Patty told me her niece in Portsmouth was friends with Zia, and that the niece was worried about Zia trying so hard to contact Kimball."

"Zia lived in New Hampshire?"

"What?" I asked. "No, sorry. Portsmouth, Rhode Island. Did you know Zia lived there?"

"Yes, but not this friend's name. Do you have a number for Ms. Harbach?"

"It'll be on her bike's work order. Want me to call Orlean and get it?"

"No, it can wait, but please get it to me this afternoon if you can," he said. "What else?"

"My brother said he overheard Cliff Vriesdorp on the phone with somebody while Derrick was in the hardware store. I'm wondering if Cliff was the one who tried to run me off the road Friday night."

"If what now?" Lincoln swore as he stared at me. "Were you planning on telling me about that little incident?"

He never swore, at least not in my presence. Maybe I should have let him know, but what could I have told him?

"The thing is, I had no information for you," I said. "Gin and I were coming back from a meeting at Zane King's. I was driving. Somebody was going way too fast behind us, and they nearly clipped my car as they passed. Thankfully, nothing happened. It was on a really dark stretch of road. Neither of us caught the license plate number. What was I going to share?" I snugged my shoulders to my ears and flipped open gloved hands. "It could have been just a reckless speeder."

"I see." He leaned his elbows on his knees and clasped his hands. "Sorry about the language, Mac. This case is exceedingly frustrating."

"I know. No worries. Gin and I both thought the

vehicle was dark, maybe black, and she said she would let any memory of the plate number percolate. I'll be seeing her in a few minutes. I'll ask what she remembers and pass it straight along to you."

"Thanks," he said.

"At any rate, it might be useful to have a word with Cliff, find out what kind of car he drives, stuff like that." Now I had to tell Tim about the incident the first chance I got. I don't know why I didn't just fill him in when the story was fresher.

"Speaking with Cliff again is definitely on my list. I did try to talk with him Friday afternoon, but he was not forthcoming. I'll certainly dig into any alibi he might have for that evening and any connections with our other persons of interest."

"Good. He came to my shop this morning, and it felt vaguely threatening, although nothing happened. So, did you get anything out of June yesterday?"

"No. She was entirely evasive."

"Too bad."

"You can say that again," he said.

"No news about Yvonne?" I shifted on the hard bench.

When his phone buzzed, he glanced at it and stood. "Gotta run. Thanks, Mac." He strode back the way he'd come, which led straight to the police station.

I also rose. Once again, I'd given more information than I'd received. With any luck, the meeting I was heading for would turn that around.

CHAPTER 41

On my way around to the side door of Salty Taffy's I paused and smiled at the sign on the front door, which read, "Gone Ice Fishing." Gin had told us to come to the side and that she was going to lock the main entrance before we arrived. We didn't need to be interrupted by candy seekers while we talked about murder.

And this place was a magnet for lovers of sweets. Gin's window displays always included baskets of saltwater taffy and giant spiral lollipops. The attention of passersby was grabbed by alluring blocks of fudge and boxes of handmade truffles, plus bins of the wrapped penny candies she sold by the pound.

Inside the workroom in the back of the shop, the book group sat on stools or chairs. Flo, as always, had her yellow legal pad on her lap. Gin was passing a bowl of wrapped saltwater taffy for us to sample, chewy candies that came in all colors of the rainbow with as many flavors to match.

I glanced around. "No Ilsa?"

Noland shook his head. "She couldn't make it. Flo,

you said you have something about Zia. I also do, but you can go first."

"Sure." Flo scrolled on her phone. "Carven is her adoptive family's surname. She grew up in Portsmouth—"

"Rhode Island." I smiled.

"Exactly," Flo said. "She graduated from high school there and did two years at community college. And then my trail hit a dead end."

"I learned similar facts," Norland said. "It's not easy to break into birth records without a warrant, but she didn't have any kind of criminal past that I could find."

I raised my hand. "Did I tell you guys about Patty Harbach?"

"Doesn't ring a bell," Flo said.

The others shook their heads.

"I've met her a few times. She's sixtyish, white hair, and lives in Bourne. She told Reba she wants to move to Westham and has joined a history club my grandma is part of."

"They're doing interesting research," Norland said. "Ilsa has gotten involved with them."

"Anyway, yesterday Gin and I attended what was billed as an informational session with Senator Kimball at the senior center." I elaborated on Kimball's reactions to all the grilling and Reba's delight at surprising him. "Toward the end of the meeting, Patty asked him if he was helping the police solve Zia's homicide, and she mentioned rumors that he knew the young woman better than he let on. He didn't like that one bit."

"Did he answer the question?" Tulia asked.

"He sure didn't," I said. "He closed the meeting right

then and there and hurried out faster than the Road Runner being chased by Wile E. Coyote. And one more thing: before Patty's remarks, June spoke against the project, couching it as a tribal objection."

"I heard about that," Tulia said. "The project has been a topic of much discussion in Mashpee. In this case, I'm not in agreement with June. Sorry, go on, Mac."

"When she was done speaking, Kimball gave her a close and possibly meaningful look," I said.

"A look indicating they knew each other?" Zane asked.

"Maybe," I said. "June went pale, turned on her heel, and headed straight out the door. Lincoln was there, and he followed her. He had told me she was avoiding him."

"So June and Kimball might be the birth parents?" Gin asked. "Maybe that's why Zia went to work for her."

"But murder your biological child?" Zane shuddered. "Why in the world would someone do that?"

He had babies at home, as did I. It was horrible to think that someone could kill their blood relation.

"We all know that murderers often act for reasons that defy common sense," Norland said. "In this case, Zia might have been threatening exposure of a past affair. Maybe she was asking for a large sum of money to keep her identity quiet."

"Remember that we also wondered if Yvonne is the birth mother," I said. "Has anyone seen her with Kimball?"

Nobody had.

"He was in the pub Saturday when Reba and I were there," I said. "But Delia told me Yvonne was out that day."

"We haven't been following up on her at all," Gin pointed out. "Does anyone know her partner?"

"I saw them on a tandem bike last year," I volunteered. "The partner seemed to be deaf or at least hard of hearing."

"I met Gwyneth," Zane offered. "Stephen and I are learning ASL to use with the babies. Our pediatrician sponsored a session, and Gwyneth was the teacher."

"Are your little ones hard of hearing, Zane?" Norland looked concerned.

"Not at all, but it's apparently easier for babies to learn sign language to express themselves than to speak, and it doesn't hinder their spoken-language development." He smiled, shaking his head. "Who knew? It's a whole new world."

"Let's talk later," I said. "I guess we should be using signs with Luca."

"Sure." Zane nodded. "You can watch videos online, but we find it more helpful to learn in person. We have another ASL session this afternoon. If I can manage to talk to Gwyneth and work the conversation around to where Yvonne was Tuesday afternoon, I will."

"I had a thought," I began. "If Yvonne was Zia's bio mom, Gwyneth might not have been happy about them having a relationship, if that was what Yvonne had wanted. Sorry, too many 'ifs.' It did occur to me, no matter how convoluted the logic."

"Hey, we're open to any and all ideas," Zane said.

Flo jotted that down. "Gin, you said you had something?"

"Maybe. Pete's Mercantile is only a few doors down

and across the street from here, as you all know. This morning I saw a big black SUV pull up to the store. Cliff got in and it drove away."

Whoa. "Interesting."

"Did you see a plate number?" Norland asked.

"Unfortunately, no. The car was too far away."

"Something occurs to me." Tulia raised a finger. "Do we know exactly how Zia died? Mac, you were the one who found her."

All eyes turned toward me. "I'm sure I've told you what I saw. Blood on the side and back of her head, and on the floor where a toy rifle was. But those things are plastic. I can't believe it was heavy enough to kill her. Alas, I never followed up on the weapon with Lincoln."

"Are there heavy objects in the toy store?" Zane asked.

"Let me see what I can find out," Norland volunteered.

"Action item for Norland." Flo again scribbled on her legal pad then glanced at her watch. "I have a meeting in ten. Anything else?"

I shook my head. "Not from me, and I need to get back, too." I checked my phone. It was already one thirty. I should be on my way.

We thanked Gin and promised to stay in touch with updates. I pointed myself toward Mac's Bikes, my pocket full of taffy and my brain a little too full of thoughts.

CHAPTER 42

As I hurried along the sidewalk, I made a spur-of-the moment decision and crossed Main Street. I felt the need for a quick kiss and a hug from my husband. I made my way into the alley a half block short of the front door of Greta's Great Grains and up to the back door of his bakery.

I was surprised to find the door to the kitchen locked. The bakery usually closed at two. Maybe this winter Monday had been slow enough to shut the business early. I sent him a quick hearts, XXs, and OOs text, just because.

I restarted my brisk walk but almost immediately came to a halt. Cliff stood with his arms folded on his chest outside the Rusty Anchor's back door about twenty yards away. Yvonne stepped into the alley, fists on her hips over a black chef's tunic.

"What do you want from me?" she demanded.

Despite the distance, the air was cold and still, and

my excellent hearing came in handy. I quickly set my phone to video and tapped the record button.

"He wants to talk with you." Cliff's words shot out as more of an order than a request.

He?

"No." She shook her head, hard. "Not doing it."

Cliff leaned in and spoke in a voice now too low for me to hear.

"Get away from me." Yvonne came in loud and clear. She set both palms on his chest and pushed.

"Hey!" He stumbled backwards. His arms flailed to recover his balance. By the time he recovered, she had returned inside and slammed the door.

What did Cliff think he was doing? It looked like he'd either threatened or browbeaten her. Good for Yvonne for literally pushing back.

Uh-oh. He caught sight of me. With a racing heart, I slid my phone into my pocket and gave him a little wave. I turned to make my way—fast—back up the passageway between the bakery and the next building.

"Hey, wait up," he shouted.

Nope, not happening. I didn't stop until I was on Main Street, where cars drove by in both directions and winter shoppers strolled past. Where I felt safe. A light snow began to fall and my shoulders relaxed. I glanced down the passageway, thinking Cliff would have followed, but he didn't appear. *Whew*.

It was past time for me to get back to a yet-safer place, my workplace and livelihood. When a big black SUV drove toward me on the opposite side of the street, my heart rate sped up again. Thankfully the vehicle didn't slow or make a U-turn. Nobody stopped to accost me or attempt an abduction. I'd never had an overactive imagination. It appeared I did now.

I skirted other pedestrians as I hustled, keeping an eye out for threatening vehicles. I waved without pausing to chat when I saw Zane helping a customer out with a case of wine. I didn't stop until I entered Mac's Bikes. My shoulders relaxed and my fists unclenched.

We got busy shortly after that. It wasn't until after Delia left that I had a minute free to text first Lincoln and then the group about what I'd seen.

Lincoln returned a terse, "Thx."

The shop continued to be quiet after that. Who was Cliff Vriesdorp, anyway? Unlike Piet's speech, Cliff's English sounded as if he'd been born here or at least had come to the country as a young child. We hadn't really talked about him in the group meeting today.

Maybe the "he" Cliff mentioned to Yvonne was Senator Kimball. But how would they know each other? I doubted a chance would open up for me to ask Piet at his store, but I could stop by on my way home and give it a shot.

CHAPTER 43

We still weren't busy at four o'clock. As my thoughts turned to closing early, my grandmother bustled in.

"Mackenzie, I've come from History Club." Her cheeks were pink from the cold air. She came around the counter and hopped up onto the stool next to mine.

"Did you all start a new project?" I asked.

"We're brainstorming possibilities, but that's not what I wanted to tell you."

"All right. I'm listening, at least until a customer comes through that door." I pointed at the entrance with my chin.

"Do you remember my friend Helene Fadiman?"

"Sure. June's mother and August's grandmother. You took me along to her house last spring."

"Indeed, we did. You've always had an excellent memory, my dear."

I kept my eye on the door and the wall clock next to it. "And? What about Helene?"

"Oh!" She laughed and tapped a finger on her temple. "Can't bring me anywhere. Yes, well, Helene and I got to talking. I know you're interested in June's involvement in this terrible homicide thing and if she had known Senator Kimball in her past."

"I most certainly am."

"It seems June and her husband and their children used to spend summers in Westerly, Rhode Island, with her husband's parents. That is, June and the kids did. The hubs only came down on the weekends."

"As happens with a number of families who own or rent vacation properties. One spouse stays back to work and mind the house on weekdays. Historically, it's been the father."

"Yes," Reba said. "As you heard yesterday, Ross Kimball's family also owns a home in the same town. Helene didn't spend a lot of time down there, but she would visit June and the children occasionally, and she met Ross more than once. Of course, he wasn't a senator then."

"Interesting."

"There's more. One summer when August was about ten, he told Helene he was sad because his mom was gone a lot during the week, leaving him and his sister with the other grandparents. When Helene asked June where she went, she was evasive."

I did a little math. "I'd say August is about ten years older than Zia. But . . . if June became pregnant with Kimball and carried the baby to term, wouldn't Helene have known?"

"Yes, except she spent that next year in India studying filmmaking and doing yoga."

"It still doesn't work." I shook my head. "Unless June went away for her pregnancy, everyone in the Mashpee Wampanoag community would have known. Tulia, Lincoln, everyone. And probably you."

"I hadn't moved to Westham yet. I was still teaching in Boston," Reba said.

"On the other hand, June was the mom of two. It's entirely possible she was simply taking time for herself on those days. Even if she was having an affair with Kimball, it might not have resulted in a pregnancy."

"Or she could have ended it," Reba said.

"That, too."

As the door began to open, Reba slid off her stool.

"Looks like you have a customer, and I've gotta run. I'll keep nosing around, hon."

Brendan appeared in the doorway.

"Hello, young man." She beamed at him. "You and the senator made a quick departure yesterday. I hope it wasn't something I said."

"No, ma'am, not at all."

"You tell your boss he's welcome to come back any time he wants."

"Certainly, Mrs. Almeida."

"Toodles, Mackie." Reba headed out.

"Good afternoon, Brendan." I folded my hands on the counter.

"Mac, I know we're late with the bicycles." His arms hung at his sides, and his thumbs ran back and forth over his first two fingers. The frown he came in with stayed in place.

"Yes, and your contract clearly states that there's a daily charge for being late. Are you returning the bikes now?"

"Uh, actually, Senator Kimball would like to keep them for several more days if that's possible." He didn't make eye contact.

"I'll check our reservations." We'd ditched the paper book and gone digital with the reservation system at the new year. The public still had to call or come in to reserve bikes and had to sign a paper contract, but we managed them in an easy-to-use application.

I brought up the screen. "Sorry, that won't be possible. Those two cycles are booked to go out tomorrow."

Brendan looked even more worried, or maybe it was nervous. "Can't you make an exception for the senator?"

"Sorry. I have an obligation to my customers. When you rent bicycles for a certain time period, I rely on you to stick to it. He might be able to find rentals in Sandwich or Falmouth, neither of which are too far from here, and certainly in Hyannis."

Also, was he even riding the bike? It wasn't exactly ideal biking weather, other renters notwithstanding.

"He's not going to be happy about this," Brendan muttered.

"That's unfortunate. Are the bikes in your vehicle?"

"No."

I glanced at the wall clock. "It's four twenty. I need them here by five o'clock, when we close."

"No." He gave his head a quick shake. "That's not possible."

"It's been snowing. Surely they didn't take the bikes on the ferry to Nantucket or Martha's Vineyard."

"Uh, no," Brendan said. "But the senator is in an important meeting."

"On his rental bike?"

He scrunched up his face. I hoped he didn't start crying. I crossed my arms and stared at him without speaking.

"Couldn't you have called us earlier?" His shoulders slumped and his voice turned into a whine.

"Young man, your boss and Ed and you all look like people who can read. Ross signed the agreement. The bikes were due back yesterday. My business model does not include chasing down the inventory." I did try to accommodate reasonable requests from customers, but this seemed like the kind of behavior powerful people and their minions try to pull all the time. I wasn't going to treat Kimball like he was royalty and I was a faithful and kowtowing subject.

"Okay. You'll have the bikes by five." He stalked out the door.

A whistle came from the repair area. I turned to see Orlean leaning against the doorjamb.

"Poor kid." She shook her head. "He's in way over his head. How much you want to bet you don't see those bikes by five or maybe ever?"

"I'm not betting, but Kimball's going to owe us a lot more than a day's late charge if he doesn't return them."

If the senator wanted to pull a power trip he shouldn't

have signed a contract. Asking to keep the bikes longer when they probably weren't even using them was the behavior of someone accustomed to controlling others. Kimball had picked the wrong person to pull that move on.

CHAPTER 44

Sure enough, five o'clock came and went. No senator, no bikes. No Brendan, no Ed.

"Let you know in the morning what I learn in Bourne," Orlean said, hat and jacket on and lunch bag in hand.

"Thanks for doing that."

She gave a little salute and let the door shut behind her.

Now what? I felt the pull of home and hearth. Was I still cut out for this sleuthing business? Finding a murderer pulled at me, too, but coming up with the time and mental energy was a lot harder now that I had a family. I was a little surprised Zane had rejoined the group only half a year after becoming a parent. What had he said? He enjoyed spending time with adults and not talking about feeding babies, changing them, and what had filled the diapers. I could relate.

I headed for the door to lock it but Yvonne pushed through before I could.

"Mac, you have to lay off."

Was that steam coming out of her ears? Her puffy coat wasn't zipped over the chef tunic I'd seen her in earlier, and she wore neither hat nor gloves. Steam or not, the woman was not happy.

"Hi, Yvonne." Locking the door could wait. I pointed at the stools behind the counter. "I'm waiting for a couple of rentals to show up. Come sit with me and we'll talk."

She took a moment to glare, but my invitation seemed to take the wind out of her sails. She sat in a huff.

"I keep a bottle of a very nice sherry in my office." I stayed on my feet. "Would you join me in a small glass?"

She didn't hesitate. "Yes, please. I mean, I need to get back to the pub, but a genteel drink might do me good about now."

"I thought Monday was a day off for you."

"Usually it is. I swapped it for Saturday. Don't ask."

I was back in a second with the bottle and two of the etched, stemmed glasses Reba had given me as a shop-warming present when I opened Mac's Bikes. I poured and handed one to Yvonne.

"This is very civilized," Yvonne said. "What lovely glassware."

"It's part of a set of eight that my grandparents received as a wedding gift a long, long time ago. Cheers."

We clinked glasses, and I took a sip. She followed suit.

"Now, what do I need to lay off?" I asked.

Her posture slumped. "I've heard rumors that you're

still asking questions like you tend to do when someone gets murdered in Westham. In this case, it was a poor young woman who deserved none of it."

I took another sip. "Why does it concern you that I'm trying to find out who killed Zia? I asked you earlier if you knew her, and you said you didn't."

"I said I didn't know anyone by that name."

"And?"

Yvonne stared into her tawny-colored drink. She took a sip, then ran a finger around the delicate rim of the glass. She sipped again. I also wanted to ask her about her clash with Cliff in the alley. One thing at a time.

She met my gaze and opened her mouth. When the door opened, she clamped it shut. Her eyes flashed with something. Whether anger or alarm, I couldn't tell.

Ross Kimball filled the doorway. "Well, well, well." He sauntered in as if he owned the place. Except he didn't.

"Ross, I hope you have the rental bikes with you." I stood.

"Yes, Mac, I do." His tone was conciliatory, but his nostrils flared. "I fail to understand how a small business like yours continues to function when you demonstrate so little understanding of the needs of your customers."

"A signed contract is exactly that." I tapped my finger on the agreement, which I'd set out on the counter. "Your card will be charged for one day's late fee. Come out with me and I'll get the bikes checked in."

"First, I need to say hello to this lovely lady. How are you, Vonnie?"

"I go by Yvonne, Ross." She tossed back the rest of her sherry. "Thanks, Mac. Gotta run." She slid off her stool.

Kimball stretched his arm across the doorway and leaned on his hand, blocking Yvonne's way.

"It's too bad about Zia, isn't it?" He stressed the name in a taunting tone.

Yvonne glared at him. "You are going to move out of my way. Right now."

He didn't budge. Her strong chef's hands formed fists. Even though it would serve Kimball right if she slugged him, it wasn't a good idea.

"Senator Kimball, I will meet you outside." I stepped in front of Yvonne.

He shrugged, turned around, and left.

"You want to go out the back door?" I asked her. "Or you're welcome to stay a few minutes until he leaves."

"I'll stay." Her voice shook. "Thanks."

"Help yourself to more sherry." I headed outside.

CHAPTER 45

Kimball was already inside the big black car. *Good*. I didn't need any more interactions with him. Brendan waited by the bikes, which he'd parked next to the building.

"These look fine," I said. "Your boss isn't very happy, though."

"No, but that's sort of his normal state." He gave a nervous glance at the car. "Can we get a receipt?"

"I'll email it to you."

"Fine. Thank you." He hurried off and climbed into the front passenger seat.

I wheeled the rentals into our storage area and locked the door. Inside the shop, Yvonne was again seated and most of the way through another glass of sherry.

"The coast is clear," I said.

"Thanks. Can I pour for you?" She lifted the bottle.

I was torn. I needed to get home—and I was dying to see if she would open up about her past.

"Sure. Hit me." It was a small glass, after all.

She filled mine and topped up hers.

"Vonnie is what Delia calls you," I said. "You two went to college together. Did you also know Ross Kimball then?"

She nodded. I waited, but she didn't elaborate.

"He seems to have known Zia," I said. "Do you know how?"

"She lived in Rhode Island?" Yvonne didn't meet my gaze.

"He's a senator. She was a young woman. How would they have met?"

"I don't know. What I do know is that Zia came to see me at the pub." She let out a long, quavery breath. "Mac, I bore a baby girl a long time ago and gave her up for adoption. Zia thought I was her birth mother."

I gave a slow nod. "Were you?"

She worked her hands in her lap. When she glanced up at me, her eyes were filled with tears. "Probably. She was about the right age. She said her parents wouldn't tell her what hospital she was born in, but one look at her face, her eyebrows, and I knew she'd been my baby."

"I noticed that too." I waited a moment, but she didn't continue. "And Ross Kimball was the father, yes?"

"He was. He leaned hard on me to have an abortion, except I couldn't bear to do that. I'm not opposed in principle to ending a pregnancy, but it wasn't right for me at the time."

"Was Kimball already married?"

"No, but he was engaged, and he already had high

ambitions for his political life." She squared her shoulders. "Before you ask about the circumstances, it was a consensual one-night stand fueled by alcohol and pot. I regretted it almost immediately, but the deed was done. Baby-making can happen when you least expect it, as it turns out."

Except for Tim and me. But that was a conversation for another time.

"If you carried the baby to term, why didn't you keep her?" I kept my voice soft.

"I was in no position to do that. Not at all. I was single. I didn't have a good job. And what if he wanted to play a part in her upbringing? No way. I wanted nothing more to do with him. She was better off being adopted by a couple who wanted her. At least I thought that at the time."

"When she came to see you, what did she want?" I asked.

"I'm not sure. She was pretty nervous. I think she wanted acknowledgment, and maybe a relationship going forward."

"Did you want that as well?"

Yvonne's shoulders sagged. "I would have loved it. Gwyneth wasn't excited by the idea, but I thought I could persuade her in time. Now I'll never have the chance."

"What about the senator? Would he have welcomed a biological daughter, given time?"

"Are you kidding? He had an affair while he was engaged to the woman he married. Having something like that come out could imperil his precious political career. No, he wouldn't have included Zia in his life." She again studied her hands.

"He must have been required to give his permission for the adoption."

"He was and he did. That was the last time I had contact with him until now. He insisted on a closed adoption, and the Carvens were fine with that. I know it seems kind of archaic now. At the time, I was a wreck, and I agreed. Now I wish I'd pushed harder for an open arrangement, at least with me."

Kimball hadn't wanted contact with the baby as she grew. "He put all the responsibility for the pregnancy on your shoulders."

"He sure did, after I refused the abortion. Listen, Mac, you need to move cautiously. That man is dangerous. He can ruin lives." She stared at me. "He has ruined lives."

"I can take of myself. I got him to stop blocking the door, didn't I?"

"You have to leave him alone."

I had my mouth open to ask her what happened with Kimball in her past when her phone buzzed. She checked it, then drank down the rest of her sherry and stood.

"Big rush at the pub. I have to get back there."

"All right. Good luck. Thanks for opening up to me."

"Be careful, Mac. That's all I'm saying. And watch your back." She hurried out.

I locked the door after her and sat there for another

minute, sipping and thinking. So Yvonne was Zia's birth mother, not June, and Ross Kimball was the father. Just . . . wow.

I drained my glass. It was time for home, husband, and honeypies.

CHAPTER 46

The snow had disappeared by the time I made my way briskly down Main Street, but more precipitation could be lurking at higher altitudes in the glowering clouds above. It was five thirty, and the sky was dark, now that the sun had set. We would spring the clocks ahead soon. After that, my walk home wouldn't feel as ominous as it did today.

I'd texted Tim that I was on my way, but I still hurried. The main drag was well lit. It was our road I didn't feel as comfortable on in the dark.

As I approached the police station, a uniformed August trotted down the front steps. He was about to turn in the same direction I was going.

"August," I called.

He paused and turned, waiting for me to catch up.

"Did you just get off shift?" I asked.

"Not hardly. I pulled a double, which means I'm on until eleven tonight."

"You mean you've been working since this morning, and you don't get off until nearly midnight?"

"Yes, ma'am." He lifted a shoulder. "It's what we do. I think it's easier on me than several of the older guys."

"I imagine." I gestured down the street. "Are you going that way?"

"Yes."

"Me too, on my way home. Let's walk together."

He shot me a funny look but began moving. He probably knew of my reputation as an amateur sleuth and was suspicious I'd start grilling him.

"How's your mom doing?" I asked.

"I'm not sure. She's glad she was able to reopen the toy store."

"She must be." We passed Tim's bakery, now dark and locked up. "My grandmother is friends with yours. Reba mentioned that Helene told her your mom and sister and you used to spend summers in Rhode Island with your other grandparents."

"We did, at the beach. I have mostly sunny memories of that time."

"Do you know if your mom was acquainted with Ross Kimball during those summers?"

"Wait a second." August stopped and faced me. "Why are you asking?"

I also paused my step. "I was at the public meeting yesterday about the wind project. Most of the people in attendance supported the proposal, but June spoke against it, from the Wampanoag perspective. When Kimball gave her a hard look, she went pale and then rushed out."

"Interesting. She has been a little hard to get hold of this week." He narrowed his eyes at me. "Mac, you do know you're not supposed to be messing around in Haskins's homicide case, don't you?"

"Of course I know. I wouldn't dream of it." I smiled sweetly.

"Right." August snorted.

We came to the town hall and library complex.

"I'm heading in there," he said. "Take care. And be safe, okay?"

"Thanks. You, too." I watched him stride around to the back of the stately brick Town Hall, which still had lights shining through its tall and wide century-old windows all the way up to the third and top floor.

What kind of business would a young patrol officer have in the town offices? Maybe he was the police liaison to a town committee or had to deliver a report to the select people. Westham wasn't a city with an elected mayor. Rather, it was governed by the time-honored New England system of three elected selectmen and -women and an annual Town Meeting in the spring. Most years the town called another special Town Meeting six months later to take up additional business.

Right now my business was to get my patootie home before the night grew any darker. I hurried to the corner and headed up our street.

As usual when it was dark and windy the rustling of the trees spooked me. Only a few dry leaves hung on from the fall, but the bare branches were almost more ominous than noises I couldn't identify. When I passed the last streetlight, I switched on my phone's flashlight and trained it on the sidewalk. The last thing I needed was to pull a spectacular trip and face-plant. The change to daylight saving time couldn't come soon enough.

I thought as I hurried on. August hadn't actually answered me about June knowing Kimball. Yvonne hadn't actually told me why I needed to butt out, unless it was because Kimball was dangerous. And I hadn't had a chance to ask what she'd been arguing with Cliff about.

Had I learned a single new thing today? Gin had seen Cliff climb into a big black car. That was new.

As the incline of the hill increased, a set of bright headlights approached in a vehicle driving way too fast for our residential street. I shielded my eyes with my hand to avoid being blinded. I kept my gaze pointed down and swung my phone light forward and back to show the driver that someone was on the sidewalk.

The car picked up speed. A crack resounded, making my heart leap into my throat. A dry branch the vehicle ran over? I hoped that was all it was. I stepped as far from the street as I could, but a stone wall marked the other boundary of the sidewalk. I pressed myself into it. The large, dark car swooshed by and was gone.

It hadn't jumped the curb, aiming at me. It was nothing more than a reckless driver in a hurry.

Or so I told myself. I couldn't get home soon enough. Tomorrow I was wearing a flashing headlamp and reflective armbands on my way home.

CHAPTER 47

By six thirty Tim and Ella and I were finishing our dinner of bow tie pasta with pesto and chicken sausages. Ella had munched down most of her carrot and cucumber sticks, but Belle had also been the beneficiary of a couple of pieces.

Ella loved fun-shaped pasta. I had fond memories of eating bow ties and corkscrews and other kinds of pasta in my own childhood. Maybe it was the mouth feel, or that the shapes sparked the imagination. We need meals to be nourishing and delicious, but if a little entertainment is also part of the package, so much the better.

Speaking of entertainment, Luca was painting his high chair tray with his remaining pieces of extra-soft pasta. He extended one hand over the side and beamed as he dropped a piece. Belle waddled over and scarfed it down.

Our experiment with letting Luca try various foods he could feed to himself was interesting but highly messy. Mostly he palmed them generally at his mouth. Some food got in, and he got used to different flavors.

I vowed to spread a plastic sheet on the floor under the high chair the next day and keep an eye on Belle. Certain foods were toxic to African grays.

I offered the baby another spoonful of applesauce without giving him access to the bowl. He clamped his jaw on the coated spoon and then grabbed it in his fist. I let him play with it.

"I think this one is all done with eating for tonight," I said.

"I am, too." Ella held one of her bow ties to her throat. "Look at me, I'm a fancy gentleman."

"Well, you do look fancy." Tim smiled at her.

The green-flecked pasta against the pink sweater was a look, for sure.

"You do look fancy," Belle muttered. "Fancy. Fancy."

Ella giggled. "All I need is a tall hat." She frowned, gesturing above her head with both hands. "What's it called, Mama Mac? You know, like the Hatter wears in Alice."

"A top hat. You would be the world's cutest and shortest fancy gentleman. Let's remember a costume like that for Halloween next fall."

Her face fell. "Halloween was when Mommy died. I wish I could see her again," she whispered.

Tim pulled her onto his lap. "We all do, sweet cheeks. We all do."

The poor thing. Ella rarely dissolved into sadness anymore, but she'd been old enough when her mom died to hang on to clear memories of Jamie.

Luca dropped the spoon on the floor. My phone buzzed as the doorbell rang.

"Are we expecting anyone?" I asked Tim.

"Not that I know of."

I checked the display. "It's Piet with a special delivery for Belle." His message also said that he hoped to have a word in private with me. I frowned at the device. All I could think of was that he wanted to talk about Cliff.

Ella brightened. "Mr. Piet? I like him." She'd been into the hardware store with me, and Piet always had a bowl of lollipops behind the counter for visiting children.

"Let's go answer the door together." I rose and held out my hand to her.

Her sad mood forgotten, we hurried hand in hand through the living room and opened the front door. The motion-activated porch light worked fine, bathing Piet in illumination.

"Hi, Mr. Piet." She gave him a little wave.

"If it isn't Miss Ella." He knelt. "Give me a high five."

She slapped his hand. "Did you bring treats for Belle?"

"I did." He pushed up to standing with a quiet groan. "Old knees." He proffered the paper bag.

I took it from him. "Thanks, but you didn't need to deliver them," I said.

"Can I take them to Belle?" Ella asked. "She's going to go to bed soon. Did you know she goes to bed before I do?"

"Is that so?" Piet asked.

She gave a serious nod. "Parrots need a lot of sleep."

"Take the treats to the kitchen, honey." I handed the

bag to her. "Use both hands, now, and tell Papa Tim I'll be right there."

"Okay." She wrapped her arms around the treats. "Bye, Mr. Piet."

"Goodbye, Miss Ella."

I stepped onto the stoop and pulled the door mostly closed behind me. "What's going on? You said you wanted to talk about something?"

"I hate to say it, Mac, but I think Clifford is up to no good. I'm aware you do that detective stuff with your group. I thought you should know."

"What kind of no good do you mean?"

"He has been wearing what looks like a very expensive wristwatch, and he's sporting a leather jacket that had to cost him many hundreds of dollars. He's not making that kind of money working for me, I can assure you." He glanced away for a moment, then back at me. "And he's all the time getting rides with someone who drives a big, black car."

Just as Gin had said.

"Is he still living with you?" I asked.

"Sort of."

"What do you mean by 'sort of'?"

"I mean, he has recently sometimes not returned home at night, with no explanation," Piet said. "I haven't heard of him having a girlfriend or anything. Our guest room has its own door to the outside, but I am a light sleeper. I would have heard if a door opened or shut."

I thought again of the creepy, shuttered motel on the beach. Was Cliff hiding out there? But why? If he had expensive new possessions, he should be able to afford a pricey hotel room if he wanted to get away from Piet's inquiring gaze.

"You said Cliff lived in Washington, DC, previously," I said. "I can't believe a single young man would want to leave there to live in little Westham. It's not like we have an exciting nightlife around here."

"I wondered the same. My cousin and I are not close, but he said Clifford had been in some difficulties down there, and the cost of living is quite high in the capital."

"It's not exactly cheap to live on Cape Cod," I mused.

"No."

"Did he grow up in DC? Is that where your cousin lives?"

"Not at all." Piet shook his head. "Their home is in Providence."

The capital of Rhode Island was only about an hour and a half's drive from Westham. I'd love to know why Piet and his cousin weren't close, but it was none of my business.

"Well, I'll let you get on with your evening. Thank you for listening." He turned to go.

"Wait." I decided to ask the question I'd been holding back. "Did you come here because you're afraid Cliff might be involved with last week's murder?"

He stared down at the sisal mat on the stoop. "Yes. Yes, I am."

CHAPTER 48

By eight o'clock, the children were clean and asleep for the night. Belle was out, too. Tim and I relaxed on the couch with mugs of herbal tea. He yawned.

"Sorry. I'm not long for this world."

"I know." I leaned into his strong, warm arm. "Poor Ella. I'm sorry I triggered her memories by mentioning Halloween, but she popped right back to her usual cheery self, didn't she?"

"She always does. At least she feels secure talking about her feelings to us."

"I'm glad for that."

"What did Piet want to talk about?" Tim asked.

"He's concerned about Cliff, the young guy who's staying with him and working at the hardware store."

"Cliff is a relative, right?"

"Yes, his cousin's son, although tonight Piet said he's not close to the cousin. He's worried that Cliff is suddenly wearing an expensive watch and a fancy, new, leather jacket and getting picked up by a big black vehicle."

"Let me guess. He doesn't pay Cliff enough for him to afford those things."

"Exactly. Earlier in the week, Lincoln seemed to know who Cliff was. I haven't learned how."

"Was that after Zia was killed?" Tim asked.

"It was. There's a little more. Today after lunch I stopped by the bakery, but you were already closed."

"I'm sorry. Was it something urgent?"

"No, no, but I wanted a quick kiss."

He draped his arm over my shoulders and squeezed me in close.

"It was nearly two o'clock," I added. "I wasn't surprised you were done for the day. Anyway, I saw Yvonne and Cliff arguing down the alley behind the Rusty Anchor. I heard her refuse to do something. Cliff apparently wouldn't let up and got too close. She pushed him away and slammed the kitchen door on him."

"Good for her."

"That's what I thought, too."

"The alley was a busy place today," Tim said. "I also spoke to Yvonne earlier. I had stepped out back for a breath of fresh air. When we're in full baking mode, our kitchen gets pretty warm."

"But it smells so, so good at those times." I inhaled, as if I could taste that yeasty, fragrant air right now.

"Yvonne was taking a cigarette break, and I wandered down to say hello."

"How did she seem?"

"Nervous," he said. "She's not usually like that. Her

hand shook a little, and she kept looking around. Is she on Lincoln's list of suspects or something?"

"This afternoon she confessed to me that she's Zia's birth mother. I don't know what Lincoln thinks about that. Being found out could make Yvonne nervous, for sure."

"I guess."

"Listen, I need to tell you about Friday night. When Gin and I were driving home, somebody came up fast on our tail and nearly sideswiped us as they passed. We were fine, the car wasn't hurt, and whoever it was drove on. That's why I didn't tell you, but I found myself mentioning it to Lincoln this afternoon, and I wanted you to know."

"Thanks for letting me know, hon. All I care about is that you stay safe and well. I don't want to go through life without you."

Whew. He wasn't upset I hadn't told him sooner.

Tim yawned again. He finished his tea and gave me a big kiss. "I'm toast, my love."

"I know. Sweet dreams."

"Thanks." He stood and stretched.

"Speaking of toast, do we have any of your bread around?"

He smiled and shook his head. "Is the pope . . . I mean, does a bear . . . never mind. Yes, my dear wife, we have bread around. A baguette in the freezer. A whole grain country loaf in the fridge, sliced. And

I brought home crusty rolls today. They're on the counter."

"You are an angel." I blew him a kiss. "Your talk about when the bakery kitchen gets too hot made me hungry for warm bread slathered with Irish butter and raspberry jam. One of those fresh rolls sounds like my bedtime snack."

He smiled all the way into the bedroom. I carried the mugs and my phone into the kitchen. I couldn't help it if I was a bottomless pit for food.

A few minutes later I sat at the table with my split, toasted, and topped roll on a plate, a couple of fingers of Scotch in a squat glass, and my phone. I swiped at and tapped the phone with my left hand while I used my right to savor the crunchy outside and chewy, yeasty inside of each bite of roll.

I needed to let Lincoln know what Yvonne told me. Should I also tell him what Piet shared with me about Cliff? I hadn't asked Piet if I could or if he planned to, but I thought I should let the detective know his concerns. Piet was clearly worried.

I pulled up Lincoln's latest text and dictated my message. I didn't want to have to type single-fingered or wipe off my buttery, jammy fingers only to mess them up again.

I repeated what Yvonne said about conceiving Zia and added what Piet told me about Cliff and his hardware store pay.

I added one more message.

Piet also said Cliff's fam is in Prov RI but Cliff had been living in DC. Could've met Kimb either place?

I sent it. I'd cleared my conscience, but that didn't mean my thoughts weren't still trying to sort through what we knew and what we didn't.

CHAPTER 49

More snow fell overnight. It was finished by the time the kids and I ventured out the next morning at eight, but the storm left several inches of slush for us to navigate. This wasn't anywhere near my favorite kind of precipitation.

I strapped on the front carrier and settled a bundled-up Luca into it. Pushing a stroller through this mess would be no fun. Ella, on the other hand, had a great time marching along in her purple boots. After my mom met us at the parsonage door, Luca and I headed out to his day care. Evan greeted us and helped me unload the baby, giving him a big smile and greeting as he took him.

"Here's his bag." I held it out. "Bottles, lunch, diapers."

"Thanks." A tic beat next to his lip. "Have you learned any more about who was responsible for Zia's . . . loss?"

"Not exactly. What about you?"

"No, but her parents were at the rooming house last night. They came to pick up her stuff."

Luca leaned toward the bright colors of the rug and

the two young toddlers playing with a big cloth basket full of balls. Evan set him down on his back.

"The parents were pretty messed up," Evan continued, "as you can imagine. They had lots of questions none of us could answer."

"By 'us,' do you mean you and her friends?"

"Yeah, and the landlord, too."

"I assume someone from the police had given permission for the parents to clear out her room."

He flipped open his hands. "I guess? The yellow tape wasn't there anymore."

"Are the Carvens sticking around, do you know?"

"They said they were. They want to visit the toy store, for one, and I think they said they had an appointment with the detective today."

"You don't know where they're staying?" I said, hoping he would.

"No. And listen, I know I said I would text you with more information. Other than what I said yesterday, I really don't know much else about Zia."

"That's okay."

One of the toddlers wrested a blue-striped ball away from the other, who sat on her tush and wailed. Another parent arrived with a baby nearing her first birthday who began crying when she saw where she was.

"You're getting busy in here." I kissed my fingers and reached down to touch my son's forehead. "Bye-bye, Lukie, sweetie."

He twisted away to watch the battle of the blue ball. No separation anxiety—yet—for my boy. *May it stay that way.* I slipped away from the chaos.

Why didn't I already know the first names of Zia's parents? Had one of the Capers learned it? Flo and Norland had originally signed up for learning more about the victim and her life. I would check back through the text threads when I got to the bike shop. I should also let them know what Yvonne said about being Zia's bio mom.

For now I thought more about where the couple might be staying. If they were coming to Westham to see where Zia had been working and hanging out, they might want to stay here. Other than a cheap motel on the outskirts, our main lodging was the Westham Hotel, the lovely facility where Tim and I had had our wedding reception a little over a year ago.

The hotel was outside of the town center, with views of the bay and lovely lawns sloping down to the water. We had married on New Year's Eve. In that season, outdoor activities weren't part of the festivities, but the twinkling lights in the trees and on the dock had been lovely, as was our first breakfast as a married couple the next morning.

Were the Carvens well-off and able to stay in an elegant place like that? Maybe they'd opted for a B and B in Falmouth or an Airbnb in Bourne, near the rooming house.

I glanced down the block before crossing Main Street. A couple peered into the windows of the Toy Soldier. The man drew the woman into an embrace for a long moment—or tried to. When she appeared to shake him off, he moved apart. With a heavy step, he followed her over to Tim's bakery, where they disappeared through the door. He wanted to be close and she didn't? That was what it looked like.

I took a moment to text Tim.

A couple just went into Greta's. If you can, find out their names? Might be Zia's parents.

Tim sometimes didn't work the front at all, but occasionally he circulated among the customers. I crossed my fingers that he might be able to learn something.

For now, I was running late to open my own place of business, not to mention changing out of my sodden, no-longer-waterproof boots into the spare shoes I kept in my office. Spending the day in wet footwear wasn't good for anyone.

CHAPTER 50

Orlean paused at the shop's retail counter when she came in at nine thirty.

"Met the dead girl's parents last evening," she said.

"In Bourne?"

"Yup. They were pretty broken up, looking at her room."

"That had to be hard for them. How did you happen to be there at the same time as they were?" I asked.

"Friends with the landlord. Used to tutor his son."

I'd been surprised last year to learn that Orlean volunteered as a reading tutor in the public schools. I shouldn't have been that shocked. She was a person of great depth, but she didn't like to talk about her personal interests or toot her own horn at all.

"Thought you might have found the two of them interesting," she added.

I waited a moment. "How so?"

"No wonder she was looking for her birth mother. The Carven mom is an icicle, if an icicle could crack a whip."

"Cold and controlling?"

"You nailed it." Her eyebrows came together. "Awful woman."

"That's sad. What's the father like?"

"Beside himself with grief, poor guy. The missus looked fed up with him."

"They raised Zia," I said. "Naturally he was sad. Too bad she wasn't."

"Raised her since her birth nearly, the dad said."

"Did you happen to catch their first names?"

"Landlord introduced them as mister and missus. As they were leaving, the mister addressed his wife as dear, but she called him Horace."

Horace Carven was a relatively uncommon name. I should be able to dig for more information on him and his wife without too much trouble.

"I spotted something curious in the room," Orlean said. "Nobody else seemed to notice."

"What was it?"

"Looked like a journal—or a diary, more so. Tucked down almost under the bed."

Ooh. "Did you look inside?"

"Nah," Orlean said. "After the parents left, he gave a heads-up about it to my buddy. When I offered, he said he'd let me hand it over to the cops." She lifted a shoulder. "Probably should have showed the father, except who knows what Mommie Dearest might have done with it."

"I think you did the right thing." I wished I'd been able to have a look at the diary before she handed it over to Lincoln, but it was more important that he have it.

A man and a woman in their fifties moseyed in.

Orlean gestured toward the repair area with her chin. "You know where to find me."

"Thanks for the update," I called as she hurried away from having to engage with the newcomers.

What she said about Zia's parents comported with the behavior of the couple outside the toy store. I hadn't heard back from Tim. If he learned something about them he would let me know when he could.

For now, I had customers. "Welcome to Mac's Bikes. I'm Mac. What can we help you with today?"

"What a great little shop you have," the woman said. "We're not biking in this weather, but I always like to bring a souvenir home to Chicago."

I showed them where we stocked our store-branded merchandise. The items ranged from water bottles to clothing, from biking wear to T-shirts to ball caps.

"What brings you to the Cape at this time of year?" I asked.

The corners of her mouth turned down. "My brother and his wife have lost their daughter. My niece was a lovely young woman. Poor Horace is beside himself."

My attention went on high alert. "I'm really sorry. Was she ill?"

"No." She lowered her voice. "It's much worse than that. She was a bit troubled, you know? But that was no reason for her to be murdered, right? Especially not right here in Westham."

The husband laid his arm over her shoulders. "We'll all miss dear Zia, sweetheart, no matter how she passed."

"I know," the wife said. "Do you think we need to worry that the murderer hasn't been caught yet?"

It was my least favorite question, but it was the one most frequently asked by visitors in the wake of a homicide.

"I don't." I repeated what I always replied. "We have an excellent state detective team on the case, along with our local police force. You don't need to be concerned."

Which was true, as long as they didn't poke around and ask questions, as my friends and I often felt obliged to do.

CHAPTER 51

"Sorry I'm late, Mac," Delia muttered as she hurried in after ten thirty. Her normally neat dark hair was mussed, and her jeans bore a smudge of dirt on one knee.

"It's all right. We haven't been too busy."

The aunt and uncle had left, and we'd had a steady trickle of business since, but no rushes. Right now the shop was empty except for the three of us.

"You look kind of frazzled," I told her.

"I am. My pooch is a bit sick, which meant I had vomit to clean up. When I went out to get in my car, I had a flat tire."

"Did you have to wait long for triple A?"

"No, I changed it myself," she said.

"That must have been messy, in this slush."

She shook her head. "I was at Linc's, and my car was in the garage. Let me drop my stuff and wash my hands. I'll be on the job in a sec."

When the restroom door clicked shut, Orlean moseyed

over. "Didn't get a chance to say that you can hand the diary over to Lincoln yourself if you want." Wearing a clean latex glove, she held up a slender book with "Diary" embossed in gold on the cover.

I stared at her. "You didn't drop it off on your way here?"

"Nope. Thought you might be interested in having a crack at it first."

"I'd love to."

"Where do you want I should put it?"

"Can you slide it into my drawer?" I pointed to a drawer under the counter where I kept a few personal items. I'd labeled it with my name, and my employees honored my privacy. I didn't keep money or ID in there, but having a lip balm, phone charger, and a few other things at hand meant I didn't have to keep running to the office for my bag. "Thanks for staying gloved."

"Sure. You want a pair? New ones."

"Yes, please."

A coat-free Delia emerged from the restroom with clean hands and tidied hair. She began to move toward us.

"I'll come get the gloves from you," I murmured.

Orlean gave me a thumbs up and nodded at Delia before returning to the back. My hands—and mind—itched to open the drawer and read whatever Zia had written in the diary. That would have to wait until I was alone.

"Want to give me an update?" Delia asked.

I blinked. Did she mean on the case? No, she couldn't be asking about that. She meant the bike business.

"So far no rentals are reserved to go out or are due in today," I began.

"Who would want to ride a bike in weather like that?" She gestured toward the window.

I glanced out at a gray, blustery sky. "Ugh. Is it going to rain?"

"It might. Or we might get the dreaded wintry mix: sleet, cold rain, and wet snow all mixed up."

"I apparently haven't been tracking the weather report. Anyway, we got in a shipment of helmets and shoes. You could unpack and price those if it stays quiet in here."

"Okay." She straightened a countertop display of lip glosses and anti-chapping salves. "So, your favorite senator was in the pub last night."

"Kimball."

"Yes. He snuck into the kitchen when I wasn't looking. I went in to pick up an order, and he'd cornered Vonnie in her office. The door wasn't fully closed. It sounded like he was browbeating her about something. They both stopped speaking when I pulled open the door."

"What happened then?" I asked. Maybe it had been about their mutual connection to Zia, but why browbeat Yvonne if their biological daughter was dead?

"I asked her if she was okay, if she needed help. He glared at me before she could speak, then he brushed past me none too gently and left through the back door."

"A senator making a more or less public scene isn't a good look."

"It sure isn't." She frowned. "What worried me is

that she wasn't pushing back. Rather than looking angry, it was like she was defeated. She and I go way back, and I know she sometimes slides into a mood of super low self-esteem, like she isn't worth anything."

"That's hard."

"I know. Vonnie is a fabulous, talented woman. I hate that Kimball made her feel that way."

"Did you happen to catch what the two of them were arguing about?"

"Not much," she said. "I heard him say something about taking responsibility, but that was it. After he left I asked her if she wanted to talk. She said she didn't and headed back to her chef stuff. Mac, I'm worried about her."

"I should think you would be. Do you work again tonight?"

"Yes, and I'll see what else I can find out."

Several customers hurried in with ruddy cheeks and wind-tossed hair.

"You might want to tell Lincoln about the incident if you haven't already," I murmured.

"I will. I got home late last night, and he left early." Her cheeks flushed as pink as those of our wind-blown customers. "I'm going to move back in with him, Mac."

I hadn't been around when their young daughter had died in an accident, but the different ways each experienced their grief had driven a wedge in their marriage. I couldn't be more delighted that time had healed both

Lincoln and Delia and brought them back together in love.

"I'm super happy for both of you." I gave her a quick hug before turning to the newcomers. "How can we help you?"

CHAPTER 52

The store was quiet by eleven. I considered sneaking a peek at the diary, but I'd have to make up an excuse to Delia for why I needed to shut the door to my office. When Norland came in, I focused on him instead.

Smelling of sunshine and fresh air, he greeted me.

"Looks like the weather has improved over the last couple of hours," I said.

He glanced at Delia, who was straightening the shirts and shorts in the retail area.

He turned his back to her. "I just stopped into the toy store," he began in a low voice as he unzipped his jacket.

"Do you have a grandchild's birthday coming up?"

"Not at all. They were born in August and November. But you might remember I signed up for an action item yesterday."

I gave a slow nod. "To check for heavy items in the Toy Soldier, right?"

"That's it. There truly isn't much someone could use as a lethal weapon."

"Because children can't lift heavy things, I suppose," I said.

"Right. The killer must have brought the heavy item with them."

"I wonder what it was. You haven't heard on your police network?"

"I haven't." Norland shook his head. "But I did some checking into Cliff Vriesdorp, even though I hadn't signed up for that."

"Ooh, good initiative, my friend. His own relative thinks Cliff might have been involved in the crime."

"Really?"

"Yes. Piet stopped by my house last night on the pretense of delivering some parrot food for Belle. He said Cliff has been wearing an expensive jacket with a watch to match, and that what he pays him to work at the hardware store couldn't fund those kinds of purchases."

"That does sound suspicious," Norland said.

"Piet also told me Cliff has been getting rides in a big black vehicle, which sounds like it could be Senator Kimball's car."

"Interesting. Well, I uncovered Clifford's arrest record."

My eyebrows flew up. "Arrested for what?" I asked.

"Assault, mostly. That is, starting fights. I kept digging. After high school Cliff started at community college but dropped out. He joined the US Army but didn't make it through the school part after basic training. Then he got a job as a bouncer at a Providence bar."

"Where he could have met Ross Kimball."

"Indeed." Norland nodded. "And maybe followed him to DC, who knows?"

"Hmm. Have you passed any of this along to Lincoln?"

Delia moseyed up. "It looks like you two are solving the world's problems. Or maybe only the ones in Westham?"

"Working on it." Norland smiled at her, then glanced at me. "My answer to that last question is not yet, but I will." His smartwatch buzzed at him. "Gotta run, ladies."

"Thanks for stopping in," I called after him.

"Were you two talking about Lincoln?" Delia tilted her head.

"His name came up." I left it at that and turned away.

If Cliff had an arrest record for starting physical altercations, he might also be the kind of person who turned to violence as a first resort for solving his perceived problems. Surely Lincoln already knew about his record, but Norland passing along the information couldn't hurt.

CHAPTER 53

We were steadily busy from then on. I didn't get a chance to mull over what Delia had told me about Kimball and Yvonne or Norland's information about Cliff, and I couldn't sneak away with Zia's diary. At a few minutes before noon, a couple came in while I was showing a man our two highest-end cycles, explaining their pros and cons.

"Mac?" Delia called. "When you get a minute, these people would like to speak with you."

"Give me one minute." I finished my conversation with the man.

He thanked me and said he'd be in touch. If he came back to purchase one of the bikes, it would be a great sale. We didn't move bikes that cost over a thousand dollars very often. I headed over to the couple while Delia moved on to assist a white-haired man looking for a specific item for his granddaughter.

"I'm Mac Almeida." I smiled at the newcomers. *Wait.*

This was the couple I'd seen down the street earlier, the ones I suspected of being Zia's parents.

The woman, taller than I and pushing sixty, gazed down the bridge of her nose at me. "My name is Sandra Carven, Ms. Almeida, and this is my husband, Horace. We understand you are a private investigator, and we'd like to engage your services. Do you have a place with any privacy where we can talk?"

"You're Zia's parents." I looked from her to him. "I'm so very sorry for your loss."

"We are, ma'am, and thank you." He grabbed my hand. "Do say you'll help us find the person who ended her life." Horace's lip wobbled, and he appeared on the verge of tears. He dropped my hand and ran his through thinning salt-and-pepper hair that was combed back from his brow.

"I would love to, Mr. Carven, but the thing is, I'm not a private investigator. As you can see, I own a bike shop. That's it." I started in on my little mantra. "We have an experienced homicide detective on the case and an excellent local police department."

His lined face crumpled. His wife, whose manner was indeed as icy as her pale blue eyes, pressed her lips together for a moment.

"I'm afraid your fame precedes you—or should I say your reputation?" She lifted her chin.

"I wish I could help you, Mrs. Carven." I clasped my hands in front of me. "I met your daughter briefly at the toy store earlier on the day she passed away. She was a lovely young woman and very helpful to me in finding the right gift for my own little girl."

Just then Reba made her way in and pushed back her wet hood. "It's a mess out there, Mackenzie." She not-so-subtly checked out the Carvens and beamed at them. "Hello, there. I'm Reba, Mac's grandmother."

"Abo Ree, this is Horace and Sandra Carven," I said.

"You poor things." She grabbed Horace's and Sandra's hands at the same time. "Your loss is enormous. My deepest sympathies to you both."

Horace's eyes finally spilled over. Reba pulled him into a hug, which he seemed to welcome.

"You poor, poor man." She released him and stepped back. "Forgive me, Mrs. Carven. I simply can't help myself from embracing those in need."

"It's not a problem, ma'am." Sandra was clearly not in need of a hug.

Horace pulled out a folded handkerchief and turned away to wipe his eyes.

"Do you have a service planned?" Reba asked. "I know several of us in the community would be happy to honor Zia's memory."

"Your so-called excellent local police refuse to release her remains," Sandra said.

"I'm sure they have to finish their investigation first," I said.

Horace nodded. "They do."

"Well, you be sure to let folks in Westham know when we can pay our respects," Reba continued. "Everyone in town loved your girl."

I gave her a quick glance, which she didn't meet. She hadn't spoken to me about meeting Zia, but that didn't mean a thing. My grandma made it her business to meet everyone, and she had a kind of radar for newcomers and people of interest, whether culturally or criminally. She happened to pop by my shop, for example, at the exact same time the Carvens were here. Still, her saying everyone in town loved Zia was a stretch. The young woman had worked here barely two months, and she lived elsewhere.

"We will, ma'am," Horace said. "I hope it's soon."

"Come along, Horace." Sandra sounded impatient. "We have other business to conduct."

"Yes, dear." To us he added, "Thank you for your sympathy." He scurried after his wife.

"That one best not visit the desert." Reba gazed after them. "Her solid-ice core might melt."

"Or not." I kept my voice low. "No wonder Zia was looking for her birth mom."

I pulled out my phone when a text buzzed in. It was from Tim.

"I want to check this message from Tim," I said to my grandma. "Did you come in with something to tell me?"

She laughed. "Not particularly, but I saw those two head in here and thought I could maybe help out."

"And you were curious, too."

"Aren't I always? Well, sweetheart, gotta dash. You take care." She squeezed my hand and sailed out the door as if carried by the wind.

I smiled to myself and tapped open the message.

You were right. They were Zia's parents, Horace and Sandra Carven. He's grieving, but she actually tried to flirt with me. WTF? XXOO

Sandra tried to flirt with Tim? I mean, he is a sweet thing to feast your eyes on. A married woman trying to hit on him while her grieving husband was at her side was entirely inappropriate for so many reasons. What the fudge, indeed.

Maybe Sandra was the kind of person who thought she could control everything. She certainly controlled Horace—except for his emotions. Having her adopted daughter leave town to search for her biological parents was hard enough. Then Zia being murdered and Sandra unable to control the investigation had to be enormously frustrating for her.

Still, something about Zia's mother made me queasy. I hoped whatever was in the diary would reveal why.

CHAPTER 54

By one o'clock the shop was quiet.

"I'm going to take lunch in my office and get a little work done," I told Delia. "Give me a shout if you need me."

"Will do."

I had the gloves from Orlean in my pocket, and earlier I'd managed to convey the diary, held in a paper towel, from the drawer out front to my office without Delia seeing me. I would have told her about it, except she was in a relationship with Lincoln, the person who needed the diary. I promised myself I would give it to him by the end of the day. Right now, I couldn't wait another minute to peruse it.

Office door shut behind me, I scarfed down half of my ham-and-cheese, then pulled on the stretchy purple gloves. I laid my hand on the book's cover. What would I find? Had Zia already discovered her birth parents? Had she written on Monday night or Tuesday, the morning of the day she would die?

I opened the book with care. It lay flat. The inside

cover was printed with the words, "Property of." She'd written her name on the provided line in a neat script.

She'd dated the top of the first page January 1, followed by the year.

"With the new year, I'm starting a new life. I have to leave Mother. I'll miss Daddy, but I have a strong need to find my birth parents. I want to start over in a place where no one knows me as that Carven girl."

She went on to describe the note she'd left her parents, saying she was leaving and would be fine but not to try and find her. She would be in touch when she could.

A smart move. That way they might not file a missing person report.

The next pages, a new day for each, detailed her finding the rooming house and the job with June. She wrote about a couple of friends she'd made, including Evan, and about how she loved talking with children when they came into the toy store.

"I hope to have my own little ones someday," she'd added.

That bit made her death still more heartbreaking. I sniffed and read on.

"June is an odd bird. I think she's snooping into my past. I don't like it, but I do a good job and just evade her questions."

Time was passing. I would get called out to the shop sooner or later. I flipped through the pages faster, scanning for changes or discoveries. At the beginning of February, I spotted Yvonne's name.

"A woman by that name worked at the hospital where I was born. She's about the right age. I found her at the pub in town and had a chance to study her face. I think we kind of look alike, but she refused to speak with me. I'll keep trying. I wish I hadn't had a closed adoption. In my heart I know she's my bio mom."

Zia had noticed the eyebrows. This entry was from a month ago. I knew from what Yvonne had told me that Zia succeeded in convincing Yvonne to talk to her, but when had that happened? I kept flipping through. A week later, I paused again.

"I dug up a newspaper picture showing Yvonne and Senator Kimball looking super comfortable with each other. It's at a charity fundraiser and was from my age plus a year ago. Been trying to reach him, but he's stonewalling me. I'm going to persist. I've been calling his office using my parents' address. I used to be his constituent. He needs to meet with me."

Wow. I turned the next page. Nothing of interest. I was about to moisten my finger on my tongue to help with turning the next page when I stopped in time. That would add my DNA to the diary, which was not a complication the book—or I—needed.

"Mac?" Delia called through the door. "Need you out here."

My shoulders slumped as I swore silently. Right when I was making progress, too. I said the only thing I could.

"Be right there." I slid the diary into my desk drawer,

stripped off the gloves and added them. Zia's book would be safe. Nobody ever came in here.

I gave the drawer a wistful glance, grabbed the other half of my sandwich, and returned to my responsible life.

CHAPTER 55

"I'm heading out, Mac," Delia said at two thirty.

"Have a good rest of your day," I said.

"Thanks."

After she was gone, my fingers itched to fetch the diary. I didn't. But since the place was quiet once again, I sent a text to the Cozy Capers. I owed my co-sleuths an update, especially since I hadn't had a chance to tell them what Yvonne had confessed. I should have done that last night, in fact.

Orlean found Zia's diary in her room, brought it to me. I read a bit at lunch in private. Zia mentioned noticing how she and Yvonne looked alike, but Y wouldn't talk to her. Zia found photo of Y and Kimball looking cozy in the right time period. Said she was trying to contact him. Then work got busy and I had to stop. Hope to read the rest before I turn it over to Lincoln. Also, yesterday Yvonne told me Zia came to see her. Yvonne is the birth mom.

I sent the overly long message. I drummed my fingers on the counter. I checked the clock. It wasn't three yet.

I twisted on my stool and gazed toward my office door in the back. Did I dare?

I wanted to find out if Zia had interacted personally with Kimball. I wanted to read what she'd written about drinking with Cliff at the pub, to see if she elaborated on June, and her reaction to speaking with Yvonne. I was thirsty to know all of it, and more.

My hopes were bludgeoned when cold air blew in through a door opened by a half dozen customers. I did a quick calming inhale followed by an exhale of negativity. I plastered on a smile and asked them how I could help.

Half an hour later, my coffers were considerably fatter. These cyclists had deep pockets and bought up a bunch of merchandise, from expensive shoes and shirts to toolkits and tubes to bottles and branded T-shirts.

If I'd thought I would have time to continue my reading, I was wrong. Lincoln replaced the shoppers. *Uh-oh.* I was sure I wore a guilty aura. What color was guilt? Dark gray, no doubt.

He glanced around. "Ah. I missed Del, didn't I?"

"Delia leaves at two thirty every day, so yeah, you missed her."

"This case is clogging up my brain. Do you have any news for me?"

He knew. He could see right through me. I swallowed.

"Um, I met the Carven parents this morning. They came in asking to hire me as a PI to find Zia's killer."

"To which you said?"

"Lincoln, you know me better than that. I told them

I'm a bike shop owner but that we have an expert detective on the case and an excellent local police force. It's my mantra. I don't even have to think about it anymore."

"I was joking." He smiled. "Those two Carvens are quite a number, aren't they?"

"He's a sweet man overtaken by his grief, and she's an iceberg."

"That's a good way of putting it. Her cold seems to go all the way down."

"Where did you meet them?" I asked.

"Mrs. Carven asked to speak with me. They came into the station at about ten this morning. She's all about appearances and giving her daughter a proper funeral."

"She didn't seem happy about not being able to take Zia's body home."

"That's an understatement," he said. "And he's nearly on his knees pleading for us to make an arrest of the horrible person who killed his little girl."

"He was in actual tears when they were here. But about Sandra—I was thinking that she's probably been able to control everything that goes on in her life until now. Her only child leaving and then being murdered has thrown not only a wrench, but an entire toolbox into the works."

"You could be right about that," he said. "Still, it wouldn't hurt her to show a little heart."

"Agreed. Have you found the murder weapon yet?" I wanted to know, but I also wanted to forestall him asking if I had anything else, as was his habit.

"I'm afraid we're still looking. The Cape and Islands

SPDU crime-scene team is down a couple of people, unfortunately."

I'd met a few members of the State Police Detective Unit back when Tim and I had found the skeleton in our wall.

"I can usually rely on their person-power," Lincoln added. "Not this time."

"Do you know if Senator Kimball is still in town?"

He tilted his head, staring at me. "Do you have reason to think he's involved in the homicide?"

"I don't know. Maybe?" I glanced at the door. This would be an optimal time to see a flood of customers come in. I could put an end to our little chat and not have to hand over the diary until later. The door stayed firmly shut.

"Mac, what else do you have for me?"

"I let you know what Yvonne told me about Zia."

"Yes, and I appreciate that," he said.

"Did you hear from Norland about Cliff Vriesdorp's arrest record? He also had a history of dropping out of college and not making it in the army."

"Those are facts we already knew, but the chief did manage to dig up a couple of sources we hadn't. Anything more?"

It was the question he always asked, and he was always referring to information. He couldn't possibly know about the diary. Still, I had to give it to him sooner or later.

"Stay right here," I said. "I do have something else."

In my office, I pulled on the gloves and gently extracted the book from the drawer.

"Here." I extended it toward Lincoln. "Last night Orlean happened to be visiting her friend, the landlord at the rooming house in Bourne, when he was showing Zia's room to her parents. After they left, Orlean spotted Zia's diary stuffed in a corner behind the bed."

Lincoln pulled on stretchy gloves and accepted the book. "And she gave it to you rather than calling the police." Steel had nothing on his expression.

"Yes, I did." Orlean sidled up. "I thought Mac might see you before I did. No harm done. Water under the bridge, Lincoln." She matched his serious look and then some.

"Very well," he said. "Mac already knows this, Orlean. In the future, should you 'happen' to find a homicide victim's personal diary, please leave it in place and call the nearest police department. Evidence needs to be tracked."

"No prob," Orlean said. "Catch ya later." She sauntered back to the repair area.

Lincoln shook his head. The phone on his belt buzzed. He answered it and listened to whoever was on the line. "Be right there."

"You're off?" I asked.

"Yes. I suppose you refrained from reading the contents of the diary, Mac. Am I correct?"

"That would be the right thing to do." I mustered my most innocent face.

He snorted. "Yes, it would. Thanks for turning it over. I won't ask how long it's been in your possession."

"Good luck. I hope what's in there helps move the case forward."

"You and me both." He hurried out.

I hadn't actually lied to him. Had I?

CHAPTER 56

I strode homeward along Main Street at a few minutes after five o'clock. Perhaps I hadn't done the right thing by reading Zia's diary, but I had redeemed myself, mostly, by relinquishing it to Lincoln. He sometimes conceded me the favor of filling me in on what I'd missed, information-wise. I hoped he would in this case.

I peered at what was happening ahead. Blue and red police lights strobed in front of a shop down the road a couple of blocks. Was it the Toy Soldier? My pace picked up on its own.

The action was, in fact, at the toy store. My heartbeat's pace also increased. *Let there not be a second murder there*, I thought, as I pictured Zia draped dead over the counter.

Up close I saw a state police SUV and cruiser as well as one from the Westham PD. I scooted in as close as I could to where a small crowd had already gathered.

"Does anyone know what happened?" I asked one of the people.

"No idea." Gin's voice came from my side.

I whirled. "Where did you come from?"

"I heard the siren and hurried down here. To answer your question, I don't know what happened, but I did see Lincoln go inside."

I patted my sternum to ease my racing heart and tried to take in a deep calming breath.

"Are you okay?" Gin asked.

"Yes." I lowered my voice. "But I was remembering being in there a week ago at this time. It was also a Tuesday."

"That was horrible for you, as it would be for anyone." She slung her arm around my shoulder and squeezed for a moment.

"It was. But I'm all right now." *Mostly*.

"Did you get to finish reading the diary?"

"Unfortunately, no," I said. "Lincoln came in an hour and a half ago. I couldn't not give it to him."

"Too bad."

"Totally, but it was in the pursuit of justice. Can't go wrong there."

Lincoln stepped out onto the sidewalk, speaking into his phone. When he was done he stashed the device on his belt. He caught sight of us and made his way over.

"Gin, Mac," he said. "Please come with me around the corner for a second."

We followed until we were out of sight of the crowd and it was quiet.

"Was there another—" I began.

"No more bodies," Lincoln said. "What I wanted to tell you is that we seem to have a murder weapon."

"You do?" I asked.

"Yes, and your daughter found it," he said.

I stared at him. "How in the world did Ella find a murder weapon? Is she in there now? Is she okay? Did it upset her?" *Why didn't Tim call me about it?*

"Hang on, Mac," he began. "No, she's not in there. Tim apparently stopped in with the kids on their way home from school. Children who are under three feet tall have a different perspective on the world than those twice their height. Little Ella saw a bocce ball mostly hidden in a corner, and she told her dad it looked funny. Tim took a gander. It looked funny because it had dried blood on it, and he called us."

"Did Ella touch it?" I asked.

"No, she said it looked yucky." A little smile played around Lincoln's lips. "And it certainly did. I thanked your husband and told him they could leave. Ella seemed fine. Tim's a great dad, by the way."

"He is." I teared up. I was itching to get home to that great dad and those beloved children. I turned away and swiped at my eyes. I'd be there soon.

"Wow," Gin said. "How did you and your team miss finding the ball?"

"We didn't," Lincoln said. "Someone left it there in the last few days, after we gave the go-ahead to June to reopen. We have her at the station now for questioning. Up to now, she hasn't admitted a thing."

"Or denied putting it there?" I asked.

"Precisely."

"Bocce balls are heavy," Gin said. "One of them could certainly do damage to anyone's head, but maybe especially to a young woman's skull."

"Right," I mused. "Zia was petite. She looked fragile, breakable." In fact, I knew nothing about how bone size related to skull thickness.

"Does June sell bocce balls?" Gin asked Lincoln.

"Yes." He nodded. "There are several sets on the shelves."

I pulled out my phone and texted Tim that Lincoln told me just now about Ella and the ball. I said I hoped she was all right and that I'd be home in fifteen minutes. It was only then I noticed a text from Tim. He had written about Ella finding the ball; I just hadn't seen the message.

He wrote back within seconds, saying she was fine and couldn't wait to see me.

When I glanced up both Gin and Lincoln were looking expectantly at me.

"What?" I asked. "Did you ask me a question?"

"I asked if you knew of any reason why June might have killed Zia," Lincoln said.

"Not exactly," I said. "But they seemed to have a prior connection. I'd love to know what it was."

"I'll see if we can persuade her to open up about that. For now, you hardworking business owners should get yourselves on home, and I'll get myself back to work."

"Thanks for filling us in, Lincoln," I said.

"Ditto," Gin said. "Free candy on me any time you want."

"You're tempting me." Lincoln smiled and hurried away.

"The case of the mysterious bocce ball," Gin said.

"Right. I wonder if June knew it was there. If not, who put it in the store?"

"I hope June isn't guilty of anything."

"Same," I said. "Right now, I'm going to speedwalk to my house and make sure for myself that Ella is all right. Talk to you soon."

Gin gave me a quick hug before we parted. "Give Ella a kiss from Auntie Gin."

"I will."

I switched on my headlamp and the flashing light on a band around my arm and headed for home.

CHAPTER 57

Coming home, as always, filled my heart to overflowing. Luca kicked his legs in his bouncy seat in the kitchen. Ella and Tim wore matching aprons. The aromas made my stomach growl at full volume. I'd never had such a happy place.

"I got to help smash the potatoes, Mama Mac," Ella told me.

"Lucky you." I smiled at her. She certainly seemed fine. "Mmm, it smells good in here. What else is on the menu?"

"We're roasting a chicken, and—" Tim began.

Ella interrupted him. "And we fried some green beans. I tried one, and it was good!"

"Apparently the first green bean she's ever liked," Tim added.

"I'm not surprised," I said. "Papa Tim is a great cook."

"I'm going to be one, too," Ella said.

"I like the sound of that." I headed for the kitchen counter where an open bottle of red wine sat next to an empty stemless wine glass. "This for me?"

"It's got your name on it," Tim said.

"I don't see her name anywhere," Ella said.

"It's only an expression, sweetheart," I told her. "He means that glass is for me." I filled it with wine and took an appreciative sip.

Tim pointed to Ella. "Stand on the other side of the table, Ella. I'm going to open the oven, and it's very hot."

"It's very hot," Belle muttered. "Very hot." She finished with a wolf whistle. "Snacks, Mac?"

After Tim extracted a perfectly roasted chicken, its skin golden and crispy, I slid by him and filled a bowl with frozen carrot bits for Belle.

"Isn't that pretty?" Tim asked. "Ella, the chicken has to rest for ten minutes to let the juices reabsorb. Let's get the table set, okay?"

"I'll do that with you, honey," I told her. "We'll let Papa Tim rest for ten minutes, too."

He shot me a grateful look. "Everything else is ready and keeping warm. I'll be back." He pulled off the apron and disappeared through the door.

Ella and I distributed silverware and plates. She sang to herself.

"I heard you found something unusual at the toy store on your way home today," I said.

"Yeah. A big heavy ball was hiding in the corner on the floor, and the ball was all yucky. Papa Tim had to call the police station, but don't worry. I wasn't in trouble."

"Of course you weren't. I bet the police were happy you showed Papa Tim what you found."

She gave a little-girl shrug. "I guess. Did you know Peppa Pig got to eat homemade ice cream?"

"She did?" Mom had let her watch an episode of the children's show, and now Ella was hooked.

"Yes, and it was strawberry. Can we make ice cream sometime?"

"Maybe in the summertime we can. It's kind of cold for ice cream right now, don't you think?"

Yes, my little girl was fine. She didn't know the yucky stuff on the bocce ball was dried blood. Finding the murder weapon hadn't been traumatic for her, and I was grateful for that.

With any luck Lincoln and team would be able to put a rush on getting the ball analyzed for DNA. Maybe it had fingerprints on it, if the killer had been stupid enough not to wear gloves. This case might finally be breaking, and none too soon.

When Tim came back in, I put all that out of my mind and feasted with my family on tender herbed chicken, garlicky fried green beans, and the comfort of buttery rough-mashed potatoes, taking small sips of wine along with it. After I fine-mashed a quarter cup of potato, Luca also ate a few bites. This was family dinner at its best.

CHAPTER 58

I settled in on the couch with my phone and a little glass of Scotch after everyone else was asleep. Several texts had come in during the earlier evening hours, but I'd ignored them. Now I dug in.

Gin had let the group know about the murder weapon find. I sent a reply saying Ella seemed perfectly fine and not bothered by her discovery of the "yucky" bocce ball. I added that I hoped the police could analyze the DNA sooner rather than later.

Tulia had also written while I was busy.

Got a chance to talk with June. Seems she suspected Zia was having an affair with Kimball cuz she was always calling him. June didn't approve.

Wow. Zia might have been phoning the senator, but it was because she thought he was her bio dad, which it appeared he was. I responded.

I heard June refer to Zia as a slut. Maybe those calls were why.

A new message came in from Norland confirming what he'd told me earlier.

Cliff V has arrest record for assault and is a serial dropout. Curious that this AM I spotted no bocce balls in toy store.

As he'd reported to me in the bike shop. So how had the heavy ball made its way into the shop?

Norland added a question.

What more did you learn from the diary, Mac?

I had to give it to Lincoln before I finished reading the most recent entries. Didn't learn anything else beyond what I texted earlier.

Flo wrote next.

I've been slammed at work, thus not helping much this time around. Sorry.

Tulia assured her it was fine, and I chimed in with the same sentiment, adding not to worry about it. Zane sent a message much like Flo's.

Same here. Not worth much in terms of investigating, but I'm following all, plus keeping eyes and ears out at work. Also locking our doors and windows.

That was a prudent practice no matter if a murderer was at large or not. What else should we talk about? I thought for a moment, then snapped my fingers and typed a message.

Zia's parents are around. Mom is total icicle, dad is super sad.

Zane responded right away.

They came into my store, bought a bottle of Tito's vodka. Drowning his sorrows? Except she seemed in charge. Maybe she's the drinker.

I should also pass along what Delia witnessed.

Delia told me Kimball intruded on pub kitchen. D found him harassing Yvonne, who wasn't pushing back. Kimball left. D was worried about Y.

Gin replied.

Entitled, much? I hate dudes like that.

I yawned. I also hated men—and women—who acted like bullies. Crashing a heavy ball on a young woman's head went way beyond bullying, but it made me think of something else to bring up.

Norland, how long do you think it'll take to check bocce ball for DNA?

It didn't take him long to respond.

Unfortunately, it could take weeks. With a rush request, and if Lincoln can pull strings, could be sooner. Because it's an active case, he might succeed. I'll see what I can find out.

I sent back a quick thanks. With nothing more from anyone, we wound down the discussion. I sat in thought, sipping my drink.

Given that the murder weapon was heavy, the most likely suspects were Kimball or Cliff. But Yvonne had the super strong arms of a chef, and I thought June was strong, too. Because the balls were sold in the store, it didn't seem as if the murder was planned out ahead of time. The killer might have been arguing with Zia and lost it, grabbing the nearest weapon-like object.

A research avenue occurred to me. Could we find out whether our various persons of interest were known to play bocce? Maybe the game had tournaments and such. Or maybe one of them had been overheard talking about the game. Otherwise, how would they know the balls were heavy enough to do the damage? On the other hand, if the killer was June, she could have simply picked up a piece of her own merchandise.

I added the question to the text thread.

We all can poke around, see if any of our suspects is known to play bocce.

Zia had certainly seemed frightened that day, and I thought I'd seen someone peering in the window. That wouldn't have been June.

I yawned again. My tired head was spinning, and it was past time to quit thinking about murder. A much better idea was to get ready for bed and slide in next to my sleeping man.

CHAPTER 59

After a breakfast-and-dressing routine more fraught than usual, I managed to drop off both children a few minutes early, by some miracle. Maybe Ella had been more affected by her find yesterday than we'd thought. She'd asked a lot of questions about the police and was contrary with things she normally didn't fuss about. I slipped a quiet word to my mom about what had happened when I left Ella in her hands. She promised to let me know how my little girl did in her care until preschool opened and if she asked any questions.

When this case was over, I'd see if I could arrange to take Ella on a tour of the police station. Everyone would love her, and it might ease her worries, however nebulous.

Right now it was only eight fifteen. I decided to pay another quick visit to Piet at Pete's Westham Mercantile.

"Hey, Piet." I smiled at him behind the counter. I loved inhaling the smell of the old wooden shelves mixed with the scents of paint, nails, oil, and all the other aromas of an old-fashioned, non-sterile hardware store. The Mercantile was here long before Piet bought it. I hoped it stayed in its current use for a good, long time to come.

"Mac, how's Belle today?"

"She's full of beans, as always. How are you?"

He frowned, glancing around. He leaned closer. "The boy says he's leaving at the end of the week. The day won't come a moment too soon."

"The boy being Cliff?" I made a note to let Lincoln know of these plans.

"The same. I have had nothing but trouble from him since he arrived. I don't know how he can be that different from my cousin, who is a fine, upstanding, moral person."

"Genes, personality, life circumstances?" I mused. "Who knows?"

"Well, that's that." He dusted off his hands as if he could dispense with Cliff as easily. "What do you need today, my friend?"

"Don't you stock a few yard games?"

"We do, we do. It's not quite the season, but I'll show you what we have. Follow me, my dear." He locked the cash drawer and hurried around the end of the counter.

I followed as he listed the game inventory.

"We have whiffle ball, croquet, diabolo, a plastic jai alai set, discs, and badminton. And the more-than-popular pickleball, but that's not exactly a yard game."

We arrived at the shelves. He studied them.

"Something's missing." His frown returned as he

pointed to an empty spot. "We usually have bocce sets, as well."

"Too bad. That's what I was hoping to pick up."

"I apologize. I can always order more in, but I don't believe we sold the set we had. Let me check in the system."

We made our way back. The bocce set was missing, and Cliff had plans to leave town. This wasn't looking good.

Piet stared at his screen. "That set did not sell. It's a nice one, too, with a compact carrying case." He muttered something to himself that might have included Cliff's name. "Would you like me to order a set for you, Mac?"

"Thanks, but I'll hold off for now. As you say, it's not exactly the season. I think Tim would love to play, though. I'll come back closer to Father's Day. This year will be his first."

Piet's expression softened. "How are those little children doing?"

"They're doing really well, thanks. Between us, my family, and the community, they're getting the love and stability they need. And we're thrilled to have them."

Piet knew the story of how Ella and Luca came into our lives, and he'd been nothing but supportive.

"Excellent." He beamed. "Here's a little flashlight for Ella, her very own." He selected a penlight from the box near the register.

"Thank you. She'll love it," I said. "Now I'd better get over to my own shop. Talk to you soon."

I'd nearly reached the door when Cliff burst in,

holding his phone in front of his face, which looked either irate or upset. Maybe both.

"With all due respect, sir, no way." His tone was low and harsh. "I'm not doing that." He glanced up to see me watching and listening. He jabbed at the phone and pocketed it. "Why are you snooping on me again?"

Whoa. "Good morning, Cliff. I just had a lovely conversation about hardware with Piet, since this happens to be a hardware store, and I was about to leave through that very door. If you'll excuse me?"

"What? Oh, sure, as if."

I raised my chin and stared at him. "Me, door." I pointed to my chest. "You, move." I pointed at him.

The door was within earshot and eyesight of Piet.

"Clifford, get out of her way," Piet called.

Cliff stepped to the side. The heat of his glare seared the back of my neck, but the door closed behind me without incident.

CHAPTER 60

After all the cold slush and snowy winds of March coming in like the lioness she was, today was the kind of day that hinted at spring lambs. The air was cool but mild, and the sun was strong. I spotted a cluster of early crocuses in a sheltered southern-facing patch of garden on my way to Mac's Bikes.

I hummed to myself as I puttered about, following the store-setup checklist that by now had become muscle memory. I headed outside but stopped short with the Open flag in my hand, stunned again to realize maybe I really was less obsessive these days. I'd been focused for my whole life on needing everything to be tidy and in its place. That need included routines like opening my business every morning.

When I first opened the bike shop, I had to be sure I checked off every item on the list, and it was an actual typed list that I laminated and kept next to the cash register. I'd done the same with the closing checklist. At the beginning I opened and closed the shop every day. The lists were for me alone. Now that I had weekend crews, I could refer them to the steps, but they didn't really need them after a few weeks. These days, neither did I.

Losing a few of my obsessive compulsions seemed like a healthy change. I reached up and slid the flagpole into the holder, then gazed at the empty blue window boxes. Soon enough I would plant them with bright-colored pansies, followed by red and white geraniums for the summer.

"Yoo-hoo!"

I'd know that cheery voice anywhere. Smiling, I turned and waited for Reba and my mom to reach my side.

"You two are up and about early," I said.

"Ella couldn't wait to tell her little friends about the policemen yesterday." Mom wore an artsy maroon beret today. "She insisted I drop her off the very moment school opened."

"Astra is coming to aqua exercise with me this morning," Reba said. "But first we thought you should know what we came across and what our plan is."

"I can't wait to hear it, but do come inside. It's still a little chilly out here." I pulled open the door and gestured for them to precede me. Inside I said, "I like the new hat, Mom."

"Thanks." She touched the beret. "Your father found it for me at that big UU ministers gathering in New Orleans he went to."

I waited. My grandmother's eyes sparkled, but that was nothing new for her. Mom wandered around, touching the handlebars of various display bikes.

"I thought you two had something to tell me." I glanced from Mom to Abo Reba and back.

"Well, we do. Reba?" Mom pointed at her tiny mother-in-law.

"All righty. So, after I heard about little Ella's discovery, why, I had myself a nice little chat with the cook at the Rusty Anchor. Did you know she's a crack shot with a bocce ball?"

"Yvonne is?"

"My word, yes. She has won tournaments and such." Reba's expression was no different from that of a cat who has recently finished consuming the best parts of a poor, doomed songbird.

I wasn't going to inquire under what pretense she had a "nice little chat" with Yvonne about the game where one carefully aims large heavy balls at an unsuspecting small ball. My only consolation was that my grandma was so tiny and gregarious, I doubted any killer would be onto her investigative ways. Anyway, after my conversation with Yvonne, I couldn't believe she'd killed Zia.

"Interesting," I said. "Did you go with her, Mom?"

"I did. She and I ventured out for a postprandial liqueur last evening, and I couldn't let her head into the lion's den alone, could I?"

"Yvonne's kitchen is hardly the lion's den," I protested.

"Well, you know what I mean, honey," Mom said.

"Do you two make a practice of going out for a drink after dinner together?" I asked.

"Not at all." Reba laughed. "But it's fun once in a while, isn't it, Astra?"

Mom smiled. "You bet."

"You said something about a plan," I prompted.

Reba nodded with enthusiasm. "We thought we might set about discovering who else among your interesting persons might have had experience with the game or had an ability with hurling those balls. I certainly wouldn't be able to heave one, but nobody else needs to know that."

My "interesting persons" had to be the several persons of interest in the homicide.

"Abo Ree, I think it would be best to leave that to Lincoln and his team," I said. "I mean, we're talking about a murderer here. Right, Mom?"

Please let her agree with me and help keep herself and our beloved Reba safe.

"The detective will do what he's able to, honey," Mom said. "But we're nothing if not good at looking innocent, aren't we, Reba? We want to lend what assistance we can."

Gah. She was no help at all. My only option was to get this killer behind bars before either of my relatives came to harm.

"Oh, and speaking of plans," Mom began, "I think we're all set for Ella's birthday party Sunday. Joseph will make the cake."

"Tim can if Pa is busy," I said. Tim would already be baking cupcakes for the Saturday party.

"You know it's tradition for your father to bake the birthday cake."

It was true: ever since I could remember, Pa had

baked and iced family birthday cakes. He'd gone so far as to take a cake-decorating class.

"Your man won't mind, will he?" my mom asked.

"Not at all."

"We're off to exercise in the water, Mackenzie." Astra kissed my cheek.

"Ta-ta, darling." Reba waggled her fingers and trundled out after Astra.

"Have fun." What else could I say?

The light streaming in the windows turned a little dimmer as I worried about my two favorite women.

CHAPTER 61

As soon as my mom and grandmother left, my phone rang.

"Sorry, Mac," Orlean croaked. "I'm sicker than a mangy mutt."

"I'm sorry to hear that."

"Shouldn't have eaten at that new clam shack over to Sandwich. Went to see my elderly cousin. Think I got bad seafood."

"I hope you feel better soon. Don't worry about here. I can handle emergency fixes, and otherwise I'll say the repair shop is unavoidably closed for the day."

"You sure?" she asked.

"Absolutely."

"Okay. Thanks. I'm sure I'll be fine tomorrow."

"Take as long as you need."

She disconnected. I considered making a sign for the door but instead, I decided I could take repair requests on a case-by-case basis. My mechanic was super well organized. I'd check the repair tickets and see if any were finished and due to be picked up today. If so,

I could make a few calls. Certain customers preferred to talk over the work with the person who did it.

I spent the next hour making those calls and helping a smattering of customers with retail items. I also completed rental checkouts for a group of five, all of which kept me too busy to dwell on bocce balls and a glowering young man named Cliff.

Flo wrote to the Cozy Capers thread at about ten o'clock and asked for a quick in-person gathering after the noon hour. Gin chimed in that we could meet in her back room again. I said I'd be there, customers permitting.

A minute later, Delia came in for her shift.

"Orlean is out sick, FYI," I said after I greeted her. "I can do minor repairs, and we can tell people to come back tomorrow if they need anything complex."

"Got it. She doesn't have something serious, I hope."

"She thinks it's a touch of food poisoning. She said she expected to be in tomorrow. How's your doggie?"

"He's fine," Delia said. "Like Orlean, he ate something bad yesterday. Dogs are better at cleaning the floor than a Hoover vacuum, except they don't have the metal stomach."

The shop was empty of customers for the moment, and I realized I hadn't talked with Delia—a longtime friend of Yvonne's—about Yvonne being Zia's biological mother.

"Delia, did you know Yvonne gave a baby up for adoption a little over twenty years ago?"

She gave her head a little shake. "Where did that come from, Mac?"

"It's complicated, but Yvonne told me she was Zia Carven's birth mom."

She stared at me. "I hope you don't think Vonnie killed the girl, because that never, ever would have happened."

"I don't. I'm simply trying to put all the pieces together."

"Hmm. Well, she and I are in our mid-forties, and we lost touch after our college graduation. I headed to the West Coast to surf and enjoy life for a while. Vonnie never returned my emails. That might have been when she joined the air force and came out, or maybe that was a little later. Like I said, we weren't in contact for pretty much the next decade."

"So, anything could have happened."

"Yep." She frowned. "You want me to ask her? About the baby, I mean?"

"No, that's okay. Lincoln might not appreciate it."

She barked out a laugh. "No kidding."

From then on, we were super busy. I had to disappoint more than one customer who came in with a complicated repair job. I was so spoiled by Orlean's expertise that I was out of practice with the intricate mechanical workings of bicycles. More than once I asked cycle owners to please come back later in the week.

CHAPTER 62

I came into the candy-factory part of Gin's shop at one o'clock, lunch bag in hand. Flo and Gin were already perched on stools, as was Norland. Zane appeared a minute later.

"I was trying to call to you out there to wait up," he told me. "But you didn't hear me."

"Sorry about that." I glanced around. "No Tulia or Ilsa?"

"Tulia's slammed at the Shack," Gin said.

"And Ilsa had a doctor's appointment," Norland added.

"Luckily my shop emptied of customers about fifteen minutes ago after a super-busy morning," I said. "But I might have to split in a hurry if Delia lets me know we have a new rush."

"Then let's get going." Flo laid her yellow legal pad on the stainless-steel island, now free of chocolates, taffy, or any of the yumminess it usually held. She hovered her pen over the paper. "Do we have any news?" she asked.

I raised my hand. "My mother and grandmother 'happened' to go out for a drink at the Rusty Anchor last night." I surrounded "happened" with finger quotes. "They had a 'little chat' with Yvonne and learned she is a whiz at bocce." More finger quotes.

Norland frowned. "They shouldn't be getting themselves involved in this, Mac."

"Believe me, I agree," I said. "They mentioned they were going to check into whether any of the suspects plays bocce. All I could do was impress on them that they need to stay safe and leave this business to Lincoln. And to us, but I didn't say that part." I pulled out my sandwich and took a bite.

"Mr. Carven came into my shop this morning," Gin said. "He implied that his wife had never really loved Zia. Their daughter had a sweet tooth, like most children, and he said he used to slip her lollipops and fudge. He told me the few times his wife discovered the sweets, she took them away and punished the girl for having them."

"Terrible mothering," Norland said. "I mean, what's the harm, really?"

"I know," Gin nodded. "He bought a pound of fudge, a giant lollipop, and two pounds of saltwater taffy in his dead girl's honor." Her eyes welled up. "It was loving and tragic."

I also blinked away tears. I hoped I never had to face either of our children dying before we did, much less being murdered.

"What if Mommie Dearest was the killer?" Flo glanced

around at us. "Furious she couldn't control this daughter she didn't share a single gene with, she came to town and offed her."

My insides went cold at the thought.

"That's too horrid to consider." Zane shuddered. "Killing the daughter she raised? I pray the mother isn't the murderer."

Flo nodded.

"It was Zia's mother who wanted to hire me as a private investigator," I said.

"That could have been her cover story," Norland began, "but a risky one."

"I turned her down, regardless. Any news on the DNA front, Norland?" I asked before taking another bite of my lunch.

"It looks like Lincoln put an urgent flag on the evidence, but I don't believe results have come in to date. I'll keep checking."

Flo added that action item for him.

"Has anyone seen Kimball in the last day or two?" Gin asked.

The response was all heads shaking and a murmured "No."

"Delia saw him harassing Yvonne in the pub kitchen, but that was Monday evening," I said. "I haven't seen him today or yesterday."

"Maybe he went back to Rhode Island or DC," Flo suggested. "I don't know if the Senate is in session. I'll see if it is, and if so, I can find out what votes might be going on." She jotted down an action item for herself on the legal pad.

"What else do we know?" Zane asked.

I swallowed my last bite of sandwich. "I stopped into Piet's hardware store this morning. He has a bocce ball set missing from the shelves, but it wasn't sold. He told me Cliff is moving somewhere else at the end of this week. When I was about to leave, Cliff came in while he was on a call. He addressed someone as "sir" and said he refused to do something. He saw me, disconnected the call, and accused me of snooping again. He was pretty irate."

Norland frowned. "That sounds volatile. You need to be super careful, Mac."

"Believe me, I am," I said. "Cliff was blocking the door. I asked nicely for him to move aside. When Piet told him to get out of my way, he did, but he wasn't happy about it."

"Unsold missing bocce balls, irate younger relative planning to skip town?" Gin posited. "Cliff sounds guilty to me."

"Have you told Lincoln about what happened?" Zane asked.

"I didn't have a chance this morning. Orlean is out sick, and we were slammed with customers until an hour ago. But I will let him know, at least by text."

When we didn't seem to have anything else to share, Flo read out our action items.

"Norland's going to keep us current on the DNA

analysis," she began. "I will check into the senator's whereabouts." Flo glanced around the group. "Anything else?"

Gin held up a finger. "I'll let Lincoln know what Mr. Carven said and our thoughts about his wife."

"So noted." Flo added that to her list and stood. "Thanks for hosting, Gin. I have to get back to the library, stat."

Zane and I agreed that we had our workplaces waiting for us, as did Gin.

"I guess I'll just mosey along enjoying life as a retired person." Norland winked. "But we'll all be in touch, yes?"

We absolutely would. There was no better group of amateur sleuths than us, at least in real life.

CHAPTER 63

After Delia left at two thirty, I was alone in the shop. While things were quiet, I straightened merchandise and put in an order for more. When the shop was mobbed with customers fifteen minutes later, I did my best to help people in the order they came in. I answered questions, rang up sales, and checked out a couple of rentals.

By four o'clock, my business was quiet again. Dark clouds had blown in outside—so much for spring lambs. The clouds meant I might be on foot in a driving rain, which was not something I'd come prepared for. *Ugh.* I would leave immediately, except we had a half-dozen rentals due in, and the agreement said they had to be returned by five o'clock. I had to stay.

I headed out front to unlock and bring in the display bikes. The Open flag flapped furiously in the wind. I jumped when a loud crack resounded. The following crash of branches at least meant the noise hadn't been a gunshot.

I hurried around to the side of the building. A large limb of the big swamp oak that stood behind the parking lot now blocked the farther half of the lot. I winced at the sight. At least no cars were parked there today; they would have been crushed if they had. The limb thankfully hadn't crashed onto the building itself.

I shook my head. That massive piece of wood was way too big for me to drag out of the way. I would call the man who plowed snow off the lot for me. He could probably hoist the broken branch into the back of his truck or cut it up. Glancing up, I winced at the gash in the trunk where the limb had been. I supposed I should get an arborist out to make sure the tree was healthy and not at risk of dropping other heavy appendages.

Sighing, I returned to my task in front of the shop, but the back of my neck prickled. Trying to appear casual, I turned to see a low-slung, silver car cruise by. It was a make that looked expensive, but I couldn't identify the brand. Whoever it was kept going, and I chalked up my neck prickles to nerves.

After the bikes were inside and stashed, I perched on a stool to wait. Between the wind, the not-yet-apprehended murderer, and being alone in the shop, I couldn't settle. My fingers drummed on the counter of their own accord, and my left foot jittered on the rung of the stool.

A few long, deep, calming breaths didn't help, either. I pulled out my phone and checked for messages. Nothing from Tim. Nothing from anyone else in my family. And, alas, not a word from any of the Cozy Capers.

Admittedly we'd gone our separate ways less than three hours ago.

I sent a quick message to my plow guy, describing the broken limb situation in the shop's parking lot and asking if he could help tonight or in the morning. He was reliable and would get back to me when he could. Or, knowing him, it was more likely he would just show up and do the work.

I slid off the stool and headed to the back to be sure the second egress door was locked. We rarely used that door, which remained locked to prevent anyone from trying to get in , but I had to be sure. In the little kitchen area, I tidied up the coffee maker and grabbed my cloth lunch bag. I wanted to leave the minute those rentals came in.

As I returned to the front, I glanced into the repair room. Orlean always left it orderly, which was something I very much appreciated about her. Even though she didn't talk much when she was here working, I felt her absence when she was out, especially today. It couldn't be helped. My weekend mechanic had other jobs he did during the work week. I couldn't call him in a pinch to fill in for Orlean.

Back on my stool, I wondered if there was anything related to the homicide investigation that I could accomplish on my phone while I waited. I thought back to the action items Flo had read off at the end of our meeting and gave my forehead a little slap. My own action item was to keep Lincoln informed about Cliff.

No time like the present. I typed out a text message.

Spoke to Piet this AM. Bocce set missing from hardware store, not sold. Said Cliff is leaving end of week. Cliff came in, told someone on phone he wouldn't be doing something. Saw me, hung up, was angry with me. FYI.

I sent it but got no reply. *Good.* I hoped that meant Lincoln had enough evidence to charge a murderer and was out making an arrest.

CHAPTER 64

My rentals arrived at four fifty, and I got the bikes checked in at double speed.

As I made my way home at a little after five o'clock, I squinted at the display windows of Gifts from the Sea, the cute local gift shop. Everything was festooned with shamrocks and green garlands. A grinning cardboard leprechaun held a bucket full of gold pieces interspersed with sand dollars and seashells.

Was Saint Patrick's Day already upon us? I supposed it was, being early March. I sighed. This Main Street business owner found the expectation to decorate for every seasonal holiday a bit exhausting. At the same time, I wanted to be a good shopkeeper-citizen. Tomorrow I would dig out the St. Paddy's Day box in the storage area and keep up my end of the bargain.

Now that we were in March, it also meant that Zia's death had happened last month—eight days ago. What was keeping Lincoln and his team from nailing down the killer's identity? Maybe a week and a day wasn't an unreasonably long time for a homicide investigation, but it felt like it.

The wind was still blowing, but the clouds hadn't begun pelting the town with rain yet. With any luck I'd be safely home before it did. I strode along briskly, increasing my pace when I spotted Brendan and Ed on the sidewalk in front of the police station. They seemed to be having an intense discussion. Senator Kimball wasn't part of the group. If he had left town, why were they still here? That might mean Kimball was around, too.

I slowed to a stroll when I neared them and kept my hearing tuned to maximum.

"We have to tell them the whole story," Ed said to Brendan. Her back was mostly to me.

His face fell. "But what if—?"

"No, Brendan," the driver said. "You know it's the right thing to do."

I sidled closer and pretended I hadn't heard. "Good evening, you two." I smiled. "Did the big boss give you the night off?"

Ed pressed her lips together and crossed her arms on her chest. She shot a quick look at the entrance to the police station.

Brendan flapped his hands at his sides. "Um, yes." He glanced left and right as if for the exit.

"I suppose he had to get back to the Senate," I said.

"They are in recess," Ed said. "Ms. Almeida, if you will excuse us, we have an appointment."

"In the station?" I used my brightest, most innocent

tone. "Cool. As do I. After you." I gestured toward the steps. I had no appointment, but they didn't need to know that.

"Do you?" Ed's razor gaze made it clear she didn't believe me.

I bobbed my head without speaking. Brendan's posture sagged, but he trudged upward. Ed followed, as did I. She made sure I was not behind her, falling back to ascend at my side. That was definitely the behavior of a bodyguard. As long as she did the right thing, in her own words, that was all I cared about. I only hoped I could eavesdrop on their appointment.

Inside, Ed asked the officer behind the glass for Detective Haskins, adding that she, Ed Kobylarz, and Brendan Lopes had a prearranged meeting with Lincoln. She slid her ID through the dish-shaped opening under the plexiglass.

I hung back. I'd never had to do that with my license, mostly because everybody here knew me. Instead, I typed a quick text to Tim saying I was delayed but fine and would be home as soon as I could.

Ed got her ID back as the inner door opened. Lincoln greeted Ed and Brendan. When his gaze traveled beyond them to me, I gave him a hopeful smile and a little wave. He shot me a frown in return.

"Please wait here a moment," Lincoln said to Ed and Brendan. He took three long steps toward me, opened the exit door, and ushered me out. "I can't talk right now, Mac."

"Please listen to this one bit. I overheard those two talking on the sidewalk a moment ago. Ed told Brendan they had to give you the whole story. He was reluctant, and she reminded him it was the right thing to do. That's all."

"Thanks," he said. "Go home. I'll be in touch."

I was about to salute and say, "Aye-aye, Captain," but the door closed before I could.

CHAPTER 65

I would have given a lot to be able to sit in on Lincoln's chat with Kimball's aides. He clearly didn't want me there, which was just as well. Tim, Ella, and Luca wanted me home, and I was headed for them, ASAP.

June was in front of the Toy Soldier reaching for her own flapping Open flag. Was a quick talk with her worth a small delay in my arrival home? Maybe.

"Hey, June," I said. "Some days it feels good to take in the flag and lock the door on your business, doesn't it?"

She squinted at me. "Maybe it feels good to you. You didn't have a girl killed on your retail counter last week."

Ouch. "True."

"You think people want to buy toys near a murder scene? You imagine you'd feel safe bringing your children in here to shop for puzzles or dolls, or sending your young teen in alone to buy a new game?"

I opened my palms. "Tim brought our kids to the Toy Soldier yesterday."

"He was one of the few parents who did. But then your daughter made a gruesome discovery. Lincoln won't let me hear the end of it."

"Do you have any idea how the bocce ball got there?" I asked.

"I . . ." She cleared her throat. "Listen, I must have been taking a restroom break in the back. The stupid ball just appeared on Tuesday late morning, right there on the floor next to the counter where it would have been if the killer dropped it. I thought the police would say I left it there."

"So you hid it behind the shelving, but Ella found it."

"Exactly," June said. "I was going to drop the ball into the dumpster behind the fast-food joint, but your girl discovered it first. I've told the whole story to Lincoln more times than I can count. He still doesn't believe me. But Mac? It's the plain truth." June's DNA would certainly be on the ball whenever those results became available, and her fingerprints as well if she hadn't worn gloves while handling it.

"It's too bad you don't have a security camera."

"But I do! The thing is, it doesn't cover every angle in front. Or maybe the villain slid in through the back door from the parking lot."

"That's not an entrance into the store that customers use, is it?" I asked.

"No. It opens onto the storage area, but I park out back and sometimes I forget to lock the door behind me when I come in."

Such forgetfulness struck me as ultra-careless behavior from a shop owner. On the other hand, Westham was generally a safe town. June might have been lulled into a false sense of security.

The shushing whir of an electric car approached. I glanced over at a sleek silver sedan cruising at a low speed. The pale license plate on the front was inscribed Rhode Island and pictured a single green wave behind a three-digit number preceded by EV. By the time I tried to see the driver, the moment had passed along with the car, and I couldn't make out anything through the tinted rear windows. The car looked a lot like the one that had been driving slowly by my shop a couple of hours ago.

June stared intently at the vehicle and let out an expletive. "That jerk needs to leave town."

"Who was it?"

"Senator fancy-pants Kimball. He's nothing but trouble."

"Thus the Ocean State license plate. I wondered about that." I watched the car drive away. With his driver currently talking to Lincoln, Kimball obviously wasn't being chauffeured in the big black SUV. Did he have the silver EV here on the Cape the whole time? Or maybe he'd gotten a ride home and came back in his personal vehicle.

"It seems odd that he would drive an electric car, as opposed as he is to another alternative power source." I looked at June. "I thought you shared his opposition to the wind project."

"I do, but for entirely different reasons. And that wasn't what I meant." Her eyes filled. "I thought—wrongly—that Zia was trying to have an affair with him. I wish I could rewind time and apologize to her.

I've learned she was trying to find her biological father. She suspected it was Kimball."

He had those light brown eyes. They weren't as golden as Zia's, but he could easily have passed down the genes for them to her. And his mouth was wide like hers had been.

"That's why she was calling and texting him so often. Now he's harassing me." June swiped at her eyes. "I've had it, Mac."

"What's he harassing you about?"

"It's complicated. I knew him a bit when I was younger."

"Like an acquaintance, or something more involved?" I asked.

She stared at me. "Not an affair. No way. But he was one of those swaggering handsome young guys." She shrugged. "We talked a bit when I was at the beach house, went for a few walks. I was married, and that's all it was. Now he's making out like it was more."

"Have you told Lincoln about the harassment? Or the Westham or Mashpee police? They need to know about it. Kimball shouldn't be allowed to do that, no matter how powerful he thinks he is."

"You're right. Lincoln would understand." She finally extracted the flagpole from its holder. "I'll let you go, Mac. Thanks for listening." She pulled the door open.

"Take care," I said. "Have a good evening."

"You as well." The door shut behind her.

I hurried along on my way, now vigilant to keep an eye out for a silver EV.

CHAPTER 66

By eight thirty that evening, everybody else was asleep. I was folding laundry, a job that never ended with two little ones in the house.

Luca was now a bit over six months old and growing fast. His six-month-sized onesies and little suits were getting tight, and I set those aside to pass along for baby Joey. Derrick and Neli had given us a big box of Cokey's too-small clothes when Ella came to live with us. I loved that we could keep the cycle going.

I'd mostly stopped dwelling on whether Tim and I would ever conceive a baby of our own, but the possibility was always in the back of my mind. I knew it was for Tim as well. After Joey was born, I had passed along Luca's three-month-sized clothes. Neli thanked me and murmured something about giving them back when her baby outgrew them.

I'd been noncommittal at the time. Keeping hope alive was a tricky thing. We didn't want to give up, but at the same time, continuing to hope could also lead to disappointment and heartbreak. Anyway, I was happy with the two children we had, and I was plenty busy with a business and a family of four.

When my phone vibrated, I set down Ella's folded flowered leggings and sat at the end of the couch next to her pile of clothes.

Not surprisingly, it was a message to the Cozy Capers group. Norland reported seeing Yvonne head into the police station as he passed by about an hour ago.

Yvonne? I hoped she was coming clean with Lincoln about her past and about Kimball's behavior in the present. She would normally be busy cooking in the pub's kitchen on a weekday evening.

I hadn't had time to report on my own police station sighting, so I typed a message about it.

Saw Kimball driver, Ed, and Brendan go into the WPD station at fiveish today to meet with Lincoln. He told me to go home. Before they went in, Ed had to convince B they were doing the right thing. Dying to know what it was.

Gin chimed in.

Eli and I walked on beach tonight to see full moon on water, just got back. Silver car parked at old motel.

A silver electric vehicle? I wrote back:

Silver EV crept past Toy Soldier today as I talked with June out front. She said it was Kimball's. Has RI plates. Same, Gin?

She wrote back within seconds.

Sorry. Didn't get close enough to see either. Thought any car there was strange.

Tulia popped in.

Place has been closed for ten years. Shd be fixed up or torn down. Total eyesore and dangerous.

For sure. Norland sent the next message.

If it's Kimball car, what's he doing at the motel? Gin, pls tell Lincoln what you saw.

Good thought. Gin responded that she would.

I sat there for a moment, phone in hand. If Gin was going to report her sighting at the beach, I should also let Lincoln know about the silver EV June said belonged to Kimball. I tacked on a question to the message about what Ed and Brendan had wanted, and a note wondering why Yvonne had gone in. Lincoln would answer or he wouldn't.

That accomplished, I stayed rooted to my seat, thinking about the group's virtual conversation of the evening. What business did Yvonne have at the police station? I wondered if she'd been summoned or had gone to unburden herself. To do the right thing, as Ed had urged Brendan to do.

And what, indeed, was a silver car doing hanging around at a long-deserted lodging at the beach? When Tim and I passed the motel last weekend, I'd been creeped out. I thought something felt different about the structure, but I couldn't pinpoint what it was.

Wait. Gin and Eli had driven out to the beach to see a full moon on the water? I rose and peeked out the window. Sure enough, the wind of a few hours ago must have blown the clouds right out of town. A fat moon now shone down from above the treetops.

I supposed whoever owned the silver car could have been at the beach for the same reason as Gin. Either way, I wasn't going to solve anything tonight. I returned to complete my folding before sleepy yawns landed me in the same place as the rest of my beloved family.

CHAPTER 67

The clear sky of last night had reverted to cloudy and windy this morning, showcasing New England's fickle weather yet again. I felt clouded over, too, as I hurried from the baby's day care to my shop.

Luca had been drooling and cranky in his high chair. Ella tried to cheer him up by singing and making funny faces, something he often chortled at. Not today. Was six months too early for him to be teething? I didn't take the time to look it up, but I supposed that could be the cause of his usual cheerful nature going AWOL.

His mood seemed to rub off on his sister. She'd refused to pick up her jammies or the book she threw on the floor, and putting her breakfast plate in the sink also didn't happen. Still, the three of us managed to get out the door reasonably cleaned up, dressed for the season, and only running twenty minutes late.

I blew a kiss at Tim's bakery. The yeasty and sweet aromas wafting from it nearly lured me off my path. I then gazed up the wide granite steps at the police station's heavy front door. I did not have time to run in and twist Lincoln's arm to bring me up to speed.

The library was across the street, which reminded me that Flo hadn't chimed in last night. She must have been busy with something. Zane hadn't either, but that didn't surprise me. Anybody with twin babies had a double valid excuse. I kept myself moving.

I wasn't sure why I felt uneasy. I guessed I was spooked by all the unanswered questions of the last week, primary among them being who killed Zia Carven. I gave myself a little shake and kept on moving until I reached Mac's Bikes.

Uh-oh. The huge tree limb still blocked half of my parking lot. Maybe my plow guy was out of town. I was going to have to find somebody to clear that wood away. I took a moment to check texts on my phone for the first time that day. The man I'd hoped would clear away the deadfall hadn't responded. I laser-focused my attention on a message from Lincoln.

He said Ed and Brendan described Kimball trying to convince them to harass Zia and make her stop trying to find her birth father. The driver and the aide had refused, but they thought the senator had hired Cliff Vriesdorp in their place. They told him they thought Cliff had killed Zia. Lincoln said they hadn't been able to locate Cliff and that I should watch my back.

My jaw dropped. Cliff had to be hiding in the beach motel. Hadn't Gin let Lincoln know about the car at the motel? Then again, if the car was Kimball's, he might have left the beach by the time the police showed up, and they might not have realized Cliff was inside the decrepit old building.

No wonder I felt uneasy. Main Street was empty of cars and I couldn't see a soul on the sidewalks on either side. I pulled out my keys, glancing over at Cape King Liquor across the road, but Zane didn't open shop until eleven o'clock.

I quickly unlocked the door to the bike shop. Fugitive or no fugitive, it was already after nine—well past time for this shopkeeper to get her rear end in gear.

I flipped on the lights and shed my jacket and bag, then headed to the kitchen area to brew a pot of coffee. Part of this morning's chaos at home meant I never got to my cherished mug of French roast. No matter. We were well stocked here with excellent dark coffee, and soon enough the four-cup machine was dripping away. In my office, I unlocked the safe and withdrew the cash insert to put in the drawer.

That done, I returned to the coffee. With the mini-fridge door open, I had my hand on the half-and-half when the shop's front door clicked shut. It was followed by another sound I couldn't interpret.

"Hey, Orlean," I called. This was early for her, but she probably wanted to make up for being out yesterday.

She didn't respond but a work boot scuffed on the floor as she headed toward the back. I frowned. Orlean didn't smoke, so why did I detect the scent of cigarettes? I poured a full mug of hot coffee and turned. My breath rushed in.

Looming over me, fists on hips and a furious scowl

on his face, was Cliff Vriesdorp. I swore silently. I was in big trouble here.

"Good morning, Cliff. I'm still setting up." I conjured a confident smile out of thin air. "What can I help you with today?" I tried to swallow down my nerves.

"It's too late to help me with anything," he growled. "If you'd butted out earlier and minded your own business, that would have been a big help. Now it's too late." He wore a black cross-body bag that bulged suspiciously. If he had a gun in there, I was in even worse trouble.

"I'm not really sure what you mean." As I struggled to keep my tone level, I thought frantically. The coffee machine and dorm fridge were in an alcove in the back of the shop, but this space wasn't a separate room. If I could get by him, I could sprint for the exit. Keeping the villain talking was such a cozy mystery trope, but maybe it would work with this actual bad guy. "I thought you were enjoying your side gig of working for Senator Kimball as well as for Piet."

"Kimball." Cliff's nostrils flared. "I never should have . . ." He caught himself. "Forget about it."

"Anyway," I said brightly, "I guess you'll be glad to move on from quiet little Westham. Piet says you're heading elsewhere."

"Not until I get you out of the way, I'm not." He reached into his bag and pulled out a dark red bocce ball. In a swift move, he raised it above my head.

Oh, no you don't. I threw my hot coffee into his face. He cried out and his hands flew to his eyes. The ball thudded to the floor. It missed my foot by inches as I leaned away. I dashed around him to freedom.

I pulled on the door to the outside, but it didn't open. Cliff let out a yell. His feet thudded toward me. I pulled at my escape route again before I saw it. That extra sound had been him turning the dead bolt on the door. My sweaty fingers fumbled with the bolt. He was almost upon me.

I whirled and grabbed the children's display bike I'd left next to the entrance. I raised it high and crashed it with all my might onto his head.

Cliff crumpled to the floor. I grabbed the flagpole and whacked him with that for good measure. When he didn't move, I turned the dead bolt and ran.

CHAPTER 68

I'd barely cleared the parking lot when a siren blared into life on a cruiser speeding toward me on Main Street. A uniformed August Jenkins sprinted toward me from the other direction. The cruiser pulled up diagonally in front of the entrance to the Mac's Bikes lot.

Lincoln jumped out of the passenger side.

"Mac, are you all right?"

Another cruiser roared up with lights flashing, completing the roadblock.

"I'm fine, mostly." I patted my chest, but my heart still raced. "Cliff is in there. He came after me with a bocce ball, but I hit him with a couple of things."

"Is the back door to the shop locked?" Lincoln asked.

"Yes." My legs began to wobble, and I wasn't sure how long they would hold me up. "I need to sit down." I stumbled over to the bench near the sidewalk and sat.

"Does Vriesdorp have a weapon?" Lincoln asked me.

"I only saw the heavy ball. After I crashed a bike on his head, he fell near the door. I also whacked him with the flagpole, and a minute earlier I threw my hot coffee in his face."

"Good work, Mac." Lincoln suppressed a smile as he beckoned to Nikki Kimuri, the driver of the first cruiser. "Kimuri, you and Jenkins secure the assailant."

"Yes, sir." Both officers pulled out their weapons and moved toward the shop. August pointed his gun with both hands in front of him as Nikki swung open the door. I listened, but I didn't hear any shots from my shop. Maybe Cliff was still unconscious.

An older model Jeep pulled up in front of Zane's liquor store. Orlean got out and moseyed across the street.

"Having a little excitement, Mac?" she asked. "Morning, Lincoln."

"You could say that," I said.

An ambulance was next to arrive.

"Are you feeling better, Orlean?" I asked.

"Tiptop. But I'm guessing Mac's Bikes isn't going to be open to the public this morning, am I right, Detective?"

"That's correct," Lincoln said. "Our prime suspect in the homicide attacked Mac. The shop is a crime scene for the moment."

Lincoln hurried over to confer with the EMTs who emerged from the ambulance, holding up a palm. He probably told them to wait until Cliff was secured.

Orlean sat next to me on the bench. "You seem kind of shaky."

"I am. Nearly getting a heavy ball slammed on your head by a murderer will do that to you."

"I guess." She gave a low chuckle. "Glad I've never been there."

"I wish I hadn't." I tried to slow and deepen my breathing. Instead, I began shivering. My warm coat was inside, and I was outside.

"Hey, that's no good." Orlean pulled off her watch cap and tugged it onto my head. She slid her warm scarf from her neck and wrapped it around mine.

"Thank you." My voice was raspy. Her caring gesture threatened to slide me into tears.

August appeared in the doorway to the shop, his gun now back in its holster. He gave a thumbs up to Lincoln.

"Hey, Linc," Orlean called. "This girl needs her coat."

One of the EMTs jogged over with a blanket that he wrapped around my shoulders. The other one headed, bag in hand, toward the shop. Lincoln held the door and followed him inside.

"Thanks," I said through chattering teeth.

"Do you need me to check you over, ma'am?" the EMT asked.

"No, I'm just cold. I wasn't injured."

"All right." He hurried toward my shop.

My grandma was next to arrive, bustling up to us with furrowed brow. "Mackenzie, darling, what in the world is going on?"

"All's well that ends well." I tried to smile. "I think."

"What she means is that a killer tried to increase his victim count and failed," Orlean offered.

I nodded and repeated what I'd told Lincoln about my counterattacks.

Reba squeezed in on my other side and rubbed my cold hand between hers.

"Goodness gracious, sweetheart," she murmured. "You do have a talent for both getting yourself into dangerous situation and then getting yourself out of them."

"Yeah." The hat, the scarf, the blanket, and most of all these two women's body heat were lessening my shivering, but I didn't feel much like talking yet.

Lincoln strode toward us as the EMTs fetched a stretcher on wheels from the back of the rescue vehicle.

"Lincoln, how did you get here so quickly?" I asked. "I didn't even have a chance to call 9-1-1."

"An alert Officer Kimuri saw Vriesdorp enter your shop," he said. "She called it in and picked me up."

"You already suspected him," I murmured.

"We did."

"Detective, dear, is Mac free to leave?" Reba asked. "She's cold and shouldn't be sitting out here."

Lincoln gave it one second of thought. "Yes. Mac, you can go. Don't count on opening today, though."

"Not a problem," I said. "Can you possibly get my coat and bag? Coat's on a peg, bag is under the retail counter." I hadn't had a chance to stash my valuables in the office.

"Vriesdorp didn't touch either item?" he asked.

"He didn't."

"Okay. Sit tight. I'll be right back." He headed for the door, pausing to hold it open for the EMTs.

They wheeled out a blanketed and strapped-in Cliff, who had one wrist handcuffed to a metal loop on the stretcher. His face was blazing red and shiny from whatever the EMTs had applied to the burn.

Lucky for me his eyes were closed. I shuddered and glanced away. The last thing I needed was to be excoriated by a homicidal maniac.

"Where do you want to go, honey?" Reba asked me.

"You know what?" I gazed at her. "I would like to go straight to Tim's bakery. I need good hot coffee, a sweet pastry, and a hug from my husband."

"Orlean, care to join us?" my grandma asked.

"Why not? My boss just gave me the day off." She nudged me gently.

Why not, indeed.

CHAPTER 69

I sipped my hot buttered rum in the Rusty Anchor at four thirty that afternoon and gazed around the corner booth's table at my fellow Cozy Capers. We had all, except Zane, who sent his regrets, agreed to gather to debrief about the case and tidy up any loose informational ends on the investigation. I had Tim's blessing to attend the gathering. He'd been more than grateful for my reporting in safe at the bakery earlier.

"What does Reba always say?" Gin asked. "All's well that ends well?" She lifted her hot toddy.

I smiled. "She does. It all ended well except for Zia."

"May she rest in peace." Ilsa lifted her mug of hot tea.

"Amen. Your daughter nearly saved my life today, I hope you know," I told Ilsa. "Nikki saw Cliff go into my shop after me. I'd barely disabled him and made it out the door before she showed up with Lincoln, plus lights and sirens."

"She's a keeper, for sure." Ilsa smiled.

"So?" Norland asked. "Did the police already suspect Cliff?"

Delia approached holding a loaded tray. She set a platter of crispy fries in the middle of the table and distributed a draft beer for Norland, a glass of red wine for Flo, and a hot chocolate for Tulia.

"I might be able to answer that," Delia said. "Last night Linc told me they had a search on for Cliff, and he had something linking both him and Kimball to the homicide."

"Maybe from whatever Ed and Brendan told Lincoln," I mused. "Thanks, Delia."

"Let me know when you need refills." She headed back to the bar.

"Mac, you have to dish on how you escaped being attacked this morning," Tulia urged. "You said you disabled Cliff. How did you do it?"

"I used what was at hand." A little shudder rippled through me. I took a sip of my drink, then held up the mug. "A cup of hot coffee, a child's bike, and a flagpole."

"I bet you had to think fast," Flo said.

"I guess. Panic and fear are great motivators. My first coffee of the day had finished brewing at that very moment, and it was good and hot. Cliff was going to crash a bocce ball on my head. I threw the coffee in his face and dashed away from him."

Ilsa shuddered, too. Norland took her hand. She hadn't been through any of our group's prior sleuthing misadventures. Hearing the details could be hard.

"Sorry," I said. "These things aren't pretty, and there's more."

"It's fine," Ilsa said. "Please go on."

"Well, when I got to the door, at first I didn't see that he'd shot the dead bolt after he followed me in. Cliff recovered enough to come raging after me, even though he must have been half-blinded by the coffee. I had a child-sized bike by the door, and I crashed it down on his head."

"I know the quality of the children's bikes you stock," Norland said. "I bought them for my grands, and they're made of decent metal. Good thought on that at-hand weapon, Mac."

"Thanks," I said. "To be sure he didn't attack me again, I gave him a whack with the flagpole, which was also right next to the door."

"And you escaped," Flo said. "Well done. None of the fictional protagonists we read about could have done any better."

"I don't know about that," I said.

Three older women came in and headed for the bar. One slowed at our table.

"Hello, Mac," Patty Harbach said.

"Hi, Patty." I smiled up at her and then made quick introductions to the group. "Are you here for happy hour?"

"At our age, my friends and I come for an early bird dinner, but happy hour drink prices are always welcome." Patty returned my smile. "I hear they've made a couple of arrests in Zia's murder. I'm willing to bet you had a hand in it."

"Uh, not really." I shook my head, hoping my fellow Cozy Capers didn't contradict me.

"It occurs to me that I never got back to you about my niece," Patty said. "She said Kimball hit on her to try to get closer to Zia."

"She was Zia's age?"

"More or less." Patty nodded. "She found the senator's behavior disgusting and told him to get lost."

"Rightly so."

"Well, enjoy your gathering." She sailed off to join her friends.

"A couple of arrests sounds encouraging," Gin began, "not to mention a young woman standing up for herself."

"I'll say." I selected a half dozen fries and savored the salty, crunchy, deep-fried crust on them one by one. The unique recipe was Yvonne's. "Norland, you said you saw Yvonne going into the police station last evening."

"I did." He gazed over my shoulder. "And here comes the man who can tell you all about it."

I twisted to see Lincoln ambling up and smiled at him. "You look more relaxed than you have in a week."

Tulia pulled over a chair from an unoccupied table nearby. "Have a seat, friend."

"Thank you." Lincoln sat. "A little birdy told me you all would be here."

"And you came to fill in all the gaps in what we know, am I right?" Flo asked.

"I'll tell you what I can. What do you need to know?"

"I'll start," Norland said. "I saw Yvonne going into the station last night."

"She did." Lincoln nodded. "She finally confirmed what Mac told me: that Zia was her biological daughter with Ross Kimball. She insisted she hadn't hurt her in any way. Her partner vouched for Yvonne's whereabouts on Tuesday. Yvonne is in the clear."

"Good," I said. "Thank you."

Delia sidled up and gave Lincoln a fond smile. He took her hand and kissed it.

"I'm going to celebrate with these folks," he said. "Can you pour me the pub's best draft beer, my love?"

That was a celebration; Lincoln rarely drank alcohol.

"Coming right up."

He watched her go, love written all over his face.

Gin cleared her throat. "Lincoln, those gaps Flo mentioned?"

Tulia elbowed him. "Yeah, quit slobbering over our waitress."

"Oh, boy." Lincoln blushed. "Am I that obvious?"

"Yes, Haskins, you are," Norland said. "And there's nothing wrong with it." He shot Ilsa an equally fond glance.

"So, two arrests?" I asked Lincoln.

"Yes. Clifford Vriesdorp decided to sing, but we were already amassing evidence against the man who paid him to kill Zia Carven."

"Senator Ross Kimball, I assume," Flo said.

Reba had been kidding on Sunday when she said *The Senator's Victim* would make a good crime novel title. It turned out to be real life, with Zia as Kimball's victim.

"Correct. The two of them were sloppy criminals in the extreme. We had a search warrant for their phone and email records. They didn't try to hide the communications. Vriesdorp was greedy for money, and Kimball assumed his prestige and power as a United States senator would protect him from being nailed for hiring Cliff to do his dirty work."

"What about DNA and such from the bocce ball?" I asked.

"That will take a while, but we'll get it," Lincoln said. "Piet Vriesdorp was also helpful. His cousin's son apparently also used the store phone to communicate with Kimball more than once. Piet gave us access to those calls." Lincoln gazed at me. "And guess where the other bocce balls from the set were?"

"In Cliff's car?"

"In Kimball's silver EV." Lincoln shook his head in disgust. "The senator has lawyered up, but we have enough to detain him."

"It was from when she spent summers in Westerly. She said he'd tried to start an affair with her, but she'd refused him repeatedly."

"Bravo to June," Tulia said. "It must not have been fun for her to have him pop up again."

"One more question," I said. "Was Cliff in fact hiding out in the old motel at the beach?"

"It seems so," Lincoln began, "although the place is

a wreck. He told us he was nervous that Piet was tracking his movements."

Delia slid a full-to-the-brim pint glass in front of Lincoln. "Our best imperial stout for the detective."

"Bless you, sweetheart," he said. "Stout is a perfect winter drink." He lifted it. "Cheers to you all, and to justice, at last."

I lifted my mug. "To justice."

CHAPTER 70

On Sunday afternoon at the parsonage, at the second party of the weekend, the strains of the happy birthday song trailed off. The first party the day before at our house had been fun and chaotic, and Ella was delighted to have her friends and her girl cousin with her to celebrate.

Today the birthday girl wore a new purple dress with rainbow-striped leggings plus a tiara that glittered in her dark curls. Her face shone in the light from the five candles on the cake—four for her years and one to grow on.

"Do I make a wish now?" she asked.

"Yes," I said, "but don't say it out loud." My own voice was nearly choked with emotion. I made my own silent wish.

"And then blow out the candles," Cokey said. "I can help you."

"Let's let her try first," Derrick said gently.

Ella squeezed her eyes shut. She opened them and took a deep breath, then blew with all her might. When one flickered, she blew again.

"Yay!" Cokey clapped.

All the grown-ups in the family chimed in with the same sentiment as we clapped. Tucker yipped. Luca, who had been napping in the bouncy seat, let out a wail. Neli patted Joey's back through the sling he was sleeping in on her chest. Tim extracted our son and stroked Luca's back on his shoulder until the baby quieted.

My mom stepped up. "The birthday girl makes the first cut." She guided Ella's hand on the cake server.

"It's a pink happy birthday cake?" Ella's eyes went wide.

"I heard strawberry is your favorite flavor," Pa said.

"It is," Ella said.

"Abo Joe bakes all the birthday cakes in our family," Cokey told Ella, with all the experience and wisdom of a six-year-old.

From cake we proceeded to opening presents. True to his word, Lincoln had returned my gift-wrapped garden supplies in plenty of time. Among the toys and books and a new stuffie picked out by Cokey, I wondered if Ella would notice what I'd picked out for her, but she was delighted with the digging tools, book, and hat.

Half an hour later, the cake-stuffed girls had been bundled up to play in the back yard with Tucker. Both baby boys slept in the arms of a parent. Several of the adults, Reba and I among them, sipped sherry while others had tea or soda.

"I understand the homicide is all wrapped up," my dad said.

"It seems to be." I nodded.

"It's partly because of your Mars transit being complete," Astra chimed in.

Sure, Mom.

"I'd say it's more due to Mackenzie's wits and persistence and the help of her book group," Abo Reba said.

"Whatever," I said. "Thank you, but I don't want to keep rehashing it. Let's celebrate family, instead." I glanced around at these people who were my rootstock, my rock, my hammock of support.

"Then I suggest a cutthroat family game of Bananagrams." Pa wore an evil grin.

"That's because you're better at it than any of us, dear." Astra rolled her eyes. "I'll fetch the game. Mac and Derrick, please clear the table."

"We're on it," I said.

"I'll just watch," Neli said. "This little guy is going to want his lunch soon."

"I'll sit out the game, too," Tim said.

"Listen," I began. "I'm betting I can beat Pa today. I'm feeling kind of lucky, you know?"

Had luck played a part in putting two killers behind bars, hopefully for good? Maybe a little. Good policing, diligent detecting, and persistent amateur efforts had played a much larger part in avenging the senator's victim.

May we Cozy Capers never need to rely on luck, wits, or our own persistence again. Life should be about family and good books. That was enough for me.

RECIPES

Oatmeal Chocolate Chip Cookies

Tim, Ella, and Cokey make these together.

Ingredients

1 cup all-purpose flour
½ teaspoon baking soda
½ cup butter at room temperature
⅓ cup granulated sugar
⅔ cup light brown sugar, packed
½ teaspoon salt
2 teaspoons pure vanilla extract
1 large egg
1½ cups rolled oats
1 cup semisweet chocolate chips

Directions

Line baking sheet with parchment paper.

In a medium bowl, whisk together the flour and baking soda; set aside.

In a stand mixer bowl, combine the butter with both sugars; beat on medium speed until light and fluffy.

Reduce speed to low; add the salt, vanilla, and eggs. Beat until well mixed, about 1 minute.

Add flour mixture; mix on low until almost combined.

Stir in the oats and chocolate chips. Chill dough for one hour to overnight.

Preheat oven to 375°F.

Use a small ice cream scooper (two tablespoons) to drop heaping tablespoon-sized balls of dough about 2 inches apart on baking sheet.

Bake until cookies are golden around the edges but still soft in the center, 8 to 10 minutes.

Remove from oven and let cool on baking sheet 1 to 2 minutes. Transfer to a wire rack and let cool completely.

Italian Vegetable Tarts

Neli brings these tarts as an appetizer for family dinner at the parsonage.

Ingredients

⅔ cup whole milk ricotta cheese
⅔ cup pesto (preferably store-bought refrigerated or homemade)
½ cup fresh-grated Parmesan cheese
¾ teaspoon kosher salt
1 (17.3-ounce) package frozen puff pastry, thawed
Caramelized onions (see following recipe)
1 cup cherry tomatoes, cut in half
1 large egg, beaten
Olive oil for drizzling
½ teaspoon black pepper
½ cup fresh basil, cut into chiffonade

Directions

Position an oven rack in the upper third of the oven and a second oven rack in the lower third of the oven. Preheat the oven to 400°F. Line 2 baking sheets with parchment paper.

In a medium bowl, mix together the ricotta, pesto, ¼ cup of the Parmesan cheese, and ¼ teaspoon of the salt.

On a work surface, unfold the puff pastry sheets and cut each of them lengthwise into 3 rectangles. Place the pastry on the prepared baking sheets. Leaving a ¼-inch border, prick the center of the puff pastry rectangles with a fork and brush the border with the beaten egg.

Spoon about 3 tablespoons of the ricotta mixture onto each puff pastry sheet, spreading within the border. Spread the onions on the ricotta mixture and add the tomatoes. Drizzle the tarts with olive oil. Sprinkle with the pepper and remaining ¼ cup Parmesan.

Bake until the puff pastry is golden brown, 18 to 20 minutes, rotating the pans and swapping them between the upper and lower racks after 15 minutes. Allow the tarts to cool for 5 minutes on the baking sheets before moving them to a wire rack.

Sprinkle with the basil and slice the strips crosswise into individual pieces before serving.

Caramelized Onions

Quantities depend on how much caramelized onions you wish to make. In this example, 5 large raw onions yielded about 2 cups caramelized onions.

Ingredients

5 large onions, yellow, white, or red
Extra virgin olive oil
Butter, optional
Sugar, optional
Kosher salt

Directions

Slice ½ inch off the stem ends of the onions and the roots off the root end. Place the onions cut side down on the cutting board. Cut them in half through the root end. Peel the skin from the onions.

Lay the onions cut side down and make angled cuts into each onion, aimed at the center, cutting almost all the way, but not completely through the root end. Make the cuts to your desired level of thickness.

The root end will help hold the onion together as you cut it, making it easier to cut. Then cut a V in the root end to cut out the tough root holding the slices together.

Use a wide, thick-bottomed sauté pan for maximum pan contact with the onions. Coat the bottom of the pan with olive oil or a mixture of olive oil and butter, if using (about 1 teaspoon per onion).

Heat the pan on medium high heat until the oil is shimmering. Add the onion slices and stir to coat the onions with the oil. Spread the onions out evenly over the pan and let cook, stirring occasionally.

Depending on how strong your stovetop burner is, you may need to reduce the heat to medium or medium low to prevent the onions from burning or drying out.

After 10 minutes, sprinkle salt over the onions. If you want, you can add a little sugar to help with the caramelization process. (I add only about a teaspoon of sugar for 5 onions; you can add more.) One trick to keeping the onions from drying out as they cook is to add a little water to the pan.

Let the onions cook for 30 minutes to 1 hour more, stirring every few minutes. As soon as the onions start sticking to the pan, let them stick a little and brown, but then stir them before they burn.

The trick is to leave them alone enough to brown (if you stir them too often, they won't brown), but not so long so that they burn. After the first 20 to 30 minutes you may want to lower the stove temperature a little and add a little more oil if you find the onions are verging on burning.

A metal spatula will help you scrape up the browned bits from the bottom of the pan as the caramelization proceeds. As the onions cook down, you may find you need to scrape the pan every minute instead of every few minutes.

Continue to cook and scrape, cook and scrape, until the onions are a rich, browned color. At the end of the cooking process you might want to add a little balsamic vinegar or wine to help deglaze the pan and bring additional flavor to the onions.

Store refrigerated for several days in an airtight container.

Bake-and-Serve Biscuits

Mac buys these from Tulia, but they're easy to make at home and have ready in the freezer for a last-minute meal.

Ingredients

- 2 cups (10 ounces) all-purpose flour, plus 1/4 cup more for dusting
- 2 teaspoons baking powder
- ½ teaspoon baking soda
- ½ teaspoon kosher salt
- 1 stick (4 ounces) unsalted butter, frozen
- 1 cup buttermilk

Directions

Arrange a rack in the middle of the oven and heat to 450°F. Grease a 10-inch cast-iron skillet and set aside.

Whisk 2 cups all-purpose flour, baking powder, baking soda, and salt together in a medium bowl.

Place a box grater over a small piece of parchment paper. Grate butter on the large holes of a box grater. When you get down to a small nub of butter, chop that nub into 5 to 6 small pieces. Use the piece of parchment paper to transfer the butter to the dry ingredients. Use your fingers to sift the butter into the flour and break up any clumps of grated butter.

Pour in buttermilk and stir with a fork until the dough comes together and pulls away from the sides of the bowl.

Transfer the dough to a lightly floured surface. Pat the dough into a 1-inch-thick rough rectangle. Sprinkle the dough with a little more flour, if needed. Fold the dough in half from top to bottom, then pat it back down into its original shape. Repeat with the folding and patting, alternating folding from each side, the bottom, and the top until you have completed a total of 8 folds. At the end, the dough should be a little springy to the touch.

Pat the dough into a 1-inch thickness. Use a 3-inch round cutter to cut the dough into biscuits. Refold and pat down the excess dough and cut more as needed. Form the scraps of leftover dough into a last lumpy biscuit.

Arrange the biscuits in the skillet. The biscuits should touch each other but not the sides of the pan. Put the skillet in the oven and increase the oven temperature to 500°F. Bake until the biscuits are golden brown. 15 to 18 minutes.

Using an oven mitt (remember, that handle is hot!), remove the skillet from the oven. Immediately remove the biscuits from the pan to a wire rack.

Fish Cakes

Tulia sells these yummy fish cakes at the Lobstah Shack.

Ingredients

1 pound firm white fish fillets
1 egg
1 ounce tapioca flour
2 tablespoons fresh dill, minced, or 1 tablespoon dried
2 tablespoons lemon juice, divided
1 tablespoon fresh ginger, grated, or 1 teaspoon dried ginger
1 tablespoon olive oil
¼ teaspoon salt
⅔ teaspoon ground black pepper
½ cup mayonnaise
½ cup whole milk plain yogurt

Directions

Preheat oven to 350°F. Line a baking sheet with parchment paper or a nonstick silicone mat.

Pat dry the fish fillets with a paper towel. With a sharp knife finely chop (almost mince) the fish fillets.

Place the chopped fish, egg, tapioca flour, dill, 1 tablespoon lemon juice, ginger, olive oil, salt and pepper in a bowl and use your hand to combine.

Using an ice cream scoop, make small (about 2 inch) balls and set them on the baking sheet. Slightly flatten the balls with your hands and bake on the middle rack for about 20 to 25 minutes or until lightly golden.

Stir ½ tablespoon lemon juice into mayonnaise and yogurt. Add salt, pepper, and more lemon juice to taste.

Serve with the lemony mayonnaise on a bun or for dinner with garlic mashed potatoes and a green salad.